THE BOOK OF SPELLS

A PRIVATE PREQUEL

KATE BRIAN

D1382518

SIMON AND SCHUSTER

First published in Great Britain in 2011 by Simon and Schuster UK Ltd
A CBS COMPANY

Originally published in the USA in 2010 by Simon Pulse,
an imprint of Simon & Schuster Children's Division, New York.

alloy**entertainment**

Produced by Alloy Entertainment
151 West 26th Street, New York, NY 10001

Simon & Schuster UK Ltd
1st Floor, 222 Gray's Inn Road, London WC1X 8HB

A CIP catalogue record for this book
is available from the British Library.

ISBN 978-0-85707-129-3

3 5 7 9 10 8 6 4 2 1

Printed in the UK by CPI Cox & Wyman, Reading, Berkshire RG1 8EX

www.simonandschuster.co.uk

THE BOOK
OF SPELLS

For Matt, who somehow lived through it,
and for Lanie, who is somehow still sane

CHANGES

Even at the tender age of sixteen, Elizabeth Williams was the rare girl who knew her mind. She knew she preferred summer to all other seasons. She knew she couldn't stand the pink-and-yellow floral wallpaper the decorator had chosen for her room. She knew that she would much rather spend time with her blustery, good-natured father than her ever-critical, humorless mother—though the company of either was difficult to come by. And she knew, without a shadow of a doubt, that going away to the Billings School for Girls was going to be the best thing that ever happened to her.

As she sat in the cushioned seat of her bay window overlooking sun-streaked Beacon Hill, she folded her dog-eared copy of *The Jungle* in her lap, making sure to keep her finger inside to hold her place. She placed her feet, new buckled shoes and all, up on the pink cushions and pressed her temple against the warm glass with a wistful sigh. It was September 1915, and Boston was experiencing an Indian summer, with temperatures scorching the sidewalks and causing the new automobiles to sputter and die along the side of the roads. Eliza would have given anything to be back at the Cape Cod house, running along the shoreline in her bathing clothes, splashing in the waves, her swim cap forgotten and her dark hair tickling her shoulders. But instead, here she was, buttoned into a stiff green cotton dress her mother had picked out for her, the wide white collar itching her neck.

Any minute now, Maurice would bring the coach around and squire her off to the train station, where she and her maid, Renee, would board a train for Easton, Connecticut, and the Billings School. The moment she got to her room in Crenshaw House, she was going to change into her most comfortable linen dress, jam her floppy brown hat over her hair, and set out in search of the library. Because living at a school more than two hours away from home meant that her mother couldn't control her. Couldn't criticize her. Couldn't nitpick every little thing she wore, every book she read, every choice she made. Being away at school meant freedom.

Of course, Eliza's mother had other ideas. If her wishes came true, Billings would turn Eliza into a true lady. Eliza would catch herself a worthy husband, and she would return home by Christmas triumphantly engaged, just as her sister, May, had.

After two years at Billings, eighteen-year-old May was now an engaged woman—and to a Thackery, no less: George Thackery III, of the Thackery tanning fortune. She'd come home in June, diamond ring and all, and was now officially their mother's favorite—though truly, she had been that all along.

Suddenly, the thick oak door of Eliza's private bedroom opened and in walked her mother, Rebecca Cornwall Williams. Her blond hair billowed like a cloud around her head, and her stylish, ankle-length gray skirt tightened her steps. She wore a matching tassel-trimmed jacket over her dress, even in this ridiculous heat. The Williams pearls were, as always, clasped around her throat. As she entered, her eyes flicked over Eliza and her casual posture and flashed with exasperation. Eliza quickly sat up, smoothed her skirt, straightened her back, and attempted to tuck her book behind her.

"Hello, Mother," she said with the polished politeness that usually won over the elder Williams. "How are you this morning?"

Her mother's discerning blue eyes narrowed as she walked toward her daughter.

"Your sister and I are going to shop for wedding clothes. We've come to say our good-byes," she said formally.

Out in the hallway, May hovered, holding her tan leather gloves and new brimless hat at her waist. May's blond hair was pulled back in a stylish chignon, which complemented her milky skin and round, rosy cheeks. Garnets dangled from her delicate earlobes. She always looked elegant, even when she was destined only for a simple day of shopping.

Standing over Eliza, her mother leaned down and snatched the book right out from under Eliza's skirt.

"*The Jungle*?" she said, holding the book between her thumb and forefinger. "Elizabeth, you cannot be seen at Billings reading this sort of rot. Modern novels are not proper for a young lady. Especially not a Williams."

Eliza's gaze flicked to her sister, who quickly looked away. A few years ago, May would have defended Eliza's literary choices, but not anymore. For the millionth time Eliza wondered how May could have changed so much. When she'd gone away to school, she'd been adventurous, tomboyish, sometimes even brash. It was as if falling in love had turned her sister into a different person. If winning a diamond ring from a boy meant forgetting who she was, then Eliza was determined to die an old maid.

"Headmistress Almay has turned out some of the finest ladies of society, and I intend for you to be one of them," Eliza's mother continued.

What about what I intend? Eliza thought.

"And you won't be bringing this. I don't want the headmistress thinking she's got a daydreamer on her hands." Her mother turned and tossed Eliza's book into the crate near the door—the one piled with old toys and dresses meant for the hospital bazaar her mother was helping to plan.

Eliza looked down at the floor, her eyes aflame and full of tears. Then her mother did something quite unexpected. She clucked her tongue and ran her hands from Eliza's shoulders down her arms until they were firmly holding her hands. Eliza couldn't remember the last time her mother had touched her.

"Come, now. Let me look at you," her mother said.

Eliza raised her chin and looked her mother in the eye. The older woman tilted her head and looked Eliza over. She nudged a stray hair behind her daughter's ear, tucking it deftly into her updo. Then she straightened the starched white collar on Eliza's traveling dress.

"This green really does bring out your eyes," she mused. "You are a true beauty, Eliza. Never underestimate yourself."

An unbearable thickness filled Eliza's throat. Part of her wanted to thank her mother for saying something so very kind, while another part of her wanted to shout that her entire life was not going to be built around her beauty—that she hoped to be known for something more. But neither sentiment left her tongue, and silence reigned in the warm pink room.

"May. The book," her mother said suddenly, snapping her fingers.

Startled, May slipped a book from the hall table, where it had been hidden from view, and, taking a step into the room, handed it to her mother.

"This is for you, Eliza," her mother said, holding the book out. "A going-away gift."

Silently, Eliza accepted the gorgeous sandalwood leather book with both hands, relishing the weight of it. She opened the cover, her eyes falling on the thick parchment pages. They were blank. She looked up at her mother questioningly.

"Today is the beginning of a whole new life, Eliza," her mother said. "You're going to want to remember every moment . . . and I hope you'll remember home as well when you write in it."

Eliza hugged the book to her chest. "Thank you, Mother," she said.

"Now remember, May is one of Billings's most revered graduates," her mother said, her tone clipped once again. "You have a lot to live up to, Elizabeth. Don't disappoint me."

Then she leaned in and gave Eliza a brief, dry kiss on the forehead. Eliza rolled her blue eyes as her mother shuffled back down the hall. Then she bent to pluck her book from the box but froze as something caught her eye: May was still hovering in the hallway.

"May?" Eliza said. Usually her sister trailed her mother like the tail of a comet.

May looked furtively down the hall after their mother, then took a step toward Eliza's open door. There was something about her manner that set the tiny hairs on Eliza's neck on end.

"May, what is it?" Eliza asked, her pulse beginning to race.

"I just wanted to tell you . . . about Billings . . . about Crenshaw House," May whispered, leaning into the doorjamb. "Eliza . . . there's something you need to know."

"What?" Eliza asked, breathless. "What is it?"

"May Williams! I'm waiting!" their mother called from the foot of the stairs.

May started backward. "Oh, I must go."

Eliza grabbed her sister's wrist.

"May, please. I'm your sister. If there's something you need to tell me—"

May covered Eliza's hand with her own and looked up into her eyes. "Just promise me you'll be careful," she said earnestly, her blue eyes shining. "Promise me, Eliza, that you'll be safe."

Eliza blinked. "Of course, May. Of course I'll be safe. What could possibly harm me at a place like Billings?"

The sound of hurried footsteps on the stairs stopped them both.

Renee rushed into view, holding her skirts up, her eyes wide with terror—the sort of terror only Rebecca Williams could inspire in her servants.

"May! Your mother is fit to burst," she said through her teeth. "Mind your manners and get downstairs now."

A tortured noise sounded from the back of May's throat. Then she quickly gave Eliza a kiss on the cheek, squeezing her hands tightly. "I love you, Eliza. Always remember that. No matter what happens."

Then she released Eliza and was gone.

SISTERS

"Elizabeth Williams?"

Eliza's foot had barely touched the platform at the Easton train station when she heard her name. A broad, straight-backed woman with a wide nose and sharp eyes approached Eliza, her outmoded black feathered cap perched firmly atop her head. Flanking her, but staying a few steps behind, were two girls about Eliza's age. The first had auburn ringlets, blue eyes, and a bright smile. She was dressed in the latest fashion, though perhaps a bit overdone for daytime, with the elaborate lace trim of her full yellow skirt perfectly matching that of the collar and sleeves of her short jacket. She wore white-and-brown buttoned shoes and a hat with a turned-down brim, just like the one May had purchased last weekend on her trip to New York with their mother. The second girl was far more understated. Her modest blue-and-white striped dress was similar to Eliza's, with a wide white collar and gathered waist. She wore sensible brown shoes and a plain blue cap over her golden blond hair. Her clear blue eyes met Eliza's, and she smiled.

Renee alit next to Eliza. "I am Elizabeth's escort."

"A pleasure to meet you," the woman said with a nod. "I am Mrs. Hodge, head maid of the Billings School for Girls. This is Alice Ainsworth, and this is Catherine White." Stylish Alice twittered her fingers in greeting, while Catherine gave a polite nod.

"Hello." Eliza lifted her chin, rounded her shoulders, and clasped her traveling bag with both hands.

"Our man has already been sent round to gather your things and bring them back to the school." Mrs. Hodge reached out a thick arm toward Eliza and flicked her fingers in the direction of a busy thoroughfare.

Eliza's heart began to pound with anticipation. This was it. She was about to say good-bye to Renee and the life she'd always known. Excited as she was, tears sprang to her eyes when she turned to the maid who had taken care of her every day since her birth.

"Good luck, Eliza," Renee said, clasping her hands.

Eliza wrested her hands from Renee's and pulled her into a hug. She inhaled her maid's familiar, comforting scent of lilac and lemon.

"Thank you, Renee," she said, her voice shaking.

Renee touched Eliza's cheek with her palm as she pulled back. "I'll see you at Thanksgiving."

Eliza nodded. As her maid walked off, she wiped the tears from her lashes and took a deep breath, her chest puffing up as she filled her lungs with the sooty air of the train station. She was free. She was really and truly free. A wide grin spread across her face, and it was all she could do to keep from spinning in a gleeful, wide-armed circle.

"You look like the cat that just swallowed the canary," Alice commented, her tone sly.

"Do I? I suppose I can't quite believe I'm actually here," Eliza said, falling into step with the two girls as they trailed behind Mrs. Hodge.

"Where are you from?" Alice asked.

"Boston," Eliza said. "And you?"

"Philadelphia," Alice replied, swinging her bag in a girlish way as she walked. Catherine opened her mouth to respond, but was cut off. "The most tedious place on Earth. Catherine here is from Georgia. She's quite quiet. Then again, my mother says I am not quiet enough, so perhaps we will balance each other out."

Alice laughed, while Catherine met Eliza's gaze and shook her head slightly. Eliza had a feeling that Catherine would have spoken if she were given the chance.

"Are you both returning students?" Eliza asked, wondering if either of them had known May last year.

"Not me," Alice said. "I spent last year at a school near home, but this year I begged to be sent away."

"I'm new as well," Eliza stated.

"Well, then, I'll have to help you two navigate the school," Catherine said, finally able to chime in. "I've been here three years. Billings is my home away from home."

Then she definitely knows May, Eliza realized, a twist of disappointment in her chest. But there was nothing she could do to change the fact that May had attended Billings first. All she could do was make sure to make her own impression. One that showed everyone she wasn't just a mini May.

Outside the station, the sidewalk bustled with travelers. A young woman took her two children by the hand as a dusty motorcar sputtered past. A few boys Eliza's age joked around next to a pile of trunks and cases, clearly waiting for their own transportation to arrive. Nearby, a couple of men in open-collared shirts and dirt-caked pants loaded up an open wagon with huge sacks of grain. One of them caught Eliza watching and gave her a wink before grabbing another bag. Eliza blushed and rushed to catch up with the others.

"Here we are, ladies," Mrs. Hodge said, pausing next to a large black coach outside. "Our driver, Lawrence, will help you in."

"She should say *adorable* Lawrence," Alice commented, quiet enough to seem as though she was trying to go unheard, but still loud enough that Lawrence did a double take. Eliza raised an eyebrow. Flirting with the help had never been an accepted practice in her world, and most servants were overlooked as if they were invisible. Eliza decided she liked Alice for noticing Lawrence's doelike brown eyes—even if the attention had clearly made the now-blushing boy uncomfortable.

Alice placed her hand eagerly inside young Lawrence's as he helped her into the carriage, grinning right at him until he looked away. Catherine was next. When Lawrence held out his hand to Eliza, though, she waved it away.

"I'm fine," she told him, grabbing the handles on either side of the door and hauling herself up under her own strength. As Eliza dropped ungracefully into the seat next to Alice, Mrs. Hodge shot her a disapproving look. But Eliza didn't care. She didn't need a man's help just to get into a coach, and now that her mother wasn't around to criticize, she wasn't about to accept it.

After Mrs. Hodge was situated up front, next to the driver's seat, Lawrence closed the door and latched it, and soon they were off, rumbling away from the train station and through the small town of Easton. The main street was flat and well kept, with new buildings in brick and wood cropping up on either side. A large general store sat at the very center of town, a mannequin in a silk, slim-bodiced evening dress in one window and a wheelbarrow in the other. Across the street, the Easton Police Station looked as if it had just been built, its redbrick façade practically gleaming in the sun.

"Oh, I'm so excited," Alice said, clapping her gloved hands as she looked out the window. "I know it's wicked of me to say, but I'm so glad to be rid of my family, especially my brothers."

"I have a brother," Catherine said. She opened a silver, oval-shaped locket around her neck and held it out for the girls to see. Eliza and Alice leaned in. The sepia photo was of a towheaded boy who looked to be about ten, grinning from ear to ear. "I miss Lincoln already."

"Pssssh," Alice said, leaning back again. "I don't believe that for a moment. I have five of those little urchins in my life, and each is more fiendish than the last. What about you, Eliza?"

"No. No brothers," Eliza replied. She didn't want to bring up her sister just yet. If she did, Catherine would undoubtedly spend the rest of the ride regaling them with a glowing account of May's illustrious tenure at Billings.

"Well, count yourself lucky," Alice said, spreading her fingers. "I am just so sick of boys and their grubby hands and their jam-covered faces and their awful habit of bringing spiders and frogs and all manner of creepy crawlies into the house."

Eliza and Catherine laughed as the carriage came to a stop at an intersection at the end of the main street.

"But I *am* looking forward to meeting the Easton Academy boys," Alice went on slyly, giving Eliza a nudge with her elbow. "I plan to have a new beau by the night of the welcome dance next week. Do either of you girls have admirers back home pining over you?"

Eliza had a feeling Alice would be shocked by the lack of romance in Eliza's past. Most of the boys in her social circle had been falling all over themselves for May since she could remember. Two summers back, Eliza had fancied herself in love with Charles Morris, a boy who summered on the Cape. But after two full months of trying to get his attention—challenging him to swim races, digging for clams and checking his crab traps with him—he hadn't even bothered to say good-bye when his family packed up their Victorian home and went back to Baltimore. When she'd complained to May, her sister had told her that acting like a boy was no way to win one.

"What about you, Cat?" Alice asked. "You seem to be quite the blushing Southern belle. I'll wager the boys are lined up for you."

"I've never had much interest in romance, to be honest,"

Catherine said, lifting a shoulder. "My mother calls me a late bloomer."

"So no beaux at all?" Alice exclaimed. "Well, then we'll have to get you one."

Catherine blushed and shifted in her seat, clearly discomfited by the subject.

"I'm sure if Catherine wanted a beau, she could get one for herself," Eliza said.

Catherine shot Eliza a grateful look. "Thank you, Eliza, I appreciate the confidence."

The coach turned up a steep hill, and Eliza spied a modest sign near the sign of the road that read THE BILLINGS SCHOOL FOR GIRLS.

"Look! We're here!" she said, sitting forward.

The three girls crowded the small square window on the left side of the coach, looking out at the sun-dappled campus. The buildings were large and imposing, constructed of gray brick and ornate moldings. Stone pathways wound through the neatly clipped grass, and the air smelled of musky lavender, probably from the field of wildflowers just north of campus. Eliza breathed in the heady scent, knowing she would forever associate it with the feeling of possibility.

"That tall building right there is the McKinley building," Catherine said, pointing to a structure with an arched doorway and several slim French windows, all of them gleaming in the sunlight. "All the classes are held on the second and third floors, except for etiquette, which we have in the parlor at Crenshaw House."

A shiver of apprehension went through Eliza at the mention of

Crenshaw. What was it that May had wanted to tell her about her new home? But she quickly shoved her worry aside. The buildings may have been a tad austere, but on a gorgeous day like this, it was difficult to imagine anything sinister happening at Billings.

"The instructors' offices are there, as well as the library," Catherine continued. "It's that smaller wing off to the side."

Eliza eyed the squat annex on the McKinley building. It was obviously a new addition, its gray bricks a darker shade than those of the original structure. The library was unimpressive and nearly windowless, but still she couldn't wait to peruse the aisles. She hoped they contained all the books she had never been allowed to read inside her mother's house.

"That long, rectangular building is Prescott," Catherine continued as the coach drove on. "To the right of the main entrance is the gymnasium, and to the left is the dining hall."

Alice wrinkled her nose. "Gymnasium? What's that for?"

"Physical fitness, I believe," Catherine joked.

"But I hate exercise," Alice pouted.

"Really? I love it," Eliza said. "Especially anything played in the outdoors."

"Ugh," Alice groaned, rolling her eyes as she leaned into Eliza from behind. "But don't you hate to perspire? It's so unladylike."

"A necessary evil, I'm afraid," Eliza said, pleased when Catherine laughed.

"Up the hill at the center of the woods is Billings Chapel. You can't see it from here. But you can see Crenshaw House," Catherine said, pointing a finger out the opposite window. "That's where all the students' quarters are. It used to be an orphanage, but the school bought it a few years back."

A lump formed in Eliza's throat, and she slid to the right side of the coach for a better look. Crenshaw loomed at the top of a grassy hill bordered by the woods, its walls an unattractive brown brick, its façade blunt and flat. It had a foreboding presence; the two large windows just above the door were positioned like glaring eyes.

Suddenly, from the corner of her eye, Eliza saw a flicker of movement in one of the first-floor windows. She looked over just in time to see a shock of blond hair, and then the curtain fell back into place. A shiver of fear ran through her heart, and she hugged her arms to her chest.

"We're separated by class on each floor, with fourth-years on the top floor and so on down," Catherine went on. "The headmistress and staff have apartments on the first floor, to keep an eye on us."

Eliza blinked. "So you can't come or go without them hearing you?"

"Exactly," Catherine replied. Then she glanced toward the driver's bench, as if Mrs. Hodge could hear their voices over the pounding of the hooves and through the thick ceiling of the coach. "But some people find ways," she added with a mischievous smile.

As the coach turned again, working its way down a slim country lane leading to the base of Crenshaw's hill, Eliza heard a distinctly male shout. Alice squealed.

"There they are! Eliza! Come see! The Easton boys!" She gasped.

Obligingly, Eliza slid back to the other side of the coach. Several boys in shirtwaists, vests, and ties were horsing around on a green lawn, their sleeves rolled up, their caps tossed on the ground.

"I knew Easton Academy was close to Billings, but I didn't realize how close," Alice said excitedly, clasping her hands together under her chin.

"The woods around Billings Chapel border both the Easton campus and the Billings campus," Catherine explained. "On weekends we're allowed to visit the Easton grounds, and the boys are allowed to visit the Billings grounds. They often come over here to play games, because we have more open space on this side of the woods."

"I say we get out and say hello," Alice suggested.

Eliza laughed.

"It's a good thing Miss Almay isn't here right now. She'd mark you for a troublemaker," Catherine warned.

Alice giggled, but Catherine didn't crack a smile. "I'm serious, Alice. Don't let her catch you mooning over the boys. My roommate was expelled last year for sneaking around with an Easton student."

"Well, she can't see me now," Alice said. Then she leaned out the open window and lifted her hand in a wave. "Hello, boys!" she called out merrily.

"Alice!" Catherine scolded, but she couldn't help laughing anyway.

Eliza leaned forward to get a better look. In the center of the group on the lawn was a tall boy with tanned skin, his dark blond hair gleaming in the sun. He grappled with a couple of other boys and managed to get the tie off one of them, then laughed as his victim gave chase. As he turned around, he looked up and his eyes met Eliza's. He stopped running and simply stared.

Eliza suddenly felt warm from her toes all the way up to the tips of her ears. Her heart pounded in a way it never had before. She knew that it was wrong to stare so boldly at a boy, but she couldn't tear her eyes away. And neither, it seemed, could he.

The owner of the stolen tie rushed him and tackled him right to the ground.

"Oof! Did you see that?" Alice giggled, covering her mouth.

Eliza sat back, her breath coming short and shallow. She had seen. In fact, she could have kept staring all day long.

NEW FRIENDS

"Eliza, Catherine, this will be your room."

Mrs. Hodge opened the door to a bright, sunlit chamber on the fourth floor of Crenshaw House, directly above the entry. They had already dropped off Alice on the floor below, which was reserved for second-years, but Alice's view had been nothing like Eliza's and Catherine's. The windows on the far side of the room looked out over the entire Billings campus and the tree-covered hills beyond. It was the sort of view that was perfect for daydreaming.

"We're roommates, then," Catherine said with a smile as Mrs. Hodge bustled away.

"Looks that way," Eliza said. "And I promise I won't be getting expelled for looking at boys."

Even as she said it, though, Eliza recalled the gaze of the boy out on the field, and she warmed from head to toe all over again. But she rolled her shoulders back and resolved not to think about him. She was not here to meet a boy. She was here to read forbidden books and be free of her mother's watchful eye.

Catherine unlatched a large wooden trunk near the wall. Down the hall girls called out to one another, chatting about their summer vacations and their day's journey. Their obvious familiarity made Eliza feel suddenly nervous. What if everyone in her class had been here all along, like Catherine? Would it be difficult to make friends?

Eliza stepped inside the room that was to be her new home. She took a deep breath and looked around, trying to keep her fears at bay. The walls were painted a lovely light blue—no pink in sight, she noted gratefully—and the lace curtains billowed in the warm breeze. Her trunk had already been placed at the foot of the bed nearest the door, and she was happy to see that her father had included a bookshelf among the furniture he had sent ahead for her. She walked over and ran her fingers along the top shelf, thinking of her father with a pang. He was currently off on a business trip in Washington, D.C., but this bookcase proved that he was thinking of her. At least someone in her family endeavored to understand her. She couldn't wait to dig to the bottom of her trunk and free her novels. They wouldn't come close to filling the shelves, but that simply meant she had room to acquire more.

"Oh, good. There's already a hook here," Catherine said from the other side of the room.

She opened her trunk and took out a wooden carving of a fleur-de-lis, which she hung on the nail above her headboard. Eliza envied Catherine's ability to feel so at home and relaxed. But then, Catherine had been coming here for years. In a few days' time, Eliza was sure she would feel just as comfortable. The key was to make the room feel like her own. She, too, had a hook above her bed. Opening her trunk, she took out the framed photograph that had hung in her room since she was little. It was a picture of her and May, taken at the farm the summer of 1907, one of the happiest weeks they had ever spent there. Neither of the girls smiled in this particular photo, as their mother forbade smiling in any pictures or portraits. "It's unbearably common," she always said. But Eliza's feet were bare in the grass beneath her formal dress, and May's blond hair stuck up a bit in back, from rolling around in the field of daisies just behind the barn. Eliza placed the photo on the wall above her own bed, happy she'd been able to bring the best part of home along with her.

Just to the left of the photograph, she noticed a small carving in the wall. "Was this your room last year as well?" Eliza asked Catherine.

"No, why?"

"Someone carved the initials CW into the wall," Eliza said, tracing the letters with her finger. "I wondered if it was you."

"There was a girl who went here a few years ago—Caroline Westwick. Perhaps this was her room." Catherine shrugged, then removed a few other things from her trunk: a long, flat wooden box, which she slipped under her bed, followed by a stack of hardcover books. Eliza peeked over Catherine's shoulder to get a glimpse at the titles: *Wuthering Heights. Jane Eyre. Mansfield Park. Evelina.*

"I love *Mansfield Park,*" Eliza exclaimed. "Don't you think it's one of Miss Austen's best, yet least appreciated, novels?"

"Oh, yes!" Catherine replied, holding the book to her chest. "I've read it at least five times, and each time I applaud Fanny Price's strength even more."

Eliza felt as if she had woken under a lucky star. Almost half of Catherine's large trunk was taken up by books. Mrs. White, it seemed, had no objection to her daughter's enjoyment of novels.

"I'm so glad you're a reader," Catherine said as she began to unpack her things. "Theresa hates when I try to talk to her about books."

"Theresa?" Eliza asked.

"Theresa Billings," Catherine replied. "My best friend."

Eliza felt a fresh twinge of envy. She had never had a best friend before, aside from May. "Billings?" she asked. "As in . . . ?"

"Yes, as in Billings School for Girls," Catherine replied, rolling her eyes slightly. "She has a single room on the top floor, even though she's only a third-year like us. She's always had a single room on the top floor."

"I see," Eliza said with a small smile.

"You'll meet her at the welcome," Catherine said, placing a few books near the end of her bed. She looked around at her plain bed and dresser. "Unfortunately, my books always end up spending the school year at the bottom of my trunk."

"That is simply unacceptable," Eliza said. "Use my bookcase."

Catherine looked at the large case on Eliza's side of the room. "I couldn't."

"You can and you will. Until I get some new books of my own, it's going to look far too lonely and sad anyway." Eliza plucked the heavy copy of *Mansfield Park* from Catherine's bed and placed it on the top shelf. "There. Much better."

"Thank you, Eliza," Catherine said, looking Eliza in the eye. "That's very kind of you."

"It's nothing," Eliza replied. "In return, you can grant me permission to read them when the whim strikes."

"Permission granted," Catherine said, with a joking bow of her head.

The two girls glanced at the open doorway as a few of their classmates traipsed by, laughing and talking of upcoming classes.

"How many students live in Crenshaw?" Eliza asked, detesting the uncertain tone in her voice.

"There are forty of us altogether," Catherine said. "Ten in each class." She glanced at Eliza, and her expression turned sympathetic. She placed a stack of books atop Eliza's bookcase and took her roommate's arm in a companionable way. "Let's walk over to the chapel together, and I'll introduce you to as many of them as we meet along the way."

Eliza grinned, relief flooding her veins. "Thank you," she said happily. "I'm glad the headmistress matched us up as roommates, Catherine White."

"As am I," Catherine replied, holding her close. "I have a feeling, Eliza Williams, that you and I are going to be great friends."

THE CHAPEL

"Oh! How beautiful!" Eliza said breathlessly as she and Catherine emerged from the canopy of trees behind Crenshaw House.

The Billings chapel stood in a clearing at the center of the woods, its bell tower gleaming white against the stark blue sky. The stained glass windows were the most intricate and colorful Eliza had seen apart from the Mission Church in Boston. Flowering shrubs bloomed along the base of the structure, their fat pink petals bobbing in the breeze.

Catherine tilted her head as she looked the structure over as if for the first time. "It is rather lovely, isn't it?"

"Catherine!"

A pretty girl with dark black ringlets and a perfectly pressed green-and-white striped dress approached Catherine, holding a matching parasol to shade her milky white skin. She held the hand of another girl, who was clearly her twin, except that the other girl wore a lavender version of the same dress and kept her eyes trained shyly on the ground.

"Viola! Bia!" Catherine greeted them. "How was your summer?"

Viola kissed Catherine on the cheek and grasped her hand. "Just amazing," she said. "All we did was travel and shop."

Catherine laughed. "Sounds like a dream," she said. "Viola and Bia Hirsch, meet Eliza Williams."

"Williams?" Viola said, her dark eyes wide. "As in May Williams?"

Catherine turned to look at Eliza as Bia glanced up with interest. Eliza blushed slightly, feeling somehow ashamed that she hadn't mentioned May to Catherine before.

"Yes, May is my older sister," Eliza said.

"Really? But the two of you look nothing alike!" Viola exclaimed.

Eliza's blush deepened. May was a renowned beauty. It wasn't the first time Eliza had been told how different she looked from her sister.

"Oh, I just adored May!" Bia said, her voice breathy and weak as she clasped her hands under her chin. "Is she well? And how is George? Oh, I'm sure she's going to make the loveliest bride!"

"Bia, you're rambling again," Viola said harshly. Bia fell silent and looked at the ground once more, while Viola moved forward and slipped her arm around Eliza's. Her grip was surprisingly tight as she tugged Eliza up the stone chapel steps. "You must tell me all about your sister's wedding clothes."

"Certainly." Eliza sighed.

"May's sister," Catherine said as they entered the chapel. "Well. This is going to be interesting."

Eliza eyed Catherine curiously. But before she had a chance to ask what that meant, a girl with plain brown hair rushed forward to greet Viola. She wore an expensive-looking gray plaid dress, which didn't entirely suit her. With her scrubbed face and her unkempt hair, she had the look of a tomboy who'd been shoved into her mother's frock.

"That's Jane Barton," Catherine said. "She, Theresa, Viola, and Bia are friends from Manhattan."

"Please find a seat, girls," Mrs. Hodge instructed from her place at the door, ushering them farther inside. "The headmistress will be here soon."

Eliza scanned the room. The air inside the chapel was at least ten degrees cooler than it was outside. Two dozen gleaming oak pews flanked either side of the long aisle, which was crowded with students. As everyone settled in, Eliza spotted Alice toward the front, gabbing away with a large girl who seemed to be eyeing Alice in a confused and apprehensive way.

Catherine beckoned for Eliza to follow her. "As third-years, we sit toward the back of the middle section."

Smiling politely at her unfamiliar classmates, Eliza trailed Catherine down the aisle. A willowy girl with milk-white skin and blond hair cut into a chic, short style approached Mrs. Hodge. She clasped the hand of a shorter, somewhat rotund girl as if desperate to keep hold of her.

"*Excusez moi, s'il vous plaît,*" the girl said to the head maid. "Petit Peu, my dog . . . he has not arrived yet?"

"Not that I know of, Miss DeMeers," Mrs. Hodge replied. "Lawrence is under strict orders to bring him here as soon as the manager at the station locates him."

"I cannot bear to think of him all alone in that crate," the girl replied in heavily accented English, looking at her friend. "He does not even understand the language!"

"Did that girl just ask about her *dog*?" Catherine whispered to Eliza as they lowered themselves into a pew.

"I believe she did," Eliza replied, intrigued. She kept one eye on the French girl as she sat, resolving to introduce herself as soon as this welcoming presentation was over. If Catherine didn't know her, then she must be a new student, just like Eliza.

Viola and Jane settled in behind Eliza as a hush fell over the crowd. Eliza turned in her seat as an imperious-looking woman walked into the room.

"That's Miss Almay," Catherine hissed, elbowing Eliza lightly.

The headmistress wore a slim burgundy dress with a high collar and held her long nose so high in the air, she could have caught a flock of birds inside her nostrils. Eliza couldn't help noting that she was old for an unmarried woman, in her fifties at least. It struck Eliza as ironic, considering how many families sent their girls here to learn how to catch a husband.

By the time she arrived at the front of the chapel and took her place at the pulpit, every single girl had found herself a seat. Everyone, that was, except for a slim, raven-haired girl who slipped in late, shedding her seersucker cape and tossing it carelessly to Mrs. Hodge, who stood next to the door. Underneath the cape, the girl wore a matching seersucker dress with a square collar and slim-cut skirt. A set of long necklaces dangled over her bosom, the kind a married sophisticate in her twenties might wear. Her eyes darted around the room until she saw Catherine, and her face lit up with a smile.

"Catherine! There you are!"

Eliza was stunned at the girl's audacity in breaking the silence in such a bold way. She walked over and sat down next to Catherine, giving her a tight squeeze and a kiss on the cheek. A huge diamond ring sparkled on her left hand. It caught the light from the nearest stained glass window and glittered spectacularly.

"Hello, Theresa!" Jane said eagerly, leaning over the back of the pew.

Theresa, noted Eliza. So this was Theresa Billings. Catherine's best friend and, apparently, an engaged woman. *Interesting*.

"Hello, Jane," Theresa said in a dismissive way before returning her attention to Catherine. "Why didn't you wait for me?" she demanded.

Catherine rolled her eyes toward Miss Almay, who was glaring at them with fire in her eyes.

"I'm so sorry, Miss Almay. You may proceed," Theresa said, earning a round of gasps and giggles from the pews.

"Well, thank you, Theresa, but rest assured I was not awaiting your cue," Miss Almay replied.

Eliza leaned forward casually, trying to get a better look at her roommate's friend.

"Who's that?" the girl asked Catherine in a loud whisper, looking appraisingly at Eliza.

"Theresa Billings, meet Eliza Williams, my new roommate," Catherine said, so quietly that she could barely be heard. She leaned back slightly so the two could see each other better.

"Eliza *Williams*?" Theresa said in a sour tone. "As in . . . ?"

"Yes," Catherine confirmed lightly.

Eliza was at a loss. She'd thought May was beloved everywhere she went, but Catherine had sounded wary when she'd learned that May and Eliza were sisters, and now Theresa seemed disgusted.

Up at the pulpit, Miss Almay cleared her throat and signaled to Mrs. Hodge.

Theresa turned away from Eliza. "I'm so sorry they stuck you with another roommate," she whispered loudly. "I told Mother to make sure you had a private room this year."

Eliza's skin burned from head to toe. Had Catherine been counting on a single? Was she bothered by Eliza's presence? Her throat tightened just as Mrs. Hodge closed the double doors with a *bang*. Eliza started. Theresa rolled her eyes and snickered softly.

"Welcome, ladies, to a new term at the Billings School for Girls," Miss Almay began. "I am Headmistress Almay. I trust you are all well rested after your summer vacations and ready to get down to work."

"My summer vacation was far more exhausting than any school year," Theresa whispered, leaning toward Catherine. "Don't you find parties to be so draining?"

Catherine kept her expression blank as Miss Almay shot her and Theresa a scathing look.

"Billings girls are the finest, most elegant, best-educated girls in the country," Miss Almay continued. "You are expected to conduct yourself with decorum at all times, and that includes when you are in the company of students of Easton Academy."

Whispers and giggles greeted this directive. As Headmistress Almay pursed her lips, clearly waiting for the noise to die down, Eliza studied her peers. All of them were perched on the edges of their pews. Alice was gripping the bench in front of her, as if to keep from running over to the Easton campus that very moment. Eliza couldn't help wondering if all the girls were here only to find a husband.

"As you all undoubtedly know, there will be a welcome dance on the third Saturday of the term, a mixer of sorts between Easton Academy and the Billings School," Headmistress Almay announced.

Alice clapped her hands together lightly at this announcement. A tingling excitement skittered over Eliza's skin at the thought of the blue-eyed boy from that morning. She shook her head. What was going on with her? Two hours ago she couldn't have cared less about boys or the dance. Now, one look at a handsome boy and her feelings were almost Alice-like.

"But remember: This dance is a privilege, not a right," Miss Almay continued sternly. "Any Billings girl who steps out of line will have this privilege revoked. Do I make myself clear?"

"We understand, Miss Almay. You hold all the power," Theresa groused under her breath.

Eliza's heart stopped as Miss Almay cast an admonishing look in Theresa's direction, but the girl didn't seem to notice. Then, out of the corner of her eye, Eliza noticed a girl creep through the double doors, closing them silently behind her. She had long, straight blond hair plaited down her back and wore a modest dress of gray muslin. Despite her plain appearance, there was something almost regal about her, about the confidence with which she held her head, about the knowing look in her eyes.

Mrs. Hodge hurried up behind the blonde and whispered something in her ear. The girl nodded and immediately set about opening the lower windows in the chapel.

Eliza widened her eyes in surprise. So she was not a student but a maid.

"Now, on to this year's curriculum," Miss Almay continued. "As always, you will be expected to complete academic courses in poetry, art, French, and classic literature, as well as practical classes in etiquette, housekeeping, and gardening. There is one change this year, however. The hours at Billings have been extended, so that you will be expected to attend six classes each day rather than five."

Viola and Jane gasped. "Whose idea was this?" Theresa demanded at full voice.

"Your father's, actually," Miss Almay shot back.

Theresa clucked her tongue, her eyes ablaze. Eliza glanced at her roommate. How could Catherine be friends with this girl? Clearly she was nothing but a self-centered, spoiled troublemaker.

Miss Almay sighed. "Are there any questions?"

Eliza's hand shot up. Catherine and Theresa looked at her in surprise, as did Miss Almay.

"Yes, Miss . . . ?"

"Williams." Eliza had the sudden, sinking feeling that she wasn't actually supposed to ask a question. "Eliza Williams, Miss Almay."

Every face turned toward her. Eliza's shoulders tensed.

"Yes, Miss Williams?" Miss Almay said.

"I was wondering . . . will we have any free time during the day?" Eliza asked.

Miss Almay leaned over the pulpit, her frown lines deepening. "Free time for what purpose?"

"For reading," Eliza replied. "Is the library open all day?"

Miss Almay narrowed her eyes, her broad shoulders squared. Eliza's heart pounded with fear. An ominous silence filled the room.

"You're May Williams's sister, are you not?" Miss Almay asked.

Eliza cleared her throat. "Yes, ma'am."

"Then I suggest you attempt to be more like her and not ask impertinent questions," Miss Almay said.

Theresa laughed. Eliza's jaw dropped slightly as humiliation poured through her, white-hot and acidic. How could asking about the library be considered impertinent? Catherine laid a comforting hand atop Eliza's, but there was no soothing this feeling away.

"May was like a goddess around here," Theresa whispered. "I suppose we don't have to worry about her second coming."

Eliza looked down at her lap, her eyes burning. She refused to cry. But inside, her heart welled with disappointment. It seemed that the

Billings School for Girls wasn't going to afford her quite the measure of freedom she had dreamed of. Just like that, all her dreams went up in a puff of smoke.

"Remember, girls—wherever you go, you are a representative of this school, and your behavior is a direct reflection on me," Miss Almay said, still hovering over her. Eliza could feel the headmistress's gaze boring into the back of her burning neck. "So rest assured that wherever you go, I'll be watching you."

ADVENTURE

That evening, Eliza sat at the card table in the center of the parlor, playing Hearts with Alice, Catherine, and Alice's roommate, Lavender Lewis-Tarrington—the stout girl from the chapel, whose quiet personality couldn't be more the opposite of Alice's. Eliza's attention, however, was not on the game. She couldn't stop replaying the incident from the chapel in her mind. Miss Almay had humiliated her in front of the entire student body on her very first day. Every time Eliza recalled Miss Almay's imperious glare, her stern words, Eliza's heart sunk a bit further toward her toes. It seemed Billings would prove to be as stifling as her home had been.

Eliza sighed, both annoyed and bored as she took in her surroundings. The large brick fireplace at the top of the room was bare, and the windows along either wall had been thrown open to afford the girls some fresh air. Small tables dotted the wood floor, and wing-backed chairs lined the walls where Jane, Viola, Bia, and some of the younger girls had gathered to pore over the latest issue of *Harper's Bazaar*. A second-year named Clarissa Pommer sat with her chair turned toward the wall, engrossed in a science book she'd brought from home. Eliza had approached her earlier and introduced herself, but Clarissa hadn't been much for conversation. In fact, she put forth a rather forbidding air altogether, with her sharp features, her two long braids pinned behind her head, and her high-necked floral dress buttoned all the way up to her chin.

In the corner, at the grand piano, Genevieve LeFranc played a classical tune, pausing every now and then to pluck a chocolate from the box she'd brought down from her room. Marilyn DeMeers sat beside her on the bench, cooing at Petit Peu, a Yorkie who'd been recently rescued from his cage. Mrs. Hodge had retired to the kitchen a few minutes earlier, leaving Helen Jennings, the young maid from the morning, sitting in a chair near the door, her hands folded primly in her lap as she kept a watchful eye on her charges.

Catherine laid down the two of clubs, so Alice laid down her ten of clubs.

"Eliza?" Alice said. "It's your turn."

Eliza blinked. She looked down at her cards, groaned, and tossed them down on the table.

"Eliza! You'll ruin the game," Lavender said, straightening her run.

"I'm sorry, but I came here to get away from the same old thing," Eliza said, pushing away from the table and standing. "And yet here we are, playing cards, just as we might do on any other night of our lives."

"What should we do? Go to the library?" Jane Barton joked, looking up from her magazine.

"Jane!" Catherine scolded, as some of the other girls laughed.

Eliza's face burned, but she ignored the girl's barb. "It's our first night here together. Shouldn't we do something . . . exciting?"

Across the room, Marilyn stopped cooing and Genevieve stopped playing the piano. Bia and Viola leaned forward with interest.

Lavender eyed Eliza timidly. Helen frowned. Only Clarissa didn't move. She simply turned the page in her book, her brow knit, the picture of concentration.

"Like what?" Catherine asked, folding her cards on the table.

"Isn't there a phonograph here? Maybe we could dance," Alice suggested excitedly.

"Or we could go visit the boys," Theresa said, walking in through the open parlor door. She wore a formfitting deep red dress with a matching cape. Her thick black hair hung loosely down her back, and she'd changed her necklaces to a set of crimson beads. Eliza fought the urge to scowl at the girl's arrival.

"I'm listening," Alice said.

"Helen. We'd like some water," Theresa said without even looking at the young maid.

The girl sighed, but dutifully got up from her chair. "Yes, Miss Billings," she said, and left the room.

"Jane, Viola, Bia, and I know some of the boys at Easton from back home," Theresa said as soon as Helen was gone. "And I happen to know that they're all going to be gathering at Gwendolyn Hall tonight. They do it every year on the first night at school."

"Ooooohh!" Alice cried, jumping up and down and clapping her hands. "Then what are we waiting for?"

"I'll go get my wrap!" Jane offered, dropping her needlepoint in her chair.

"How would we get there?" Viola asked.

"There's a tunnel not far from Crenshaw, at the edge of the woods. It will take us right there," Theresa said, her dark eyes gleaming as she placed both hands on the back of Eliza's vacated chair. "I overheard my father and his friends talking about it at cards. It's amazing the things you learn about men when they think they're on their own."

"So you want us to sneak out of here in the dark and take some tunnel to Gwendolyn Hall to meet the boys?" Eliza asked skeptically.

"Precisely."

"Are you sure about this?" Catherine asked, crossing her arms over her chest. "If we get caught, we'll be forbidden from the welcome dance. And that's the best-case scenario."

"Helen already overheard your plan," Clarissa pointed out from her chair.

"Helen just heard me suggest it," Theresa replied. "She won't report us unless she sees us leave."

"But I do not wish to be kept from the dance," Genevieve said. She placed the top on her box of chocolates and tucked them away into a quilted bag she had slung over her shoulder.

"Nor do I," Marilyn added, her accent even thicker than

Genevieve's. According to Alice, the two of them had grown up together in Paris. Eliza hadn't seen them leave each other's side all day.

"Oh, come on, girls. What she doesn't know won't hurt us," Theresa said, waving a hand. "Besides, I own this place, remember? If she threatens us, I'll just telephone Father. He owes me after insisting on that change to our curriculum." She walked to the door and grasped the brass doorknob. "Now, do you want to stay in here under lock and key all night, or would you rather go on a little adventure?"

Though she hated to admit it, excitement pounded through Eliza's heart at the word *adventure*.

"Is the tunnel safe?" Lavender asked.

"Of course it is," Theresa replied, rolling her eyes. "My grandparents and the Eastons had it built as a hiding place for runaway slaves back in the day."

"The Underground Railroad?" Eliza asked.

Theresa nodded. A few of the other girls wrinkled their noses and shuddered, but Eliza was intrigued.

"Not that you'll be coming along, Eliza," Theresa said, looking her up and down.

Eliza blinked. "Why ever not?"

"Why, you're a Williams," Theresa said with a snort, looping her arm through Catherine's. "The faculty might have revered your sister, but that girl wouldn't know an adventure if it jumped out of a bush and bit her. Given your love of libraries, I have to assume you're cut from the same bland cloth."

Eliza's jaw dropped, and Theresa turned to face the room. "The rest of you, go get ready. I'll wait for you outside. But hurry. Helen will be back soon. Perhaps Eliza can tell her we all went up to bed."

Catherine eyed Eliza sympathetically. Eliza felt as if her insides were about to burst.

"I'm coming with you," she said in a determined voice.

Theresa paused. She turned around and raised her eyebrows. "Really?"

"Yes, really," Eliza said firmly. "I am *not* my sister. I'm always up for an adventure."

"We'll see about that," Theresa said.

AGREED

Runaway slaves walked these steps, Eliza thought excitedly. *They touched these walls.* Of course, the runaway slaves probably didn't have Petit Peu barking nonstop behind them, his high-pitched yap echoing off the walls. Genevieve and Marilyn had finally agreed to meet the boys, while Clarissa had stayed behind, listlessly promising to tell Helen that the others had gone to bed.

"Theresa Billings, if this tunnel doesn't end soon, I'm going to go right back to Headmistress Almay and have her telephone your father," Viola said, her voice tremulous. She gripped Eliza's arm tightly.

"She can telephone all she wants. My father's currently on a steamer bound for Portugal," Theresa said, holding her lantern aloft.

"But didn't you say that if we got into trouble, you'd phone him?" Lavender asked. She had insisted on bringing up the rear so she could keep an eye on everyone.

"I say a lot of things," Theresa replied under her breath.

Suddenly Eliza heard a scrabbling sound, as if claws were scraping against the stone floor. She froze.

"*Turn back,*" a voice whispered in her ear, so close that a shiver raced down her spine.

"We can't turn back now, Viola," Eliza said. "I'm sure we're almost there."

"Huh?" Viola said with a confused look. "Why are you telling me?"

"You just said 'Turn back,'" Eliza replied.

"No, I didn't," Viola said.

"Yes, you did. You whispered it right in my ear."

Viola's face paled. "I didn't say anything. Did you say anything?" she asked her sister.

"No," Bia whimpered.

Suddenly everyone was whispering in a panic. "It's a ghost. A slave ghost," Viola said, grasping her sister even tighter as her eyes rolled around wildly, looking for the ghoul. "Oh, Bia. We have to get out of here."

"Yes. Let's turn back," Genevieve said. "I did not come all this way from Paris to be murdered by a ghost."

"There are no ghosts down here!" Theresa blurted in frustration, waving her lantern around. "Look what you've started, Eliza!"

"But I'm sure I heard something," Eliza replied, her pulse racing. "Somebody said 'Turn back.'"

Theresa clucked her tongue impatiently. "You just want to be the center of attention. Just like the mighty May."

Eliza felt as if she'd been slapped. She had just opened her mouth to defend herself when Catherine stepped forward and took the lantern from Theresa.

"Girls, we're almost there," she said firmly. "Follow me."

To Eliza's shock, the girls fell almost entirely silent and did as they were told.

After several long minutes, Catherine paused. "I've found a door!"

She held the lantern up. Sure enough, it illuminated the grainy wood surface of a slated door set into the stone wall just ahead.

"Welcome to Gwendolyn Hall, ladies," Theresa said.

Alice let out a squeal and rushed forward, shoving a few girls aside in order to be the first through the door. Theresa, however, had other ideas. She blocked Alice's forward motion with one arm, then reached past Catherine to open the door herself. Instantly, warm light and the sound of deep voices filled the tunnel. Despite herself, Eliza's heart took a few extra spins as she recalled their true reason for being here. She couldn't help but hope to see the blond-haired boy from the great lawn.

"Hello, gentlemen," Theresa said. "Do you have room for a few more?"

Whoops filled the air. Alice, Theresa, and Catherine stepped inside. Viola lifted her skirts up a good foot from the ground to keep them clean, dragging her sister and Eliza inside with her.

They emerged in the basement of Gwendolyn Hall, a wide, low-ceilinged room that was nevertheless spotlessly clean and bright. Its walls were made of white plaster, its floor of dark gray cement. The boys had lit several lanterns and candles, all of which were set on a high shelf that ran clear around the room, their flames flickering jovially. Most of the boys were still in their formal day attire, but a few had tossed their jackets aside and undone their collars, taking on a far more casual appearance.

One of these was the boy from that morning.

As soon as Eliza saw him, she found she couldn't move. He was laughing uninhibitedly with a group of his friends, and she had a moment to enjoy the sound, to let it fill her from the tips of her ears to the tips of her toes. Then he turned from his companion and found her with his eyes. His laughter stopped. Eliza's knees all but gave out on her at that moment, and she was grateful to have Catherine at her side to support her.

"Eliza, do you feel faint?" Catherine shot her a worried look.

"No, no, Catherine. I'm fine," Eliza said, blushing furiously.

At that moment, the boy's companion turned around. His entire face brightened.

"Eliza Williams!" he said in a booming voice.

It took Eliza a moment to focus on this person who'd said her name. His pinstriped shirt barely contained his broad shoulders, and he wore a formfitting tweed vest. His tie was loosened, his sleeves buttoned at the wrist. His face seemed slightly square, which might have been due to an obviously fresh haircut that left him nearly shaven around the ears, but his smile was kind and his brown eyes warm.

"It's Jonathan Thackery," he said, bringing a large hand to his own chest. "We are to be brother and sister, once May and George wed."

"Mr. Thackery, of course!" Eliza stepped forward and extended a hand, which he clasped in both of his. She had met Jonathan at the engagement party his parents had thrown for May and George over the summer, and they had spent nearly the entire next day sunbathing with their siblings on the lake near the Thackerys' summer home.

"Allow me to introduce you to my friend here," Jonathan said, slapping his hand on the blond boy's back. "Eliza Williams of Beacon Hill, Boston, this is Harrison Knox of Manhattan, New York."

"It's a pleasure to meet you, Miss Williams," he said, looking her in the eye. "Welcome to Easton Academy."

Eliza opened her mouth to reply, though she wasn't certain she would be able to get any words past the sudden tightness in her throat. "Thank you," she finally managed. "Do you two know my friend Cath—" She turned to introduce Catherine, but the girl had slipped away. Eliza's brow knit as she turned back to the boys. "Perhaps she was an imaginary friend," she said, joking over her embarrassment.

Both Jonathan and Harrison laughed.

"Well, how did you find our tunnel, Miss Williams?" Harrison said, turning to the side slightly and, in effect, edging Jonathan out of the conversation. Jonathan joined a much more raucous group of boys who had formed a loose circle around a grinning Alice. "I hope the spiders and mice weren't too unpleasant for you."

"It takes more than mice and spiders to intimidate me," Eliza replied. Feeling warm, she wished she had a fan of some sort, although such an item might have seemed out of place in a damp, windowless basement. "On the contrary, I enjoyed it. It reminded me of something out of an adventure novel."

Although I could have done without the eerie whispers, she thought with a shiver.

Harrison's handsome jaw dropped slightly. "You read adventure novels?"

"Doesn't everyone?" Eliza asked.

Harrison considered this. "Everyone worth talking to, I suppose."

Eliza smiled as he held out a hand toward a pair of chairs near the wall. She sat down, tucking her skirt beneath her legs. Her heart fluttered like mad as he sat next to her.

"What have you read?" he asked with genuine interest.

Eliza hesitated. Her mother would have a fit worthy of Marie Antoinette if she knew that Eliza was even considering telling him about the novel she had smuggled to school in her travel bag. She sat up a bit straighter and looked Harrison in the eye.

"I'm in the middle of *The Jungle* by Upton Sinclair," she replied.

His eyebrows shot up and he turned fully sideways in his chair, the soles of his shoes scratching against the cement floor. "I've just finished that one. What do you think of it?"

"I adore it," Eliza gushed. "It's horrifying in its vivid details, and the tragedy just mounts from page to page."

Harrison smirked. "You enjoy tragedy, do you?"

"Of course not. But when Mr. Sinclair wishes to make a point, he's certainly deft at making it."

"Has he turned you socialist, then?" Harrison asked, a bit of a challenge in his voice.

"Hasn't he turned you?" Eliza asked.

"Not I," Harrison said with a laugh, shaking his head. "But I'm glad his work caused the government to start regulating the working conditions in our factories."

"But do you really think it's enough?" Eliza asked. "What about the monopolies and the gang-run city governments? Just regulating wages and hours and cleanliness isn't going to solve all the evils brought about by big business!"

"My word, Eliza Williams. You've certainly thought a lot on this subject," Harrison said.

Eliza's heart skipped an awful beat. "You're teasing me," she said, turning to face forward. The rest of her friends were just starting to feel comfortable enough to insert themselves among the boys.

"No, I'm not," Harrison said, holding his hands up in surrender. "I'm just . . . impressed."

She dared a sideways glance at him. He nodded toward the rest of the party. "How many of them do you think are discussing politics and literature right now?"

Eliza scanned the basement. Alice was batting her eyes at no fewer than four boys, while Theresa and Jane were listening to two others in the corner. Lavender and Catherine sat alone together, conversing in low tones. The rest of the girls were giggling and casting glances at the various groups of boys.

"My guess would be none," she said, smiling and looking down at her hands. "My mother would tell me to turn the topic toward the weather, or ask you about your family or your aspirations."

"The weather is fine, thank you. My family is boring, and I aspire to keep talking to you for as long as possible, if you'll agree to not mention any of those dull topics again," Harrison said lightly, looking intently at her.

Eliza grinned. "Agreed." For a long moment she held his gaze.

"Miss Williams, would it be too bold of me if I said that you have the most beautiful eyes I've ever seen?" he said quietly.

Eliza couldn't breathe. She could barely even think. Somewhere in the back of her mind, she heard her mother teaching her the proper way in which to react to a compliment: Cast her gaze down, blush, and either thank the boy politely or protest. But as Eliza looked into Harrison's dark blue eyes, another answer came to her.

"Likewise, Mr. Knox," she said.

He grinned.

"There you are, Harry! I've been looking all over for you!"

Harrison nearly jumped out of his chair. Theresa was cutting across the basement purposefully, a hand outstretched toward Harrison, the engagement ring upon it twinkling in the candlelight.

"Theresa. You look lovely as always," he said. He took her offered hand and kissed it, an everyday gesture that nevertheless made Eliza's stomach twist into knots.

Theresa chuckled and slipped her arm through his, pulling him proprietarily to her side. Together they faced Eliza, who rose belatedly from her own chair.

"You're ever the gentleman." Theresa reached up and brushed an errant lock of blond hair off his forehead. The knots in Eliza's stomach tightened. "I see you've met Billings's newest student, Eliza Williams."

"Yes. We've just been discussing our aspirations," Harrison said, his tone suddenly formal.

Eliza stared at Theresa's hand on Harrison's arm. "How do you two know each other?"

"Oh, Harry didn't tell you? He and I are engaged to be married," Theresa said, thrusting her ring toward Eliza's nose.

The entire world dropped out from beneath Eliza's feet. She tore her eyes from the diamond long enough to glance at Harrison. He looked away sheepishly.

Engaged. He's engaged. And to Theresa? How could he be engaged to someone so awful?

A sour desperation spread through Eliza's gut. She knew she was to congratulate the pair and ask what season they planned to wed. But her mouth felt glued shut, and her thoughts were a confused tangle. Harrison had complimented her taste in books, her thoughtfulness, and her eyes. Was that standard behavior from an engaged man? Obviously she had misinterpreted his interest in her. Suddenly Eliza felt awkward, naïve, and pathetic.

"We're thinking a spring wedding, right, Harry?" Theresa said, smiling up at him.

"Spring, yes. Spring would be . . . fine," he said in a strangled voice.

And just like that, something snapped inside of Eliza. Anger crowded out her desperation—anger not at Harrison nor at Theresa, but at herself. She had promised herself she wouldn't turn into May and sell her soul for a boy, yet here she was, on her first night, ready to cry over the first one she'd met. What had gotten into her?

She drew herself up and lifted her chin. "Congratulations," she said. "I'm sure the two of you will be very happy together."

Then she turned and strode over to join Jonathan, Alice, and two tall boys, resolving to put Harrison Knox and Theresa Billings entirely out of her mind. He was a flirt, and she was a witch. As far as Eliza Williams was concerned, they deserved each other.

MY HARRISON

"Everyone, stop here," Theresa said as they emerged from the tunnel. She paused at the edge of the woods and glanced up at Crenshaw House, which stood just across an open expanse of the hill. The rest of the girls crowded behind her, camouflaged by the trees. Eliza stood at the back of the pack with Alice, her pulse pounding in her temples. She couldn't stand how Theresa kept taking charge of every situation, how everyone looked to her as though she was some sort of messiah. All Eliza wanted to do was get inside her room, pull the covers over her head, and pretend this night had never happened.

"We'll go across in twos," Theresa said. "When you get there, keep to the wall and out of sight. I'll go last and let you all in."

Everyone nodded their agreement.

"Viola, Bia, you go first."

As the two sisters sprinted off across the grass, grasping each other's hands, Alice leaned in toward Eliza's ear.

"I need your opinion on the boys," she whispered.

"What boys?" Eliza asked, keeping one eye on Theresa. She was walking along the line of girls like some sort of army general.

"Jeff Whittaker and Christopher Renaud!" Alice said, wide-eyed. "You met them."

"Right. Of course," Eliza said, remembering the names of Jonathan's other friends. Theresa glanced in her direction, then turned and walked back to the front, urging Genevieve and Marilyn to go next. A cool breeze rustled the leaves overhead, stirring up the scent of freshly fallen pine needles. In any other circumstances Eliza would have been taking in the scenery, enjoying the rare treat of being outdoors at night, but thanks to Theresa—and Harrison—she just couldn't seem to relax.

"I'm deciding which one of them I'm going to allow to escort me to the welcome dance," Alice said breathlessly. "You seem like a level-headed girl, Eliza. Whom do you think I should choose?"

Alice grasped Eliza's hand, and Eliza felt a rush of sudden and unexpected affection. Alice was almost like a little girl—a little sister, which was something Eliza had never had.

"Well, Jeff might be better for conversation, with his recent travels to talk about, but you and Christopher have similar coloring, so . . ."

"Oh my goodness, I hadn't thought of that! We would make a handsome pair, wouldn't we?" Alice gasped. "But Jeff is so attentive. He actually noticed my shoe had come undone and risked his pant leg on that musty floor in order to refasten it for me! Oh, why does this have to be so hard?"

She looked up into the boughs overhead as if the trees would offer some sort of answer. Nearby, Catherine stifled a laugh.

"I'm sure you'll make the right decision in the end," Eliza said, squeezing Alice's hand. "Perhaps you should go see Christopher at Easton tomorrow and ask where he summers. That may help tip the scales."

Alice nodded solemnly. "Of course. Thank you, Eliza. I knew you were the right person to talk to."

Catherine turned around then, clearly unable to stay away any longer. "She's right, you know, Eliza. You may claim to have had no beaux, but clearly you understand the perils of romance," she teased.

"Thank you, Catherine. I do consider myself a student of the human condition," Eliza replied, feeling Theresa's eyes on her as she sent Jane and Lavender off into the night.

Catherine laughed quietly. "That reminds me! I wanted to ask you, have you read *The Canterbury Tales*?"

"Oh, it's one of my favorites!" Eliza held a hand over her heart. "The language, the imagery, the dialogue! Don't you feel as if you're right there with the characters?"

Suddenly, Theresa cleared her throat. She eyed Catherine and Eliza, her hands behind her back. "Catherine, Alice, you may go."

"What?" Catherine said. "But I—"

"I know we always stick together, Catherine," Theresa said as if humoring her, yet in a somehow condescending tone. "But I'd like to get to know our new charge a bit better." She looked Eliza up and down in a way that made Eliza's blood curdle.

Catherine gazed at them for a moment, then shrugged.

"All right, then. But play nice," she added, giving Theresa a shrewd look. She took Alice's arm and turned around. "Shall we?"

"We shall!" Alice said.

Theresa watched the two girls race off into the night, then turned toward Eliza. She placed the lantern down on the dirt path. The flame cast dancing shadows along the ground, but Theresa's face was shrouded in darkness. Eliza's pulse began to pound with apprehension.

"You and Catherine seem to be getting along," Theresa stated.

"We're roommates. I should think getting along would be a good thing," Eliza replied, casting a glare at Theresa. She refused to appear intimidated.

"Of course it is," Theresa shot back. "There's no need to be so defensive." She took a step toward the lantern—toward Eliza. "So, what did you think of my Harrison?"

Eliza clenched her teeth, the words *my Harrison* ringing in her ears. "It looks as though Alice and Catherine have arrived at Crenshaw," she said coolly. "Shall we?"

Theresa took another step. A shock of fear went through Eliza's veins. "You didn't answer my question."

"I found him to be quite . . . polite." Eliza held perfectly still.

"And handsome, of course. You found him handsome," Theresa prodded, moving closer still. So close that Eliza could now make out every feature of her beautiful face—every suspicious feature.

Eliza's face burned and she could only hope that, in the darkness,

Theresa couldn't tell. She cast a glance over the girl's shoulder at Crenshaw, where all their friends waited impatiently.

"I suppose," Eliza replied finally. "Shouldn't we go? We don't want to get caught."

"I think he's the most handsome boy in all of New York," Theresa said in a wistful tone, gazing off toward the towering shadow of Crenshaw House. "He's been promised to me since we were children—just a silly agreement between our parents, who are lifelong friends. But over the summer he made it official." Theresa lifted her hand to gaze admiringly at her ring. "He went down on one knee and everything. The boy, I'm afraid, is completely in love with me."

Eliza stared at Theresa. If the girl was expecting Eliza to break down crying and confess that she was pining for Harrison—well, that was not going to happen. Eliza had just met the boy.

"I'm so happy for you, Theresa, really," Eliza said firmly, putting on a huge smile. She reached out and squeezed Theresa's hands for good measure, even though the gesture made her own skin crawl. "I wish you and Harrison years of marital bliss. Now, can we please go?"

Theresa tightened her grip until she was squeezing so hard, Eliza feared for her fingers. "Of course!" Theresa said with wide-eyed innocence. "Why have you kept me out here so long? Our friends must be dying of fright."

With that, she dropped Eliza's fingers, grabbed the lantern, and sprinted across the grass. Eliza's jaw dropped. For a moment she was stunned over Theresa's accusation that she'd been the one to stall them. But as the pitch darkness closed in around her, Eliza recovered herself and ran. Theresa was at least ten paces ahead. Eliza lowered her head and sprinted as hard as she could, determined to catch up with her rival before they reached the dormitory. Determined to win. At least at this.

Theresa let out a yelp of surprise as Eliza drew up even, then passed her. Eliza drove her hands into the rough brick wall of Crenshaw at least three yards ahead of Theresa. She turned around, leaned back, and smiled over her triumph.

"Congratulations, Eliza," Theresa said slyly, her chest heaving as she arrived. "You must be very proud."

Eliza opened her mouth to respond that yes, she was very proud, but at that moment, the double doors at the front of Crenshaw House swung open, letting out a loud, ominous squeal. Lavender instantly stepped in front of the other girls as if she was readying herself to protect them.

"Hello, ladies," the headmistress said, staring down her nose at Lavender. She smiled grimly at the collective gasp that met her greeting. "Kindly come inside so that I may take down your names." She stepped aside to let them all through the double doors, but for a long moment, no one moved. Eliza looked at Catherine, whose face was deathly pale, her mouth set in a pained line.

"Good evening, Miss Almay," Theresa said confidently. "And might I say, you look lovely in your dressing gown. Is that silk?"

Some of the girls laughed halfheartedly, but Miss Almay's frown lines only grew deeper.

"Inside, Theresa. Now."

Theresa strode through the door, her head held high. Slowly, the other girls followed, their eyes trained on the ground. Eliza brought up the rear, right behind Catherine, her heart heavy as she imagined her mother's reaction upon hearing that her younger daughter had been expelled from the Billings School for Girls on her very first day.

Just as the door slammed shut behind her, a breeze curled around Eliza and tickled her ear. "I told you that you should have turned back," the same low voice from the tunnel whispered. Eliza's breath caught and she whirled around. But no one was there.

TREASURE

"Miss Almay is simply evil for making us toil in this heat," Theresa groused, shoving her spade into the dirt in the garden behind Crenshaw House. She pried out a dandelion by the roots and tossed it aside, then wiped the back of her hand along her perspiring brow. Even Eliza had found herself close to complaining as she worked under the relentless sun, but each time she'd held back. She didn't want to sound as petulant as Theresa had sounded all morning long. Eliza could tell that Catherine, who was weeding a row of carrots a few feet away, was also biting her tongue.

Theresa tossed another dandelion. "And do you know that Viola and Bia haven't spoken to me at all since last night? As if it's somehow my fault we were caught."

Viola, Bia, and Jane were gathering apples under the watchful eye of Mrs. Hodge; the cook was to use the fruit in her fritters and pies. Helen, meanwhile, had been charged with keeping an eye on the garden workers. The young maid sat nearby in the shade of an elm tree, her gaze trained on Eliza and her friends like a hawk stalking its prey. Eliza wondered if she'd been scolded for allowing the girls to sneak out on her watch.

"It wasn't your fault," Alice said, sitting back to fan her face under the wide brim of her straw hat. "We all wanted to go. I just can't believe she's also forbidden us from attending the dance. Isn't it punishment enough that we're being forced to weed the gardens and sweep the walks like common servants?"

"I rather enjoy this." Eliza grabbed a weed at its base, yanked it out, and tossed it into the basket, which was rapidly growing full. "Being out in the sun, getting some exercise."

"But don't you care that we're not going to get to go to the dance? All the other girls will get to talk and dance with the boys," Alice said, her shoulders curling forward as she gazed longingly toward the woods that separated them from the Easton campus. "We're going to be at such a disadvantage."

"It's not a contest," Eliza said lightly.

"Not for me at least," Theresa said. "I've already won the most worthy boy."

Swallowing a groan, Eliza took hold of a large weed with both hands and tore it fiercely from the ground. The sound of male laughter caught the girls' attention.

"There are some of your conquests now," Catherine said, nodding in that direction.

Sure enough, off in the distance, Eliza could see Jonathan and

Harrison walking along with Jeff and Christopher, their confident strides a measure of their assured place in the world. Alice scrambled to her knees, soiling the skirt of her pink dress as she angled for a better look. Theresa shielded her eyes and smiled.

"Forget spring. I think we'll have an autumn wedding," she mused, her eyes on Harrison. "This would be a beautiful sort of day to exchange vows, don't you think?"

Eliza took up Theresa's forgotten spade and drove it into the earth, ignoring the question.

"I rather think not," Catherine said.

All three girls glanced at Catherine, surprised.

"You said it yourself. It's too hot," Catherine continued, looking, for some reason, at Eliza. "Your wedding cake would melt into a puddle of sugar and eggs."

"In your opinion," Theresa said, sitting back down on her gardening stool.

"Which, if I'm not mistaken, you asked for," Catherine replied.

Stifling a laugh, Eliza drove the trowel into the dirt again. It slammed into something hard, making a loud scraping noise that set her teeth on edge.

"What was that?" Alice asked, peering over Eliza's shoulder.

"Probably a rock," Eliza replied.

She dug up a few shovelfuls of dirt, expecting to see another of the small, fist-size rocks they'd found so many of during their past hour of gardening. But instead, the surface of whatever she had found just seemed to grow on either side of her shovel. Eliza dug and dug until she'd uncovered what appeared to be a long wooden box. Some kind of metal band was wrapped around it, clasped with an ornately carved latch.

Eliza stole a quick glance at Helen. The girl was standing now, and Eliza's heart skipped a nervous beat. She positioned herself so that her back was to the maid, entirely shielding the hole and its contents from view.

"Girls! Don't look now, but I've found something," Eliza whispered.

Catherine abandoned the carrots and moved closer to Eliza, starting to dig casually just a foot away. Alice and Theresa angled themselves so they could see inside the hole as well.

"What is it?" Alice asked, looking over her shoulder at Helen.

"I don't know," Eliza replied. "Who would bury something here?"

"Who cares? Just dig it up," Theresa ordered.

It was an order Eliza didn't mind taking. After using her trowel to clear away some more of the dirt, she dug in with her fingers. Finally she was able to pry the box from the ground. The case was about a foot long and flat, only two inches in height. Eliza whipped a handkerchief from the pocket of her apron and dusted the dirt from the grooves and crevices of the carved latch. It was some sort of symbol, with circles swirling together to make an exotic design, but there were no letters or words to identify the owner.

"Let's see what's inside!" Alice whispered fervently.

Eliza laid the box on the ground next to the hole and glanced over at Helen again. The girl was walking toward them. Eliza's heart all but stopped.

"She's coming," she whispered, turning around again.

"Oh, Lord," Theresa said.

"Theresa! Don't take the Lord's name in vain!" Alice scolded.

Everyone looked at her, surprised.

"Forgive me, Sister Alice," Theresa said sarcastically. Then she sat up and called out, "Helen! Would you mind getting us some water? We're parched, and I'm certain Headmistress Almay wouldn't appreciate it if we all ended up dehydrated in the infirmary."

Helen stopped in her tracks. She looked at Crenshaw House, then back at the girls, an almost desperate look on her face. "Of course, Miss Billings," she said finally. But she cast a furtive look over her shoulder as she went inside, as if her conscience was telling her to stay.

As soon as the door had banged shut behind the maid, Eliza opened the box, her hands shaking with excitement. Inside was a folded piece of dusty, frayed velvet. Quickly Eliza removed her gardening gloves and unfolded the scrap of cloth. Tucked within was a large, perfectly round gold locket. Etched into its face was the same swirling circle design as on the box's lid.

"A buried treasure!" Alice announced excitedly.

Theresa and Eliza reached for the locket at the same time, but Catherine grabbed Theresa's hand.

"It's Eliza's. She found it," Catherine said.

Theresa clucked her tongue. "What's gotten into you today? You'd think *she'd* been your best friend for the past two years." Eliza half expected Theresa to walk away for a pout, as many girls in Eliza's and May's small circle back home would have done, but surprisingly, she stayed put.

Eliza scanned the hillside leading down to the campus lawn.

Helen's empty chair sat beneath the huge elm. Down the hill, Mrs. Hodge was busy yelling at Bia for eating one of the apples. A hawk swirled overhead. No one was paying the four girls in the garden any heed.

Eagerly, Eliza lifted the necklace and opened the locket. A piece of parchment paper, creased into a tiny square, dropped to the ground. Theresa seized upon it hungrily. She dusted the dirt off the square and unfolded it.

"It's all in Latin," she said, frustrated. "Does anyone read Latin?"

"I do." Catherine reached for the parchment, but stopped. "Wait. There's something else in the box."

Eliza looked down. A warm breeze tickled the back of her neck, and even in the heat, she shivered. Sure enough, another piece of parchment peeked out from beneath the velvet covering. She tugged it out and opened it. The other girls leaned in around her shoulders, and Eliza felt the same rush of anticipation she'd had as a child whenever May had proposed a new scheme.

"What is it?" Catherine asked.

Crude illustrations of structures, streets, and bodies of water covered the page. There were also short lines of handwritten text indicating paths to a series of various destinations. Right near the center of the page was a big, dark X.

"It's a treasure map," Eliza said.

The four girls looked at one another, a sizzle of excitement rushing between them.

"Look. This must be Crenshaw," Theresa said, grabbing the map

THE BOOK OF SPELLS

out of Eliza's hands. She pointed at a drawing of a square building at the top of a hill.

Suddenly Eliza wished Theresa had been anywhere but here when she'd found the box. Clearly the girl was going to try to dictate this situation, just as she did all others.

"*X* marks the spot," Catherine said, pointing to the middle of the page.

Theresa opened her mouth as if to speak.

"I say we follow it. Tonight," Eliza announced quickly.

Theresa shot her an annoyed look, and it was all Eliza could do to keep from preening. Clearly she'd stolen the words out of Theresa Billings's mouth.

"But we're already under probation," Catherine said, glancing over her shoulder at Crenshaw House, as if she expected Miss Almay to be standing in the doorway.

"But we must," Eliza said. "Imagine what we might find!"

Theresa's eyes shone. "It could be gold or diamonds or—"

"I don't know. What if we get caught?" Alice said fretfully.

"Oh, grow up, Alice. We're going," Theresa said, folding up the map. "Besides, Miss Almay can't forbid you from the dance *again*."

Just then, the front door to Crenshaw House slammed, and out walked Helen with a tray of water glasses, the ice cubes clinking together loudly in the stillness of the afternoon.

"Hide it!" Theresa instructed, lifting up Alice's wide skirt. Eliza stuffed the locket and map back into the box and shoved the whole thing toward Alice's feet. Alice dropped her skirts down to cover the box, then sat on her gardening stool again and grabbed her trowel. Catherine, meanwhile, folded the small parchment inside her fist.

"If you two won't go, Eliza and I will go without you," Theresa hissed.

Eliza clenched her jaw at Theresa taking charge once again—and so offhandedly ostracizing not only Alice but also Catherine.

"No. We were all here when we found it. Either all four of us go or none of us go," Eliza said. Helen was only fifty feet away now.

Theresa scowled, but Catherine seemed moved. "All right. If it means so much to you two, I'll go."

Alice let out a whimper, bouncing her knees up and down as she looked from Helen to Eliza and back again.

"Your water, girls," Helen announced, standing on her toes as she called to the girls. "I don't believe Miss Almay would object to you all taking a slight break."

"We'll be right there," Theresa yelled back.

"Alice! It's to you," Eliza whispered.

"All right, fine. But only because you mentioned diamonds," Alice said.

"We meet at midnight underneath the old elm," Theresa said, nodding toward the tree under which Helen was now placing the tray. "Agreed?"

"Agreed," Eliza said, placing her hand in the center of their circle. Catherine immediately clasped it, and Theresa did the same.

Reluctantly, Alice reached up from her seated position and placed her hand atop the others. "Agreed," she repeated.

LATE

That night Eliza and Catherine were silent as they dressed for the treasure hunt. Eliza donned her drabbest dress—a black, shapeless, long-sleeved frock her mother had bought her for her elderly neighbor's funeral—and her fingers quaked as she fastened the buttons. Somehow she managed to clasp the gold locket around her neck, but not before dropping it four times.

Get a hold of yourself, Eliza. This is exactly the type of adventure you crave, she told herself.

A sudden rap on the door startled her out of her wits, and Catherine actually yelped. They looked at each other and then laughed.

"I suppose I'm a bit on edge," Catherine said, blushing.

"As am I," Eliza admitted. "Come in!"

Helen opened the door, holding a package wrapped in plain brown paper. "This came for you, Miss Williams," she said.

"For me?" Eliza asked with surprise as she accepted the package. She could tell by its weight that it was a book.

"Who's it from?" Catherine asked, tilting her head to see the package.

"It doesn't say," Eliza replied. "But if it's a book, it's probably from my father."

Helen hovered in the door, eyeing Eliza's and Catherine's dark dresses with suspicion. Eliza's heart gave an extra thump. "Thank you, Helen," she said firmly.

Helen flinched, then quickly curtsied. "You're welcome, miss." Then she was gone.

"You don't think she'll tell Miss Almay we were dressed this way at this hour, do you?" Catherine asked.

"Your friend Theresa seems to trust her," Eliza said as she sat on her bed. "Isn't that enough?"

"You don't like Theresa much, do you?" Catherine asked. There was no trace of an accusation in her tone. She simply sounded curious. "Not that I'm surprised, considering."

"Considering what?" Eliza asked, tearing the brown paper from the book.

Catherine hesitated. "Nothing. Just . . . nothing."

"Oh my goodness!" Eliza exclaimed. All thoughts of Theresa Billings vanished from her mind the second her eyes landed on the book's title. "*A Tale of Two Cities*! I took this book out of the library last year, but my mother found it and made me return it. She said the contents were far too scandalous for a young girl."

"Oh, it's an incredible story," Catherine said, "I like your father already."

Then Eliza noticed something odd. The book, it appeared, was used. The corners were frayed, and one of the pages near the front had been bent down. It looked as if it had been read several times over. But it was not at all like her father to buy her a used book. She opened the cover to see if he had enclosed a note, and her heart stopped, for the bookplate secured inside the cover read PROPERTY OF HARRISON B. KNOX.

Instantly, Eliza tilted the book so that Catherine would be able to see only the cover. She turned the page and once again, her heart caught. Harrison had written her a message near the top left corner of the cover page.

For my favorite tragedy lover. There will be something to interest you on every page. Enjoy it. Harrison Knox.

My favorite tragedy lover, thought Eliza. *He used the word* my. *He implied that I am his! Harrison touched this book. He read these very pages.*

Eliza was nearly breathless with bliss. She could think of no gesture more romantic. Then, suddenly, she felt foolish. Harrison was in love with Theresa; they were engaged to be married. He couldn't have realized what this book would mean to Eliza. He was probably just passing along a favorite story to another book lover.

"What is it, Eliza? You look positively feverish," Catherine said, rushing to her friend's side.

"It's nothing," Eliza said, slamming the book closed. "Just a note inside from my father."

Catherine nibbled on her pinky finger for a moment, looking as if she was on the verge of saying something. Then she turned away and grabbed her black felt hat.

"Shall we be off, then? You can only imagine what a bear Theresa can be when people are late," she said.

"But she was late to the welcome," Eliza said, placing the book on the top shelf of her bookcase as she stood.

"Yes. It's perfectly fine for her to keep others waiting, but heaven forbid the rest of us should attempt it," Catherine said with a fond smile.

"Are you sure about this, Catherine?" Eliza asked, reaching for her new friend's hand. "You were the first to protest the plan this morning. I didn't intend to force you into it."

Catherine shifted her feet nervously. "It's all right. No one forced me. I'm going of my own accord." She looked Eliza in the eye steadily.

"All right, then," Eliza said with a resolute nod. "How are we to get out of here without being noticed?"

"We must take the servants' stairs at the back," Catherine replied as she reached for the door. "They go right by the kitchen, where Mrs. Hodge and Helen spend most of their time, but it's the only way. If we walk out the front, Miss Almay will surely spot us. She spends most of her time at the window."

"But won't the maids hear us?" Eliza asked.

"We'll just have to hope they're washing dishes or scrubbing the floor," Catherine said. "Theresa does this all the time."

That was all the motivation Eliza needed. If Theresa could do it, so could she. "Then we'll just be as quiet as mice."

Eliza took the door handle and slowly opened it. The hallway was empty. She slipped out of the room, gesturing for Catherine to follow. Catherine closed the door with the faintest of clicks, but still winced at the sound.

"Which way?" Eliza whispered.

Catherine gave a nod to the right, and Eliza tiptoed down the hallway, past the closed doors of her slumbering classmates. Around the corner at the end of the hall was a slim door. It let out a loud creak as Eliza opened it.

"Shhh!" Catherine said automatically.

Eliza slipped inside and found herself on the wooden landing of a rickety set of stairs. Catherine tumbled in behind her and closed the door.

Catherine, to Eliza's surprise, was giggling. "I can't believe I just shushed a door."

Suddenly Eliza's nerves took over and she couldn't help laughing as well. She covered her mouth to stifle the noise, but then a sudden creak down below stopped her cold. She grabbed Catherine's arm.

"What was that?" she whispered.

Catherine shook her head mutely, her eyes wide.

Then came a whisper. "Eliza? Is that you?"

Eliza breathed a sigh of relief. It was just Alice. Eliza looked over the railing and saw the younger girl staring up at her, holding a candle in her tremulous hand.

"We're coming!" Eliza whispered. Catherine grabbed Eliza's hand as they started down the stairs.

"I nearly died of fright when I heard someone on the stairs," Alice said when they reached her. She clutched Eliza's other hand.

"It's all right. We're together now," Eliza assured them, feeling a rush of pride over their confidence in her. "Let's just get out of here as quickly as we can."

Catherine and Alice nodded. Hand in hand, the three girls tiptoed to the foot of the stairs, where there were two doors. One undoubtedly led to the kitchen, the other outside. But Eliza was so nervous and turned around, she couldn't tell which was which. If she chose wrong, they were as good as expelled. She looked up at Catherine, but before she could pose the question, there was a huge clatter from behind the door to her right.

Eliza's heart hit her throat.

"Mary and Joseph!" Mrs. Hodge shouted from behind the door. "These hooks are about as useful as two left shoes!"

She began to bang pots and pans around, making enough racket to wake the dead. Eliza grabbed the doorknob on the opposite door and shoved it open.

"Go! Go now!" she whispered to her friends.

The two girls raced past her, now holding each other's hands. Eliza stepped out after them, closing the door as quietly as she could before running blindly into the night. Alice extinguished her candle, but the moon was bright and Eliza was able to see her friends' shadows as they made for the elm tree. She ran after them, ducking under the lowest branches just in their wake.

"Oh my goodness!" Eliza exclaimed, hand to her heart. "I was sure she was going to catch us."

"I think I'm going to faint," Alice said, clinging to a branch.

"We made it," Catherine said, breathless. "That's all that matters. But where's Theresa?"

"Right here." Theresa stepped out from behind the thick trunk of the tree, dressed head to toe in black, holding a candle in front of her face. Alice screamed, and Eliza slapped her hand over the girl's mouth.

"Theresa!" Catherine scolded, hand to her forehead. "Are you trying to scare us to death?"

Theresa narrowed her eyes. "You're late." Then she blew out her candle, plunging the girls into darkness.

TREASURE HUNT

"I don't like this. I don't like this," Alice repeated, holding on to Eliza's arm.

Cicadas hummed in the grass. A cloud passed over the moon, casting jagged shadows over the Billings campus. And as the four girls approached McKinley Hall—Theresa leading the way, of course—a stiff wind whipped through the building's eaves, creating an unsettling howl.

Eliza gripped Alice right back and could only hope the girl thought she was trying to be comforting. "It's all right, Alice. Look how well we're doing," she said. "We've already solved two clues. There are only two more to go."

"But are you sure that last rhyme was intended to lead us here?" Alice whispered. "It could have meant Prescott."

"No," Catherine replied from behind them. "It said 'due west.' McKinley is directly west of the old oak."

Up ahead, Theresa pressed her back against the side of the steep stairway leading up to the front door to McKinley. She motioned for the other girls to follow her. Catherine glanced over her shoulder as if she'd heard something, and for a moment Eliza stopped breathing, but Catherine said nothing and they all ducked down together.

"Eliza. The map," Theresa whispered.

Eliza bit her tongue as she unfolded the map and held it in front of them. Theresa's bossy manner was beginning to grate on her very last nerve. She ran her finger over the page until she found the McKinley building.

"'At my base a malignant weed keeps away the flowering seed,'" Eliza read. "'Find the stone marked by decay, its etching sends you on your way.'"

"Malignant weed?" Alice said, shivering. "I don't like the sound of that."

"It probably just means poison ivy," Catherine said. "Theresa, remember last year when Glenda Pearson fell off her bicycle at the back of McKinley and ended up with that awful case of poison ivy?"

"That's right! Ugh. That awful sycophant deserved it," Theresa said, rolling her eyes.

"Who's Glenda Pearson?" Eliza asked.

"She's in my year," Alice replied, scrunching her nose. "I try to find something to like in everyone, but even I can't find anything to like in her. She's already tattled on me three times in class for doodling in my notebook."

"Well, at least she's good for something. Thank you, Glenda, for falling in the poison ivy!" Catherine said with a laugh. "Come. Let's go around back."

The girls pushed themselves to their feet and crept around the base of the building. Theresa held the lamp low at the back of the structure, but the ground around it was bare. There wasn't a weed to be found.

"They must have torn it all out," Catherine whispered.

"All the better for us," Theresa said. "I was going to make one of you girls walk through it to find this decaying stone."

"Why not you?" Eliza demanded.

"I'm highly allergic," Theresa snapped in reply, as if Eliza shouldn't have even asked. "If I get poison ivy, I could die. Do you want me to die, Eliza?"

Maybe, Eliza thought, then immediately admonished herself. She didn't want anyone to die. Not really. But she wouldn't have minded seeing Theresa covered in poison ivy welts, scratching her skin like mad.

"There!" Catherine gasped. "That stone near the drain. It's far more decayed than the others."

Eliza dropped to her knees to get a better look, swiping away some of the grime from the rotted brick. Her fingertips grazed several indentations. They felt like numbers or letters, but she couldn't quite make them out. Overhead, the wind whistled again, and for a moment all four girls froze. When the noise finally died down, Eliza spoke again. "Theresa! The candle!"

"Well, look who's suddenly issuing demands," Theresa said, pulling a matchbook from her pocket and lighting the candle.

Eliza rolled her eyes, then held the candle right up against the brick wall of the building. Squinting, she could just make out an uppercase E. She used her fingernail to scratch the dirt out of the next few numbers and letters, then leaned back to read what she'd found.

"E 150 p. N 100 p.," Eliza read. "What could that possibly mean?"

Catherine swung around and looked back in the direction from which they had come. "East and north! The E and the N probably mean *east* and *north*."

"You're right! And the numbers must be paces. That's what the p stands for," Eliza said, feeling an exhilarating tingle as the answer dawned on her. "It means we are to walk one hundred fifty paces to the east, then one hundred paces to the north."

"It can't be," Theresa said. "Everyone's paces are different. What kind of direction is that?"

Clenching her jaw in frustration, Eliza was about to protest. But then, suddenly, she heard a window slamming, and the sound obliterated every thought in her mind. Someone had seen them. Someone was coming. She looked up into the terrified eyes of her friends and could think of only one word.

"Run!"

GOD'S HOUSE

Eliza pumped her arms as she ran. Her breath was so loud that, combined with the ridiculous pounding of her heart, she could hear nothing else. As she raced up the steep hill, the locket bounced against her chest. All she could think about was making it to the tree line through which her friends had just disappeared. She felt that if she could only get there, somehow she would be safe.

Pressing her lips together against a panicked sob, Eliza hurtled herself into the woods and right into Catherine's waiting arms.

"It's okay," Catherine said in her ear as Eliza's chest heaved. "It's okay. No one's there."

Alice, meanwhile, leaned back against a tree trunk, sobbing softly. Clearly she had reached her limit.

"No one's there?" Eliza repeated, relief flooding through her. She turned around to look back toward McKinley. The moonlight bathed the entire campus in a white glow, and she could see now that the campus was deserted. "Thank God," she said, leaning into Catherine's side. "I thought we were done for."

"So you doused us in darkness?" Theresa demanded, ripping the candle out of Eliza's hand. "That was my last match."

"I didn't want us to be seen!" Eliza replied, stung.

"And now *we* can't see anything," Theresa shot back.

"I did what I thought I had to do, Theresa!" Eliza half whispered, half shouted. "Why are you the one who always decides what is right and what is wrong?"

"Girls," Catherine said.

"I get to decide because I know best," Theresa replied.

Eliza blinked. She couldn't be serious. "And who decided that you know better than everyone else?"

"Girls!" Catherine shouted.

"What?" they both demanded, whipping around to face her.

"I just thought you might want to know we just ran one hundred and fifty paces east," Catherine said with a smile. "Approximately, of course."

Eliza's jaw dropped. "How do you know that?"

"I counted while I was running," Catherine said. "Just in case."

Theresa and Eliza looked at each other, for a moment united in their awe. "Well, then," Theresa said. "I suppose we should walk one hundred paces north and see where that gets us."

"We're still doing this?" Alice wailed.

"Oh, hush," Theresa told her. "Follow me."

She counted the paces quietly as they made their way along a makeshift path through the woods. Eliza breathed in and out slowly, trying to regain her normal pattern after the terror of her run. She couldn't help wondering who had closed that window back at McKinley. Whoever it was, what was the person doing there so late at night? And if he or she had seen Eliza and her friends, why not come after them?

"That's fifty," Theresa said as they came to the edge of the woods.

"Oh, no," Alice intoned.

Eliza joined the other three girls on the grass just beyond the tree line and stared up at the stark white façade of the Billings Chapel.

"Another fifty paces will take us right to the door of the chapel," Catherine stated.

"This isn't happening," Alice whined, leaning into Eliza's side.

The wind kicked up, swirling around the four girls and lifting their skirts. Eliza clung to the map with one hand and held her hat to her head with the other.

"What does it say after that?" Theresa asked. "Once we walk the hundred paces north, where do we go next?"

Eliza looked at the map but couldn't make it out in the darkness. "I can't tell," she admitted. "The moon is strong, but not strong enough to make it out."

"Perhaps if we still had the light . . . ," Theresa said sarcastically.

"Theresa, please," Catherine said.

Theresa clucked her tongue but said no more.

Catherine took a step forward and looked up at the spire of the chapel. "Perhaps there are matches inside."

"Then let's go inside," Theresa said, starting ahead.

Alice grabbed her arm. "No! You can't!" she pleaded. "That's a sacred space! You can't just traipse through there alone in the dead of night!"

Theresa glared down at Alice's hand until the girl finally released her. "Control yourself, Alice Ainsworth," she said, her tone clipped and impatient. "It's just a building."

Alice's skin was so pale, Eliza feared her friend might faint. She forgot about her hat and reached around Alice's slim waist, holding on to the girl in case she crumbled. The proximity to another warm body helped calm Eliza's own nerves a bit.

"It's not just a building," Alice said, her voice low and firm. "It's the house of God."

Theresa rolled her eyes. "Well, my pastor is always saying that we're welcome in God's house anytime."

And with that, she turned on her heel and walked purposefully toward the chapel, hitching up the skirt of her black dress and taking the lantern with her. Catherine stepped closer to Eliza, but other than that, none of the remaining three girls moved. Alice let out a quiet wail as Theresa shoved open the gleaming, arched door. The motion produced a loud, ominous creak that could just be heard over the whistling winds.

"Girls! Where's your sense of adventure?" Theresa shouted from the open doorway. Then she disappeared inside, letting the heavy door slam behind her.

An owl hooted nearby, and Alice mewed pitifully. But Eliza swallowed back her fear. "I'm going in," she said, stepping away from the others. She didn't want Theresa to think she was afraid.

"No! Eliza!" Alice attempted to cling to her, but Eliza shook off her grasping fingers.

"Would you rather leave Theresa in there alone?" Eliza asked, the wind tugging her hair out from under her hat.

Alice hugged herself, her bottom lip trembling. Eliza looked to Catherine, pleading with her eyes.

"She's right, Alice," Catherine said. She took Eliza's arm and started for the chapel.

"So now you're leaving me out here alone?" Alice wailed.

"Come with us!" Eliza hissed. Alice clasped and unclasped her hands, looking from the chapel back toward campus—gauging, it seemed, whether going inside with her friends or walking back alone was the worse of the two evils. The very idea of Alice trying to get back to Crenshaw House by herself without fainting or going into hysterics seemed impossible.

"Wait here," Eliza said to Catherine.

The wind was growing fierce now, forcing tears from her eyes as she hastened back toward Alice. "Look at me, Alice," Eliza demanded, taking her friend's hands. The wind tore through the trees around them, creating a vortex of green and brown leaves.

Alice took in a shaky breath, glancing about warily as a gust pushed her forward.

"If you come inside with us, I promise to not let anything bad happen to you," Eliza said.

"But . . . how can you promise that?" Alice asked, her bottom lip quivering.

"Because I'm your friend and I would never put you in harm's way." Eliza had to shout now to be heard over the whistling wind. "I would never put anyone I loved in harm's way."

Alice's expression softened slightly, the creases of anxiety disappearing from her forehead. She looked at the chapel again uncertainly. The wind shoved her forward once more, and she staggered into Eliza. Eliza wrapped her arms around the girl, holding her steady.

"Come along. Theresa is waiting for us," Eliza said.

She breathed a sigh of relief when Alice's feet finally started moving. They rejoined Catherine, and the three of them walked with the wind at their backs. Eliza shoved open the door to the chapel, and together they tumbled inside.

"What took you so long?" Theresa asked.

Standing at the center of the aisle, between the two rows of polished oak pews, and framed by the gorgeous stained glass windows above the pulpit, Theresa held two lit candles that she had no doubt taken from the wall sconces.

"Bring the map here," she instructed.

Eliza did. Theresa handed the candles to Catherine, then bent toward Eliza so she too could look over the map. But there was no text left to read, just simple drawings: arrows and doors and a staircase.

"The arrows seem to be pointing down the aisle and then to the left side of the chapel, where there is to be a door," Eliza said. "And behind the door, some sort of square room."

"Then let's go," Theresa said, starting in that direction.

Eliza folded the map and followed. The chapel was all creaks and wails on such a windy night. Catherine and Alice brought up the rear, and Eliza could hear Catherine whispering soothing reassurances to Alice as they moved.

Through an arched doorway at the front of the chapel and down a short hall, Theresa and Eliza came to a solid, six-panel door.

"Shall we?" Theresa asked, shadows dancing across her face.

Before Eliza could speak, Theresa had tried the brass knob, and the door swung open to reveal a small, square office. Just like in the drawing.

"Huh. No ghosts or goblins or mummies," Theresa joked. "I'm almost disappointed."

Alice let out a groan as Theresa and Eliza stepped over the threshold into the chamber. The walls were a modest white, and oak beams lined the ceiling. At the center of the room was a plain wooden desk, and bookcases lined all four walls. A huge cross, whittled out of what appeared to be maple, hung on the wall behind the desk.

"This is the chaplain's office," Alice whispered from the doorway. "We shouldn't be trespassing."

"Oh, Alice, hush," Theresa said, walking behind the desk. "He'll never even know we were here."

"But God will know," Alice said.

Eliza and Theresa looked at each other and for some reason, even though Eliza knew that what they were doing could be considered blasphemy, and even though she was irritated with Theresa beyond all measure, all she wanted to do was laugh.

It's just my nerves, Eliza told herself. *I'm not a bad Christian for being here. If God didn't want me to be an adventurer, he wouldn't have built me this way.*

"I see no other way out," Theresa said, turning in place.

Catherine brought the lamp over and lit it from a candle, and Eliza unfurled the map once more. "It doesn't make sense," Eliza said. "There's a drawing of a set of stairs on the west wall of the office."

All three girls turned around to face the west wall and were met with an imposing bookcase full of Bibles and other religious works. Had they come all this way for nothing? Had it indeed been nothing but a grand hoax?

"Let's get out of here," Alice whined. "Please. Let's just go."

Eliza moved around to the side of the bookcase and ran her hand along the corner between case and wall. Her fingertips found something metallic and grooved.

"Girls, you'll never believe what I've just found," she said. Her mouth was dry as she tried to swallow.

Catherine peeked around the bookcase, shining the lantern at the wall. Sure enough, three huge brass hinges were affixed to the bookcase and the wall.

"Does it open?" Theresa asked breathlessly.

"Let's see!" Eliza replied.

Catherine placed the lantern on the desk, and the three of them tugged at the opposite side of the bookcase. When Eliza first felt it give, she let out a gasp of surprise. Slowly the bookcase swung free, revealing a small white door set into the wall. Sitting in its keyhole was a large brass key, with a purple ribbon dangling from it.

FULL CIRCLE

"This is just like *Journey to the Center of the Earth*," Eliza said breathily, tingling from head to toe. She instantly thought of Harrison and wished for a brief moment that he could see her right then. But then she realized he'd be seeing Theresa, too, and she quickly banished him from her thoughts.

As Theresa went to open the door, Alice let out another pained wail and leaned against the doorway between the office and the chapel.

"Are you sure about this?" Catherine asked, her eyes concerned.

"We can't stop now," Theresa said, as though it was the most obvious argument in the world.

"She's right," Eliza confirmed. "We're so close."

"Wait," Catherine said. Both Theresa and Eliza looked at her, exasperated. "I don't mean to be the dull one," Catherine continued. "I just want to make sure we're not doing something we're going to regret."

Theresa reached for Catherine's hand. "I don't mean to offend you, Catherine, but if you live your entire life wondering what you're going to regret later, you'll never truly live it."

Eliza blinked, surprised to agree so wholeheartedly with Theresa's words. Catherine appeared taken aback as well. She knit her brow for a moment and then nodded, her chin set with determination.

"All right, then," she said firmly. "No regrets."

"Let me get another candle," Eliza said. She turned and removed one from a sconce on the wall, then held the wick against Theresa's flame to light it. "All right," she said with her face newly aglow. "Go ahead."

Theresa reached out and turned the key. It let out a reverberating click that brought forth another wail from Alice. Theresa tried the knob, and the door swung open easily, soundlessly. Cold air rushed up from the dank depths below, taking the breath right out of Eliza's lungs. Eliza held her candle aloft, and Theresa and Catherine followed suit.

"What is it?" Alice whined tremulously. "What did you find?"

"It's a staircase," Eliza replied. "Just like the map said."

"A staircase?" Alice managed to pry herself away from the door and join the others. She peered down into the darkness. The winding staircase disappeared around a bend after only five steps. "No," she said. "No, no, no. You can't be thinking of going down there. All you're going to find down there is death and damnation, you realize that, don't you? That staircase was not meant to be found!"

Eliza clenched her teeth. "Let's go."

She took the first step onto the top stair, which moaned beneath her weight. Catherine stayed close behind her and Theresa brought up the rear as they continued down the winding stairs. All three flames seemed to wax and wane as they went, disorienting Eliza. Each time the light started to dim, she clutched Catherine more tightly, terrified of falling.

Then, from out of the darkness, a voice whispered in Eliza's ear.

"Turn back."

Eliza stumbled. Catherine bumped into her from behind. Theresa swore under her breath.

"Eliza! You need to warn us if you're going to do that!" Theresa admonished.

"Did you hear that?" Eliza said, her breath ragged.

"Hear what?" Catherine asked, her voice thin and high.

Eliza looked past her at Theresa, who shook her head slightly as if she thought Eliza was going insane.

Perhaps I am *going insane,* Eliza thought tremulously. *Hearing voices that aren't there.*

"It was nothing. Probably just an odd creak," Eliza told them, with more confidence than she felt.

"I can't see you anymore!" Alice cried out from above. "Are you still there?"

"We're fine, Alice!" Catherine shouted back. "Calm down!"

"I can't calm down! What if you don't come back?" Alice whined.

"We're coming back," Theresa said through her teeth. "Now kindly shut up!"

Alice let out a whimper but said nothing more. Seconds later the girls reached the bottom of the stairs.

Eliza moved aside, her shoes scratching across the floor as if it was covered in sand or grime. Theresa and Catherine joined her, holding out their candles and the lantern in front of them. With a deep breath, Eliza realized that there was nothing to be afraid of in the basement room. No devils or demons or mummies or ghosts. It was simply a small, circular room with no furniture save for a large wood trunk at its center.

Slowly Theresa walked around the trunk. After a moment, Catherine and Eliza followed. All three of them crouched in front of it, tucking their skirts around their knees. The trunk was made of a plain but sturdy wood. Its latch was simple and gold, and etched into the panel just above the latch was the intertwining circle symbol now so familiar to Eliza. She touched the locket around her neck, then reached out and traced the symbol on the trunk with her fingertips. Despite the cool air of the chamber, the wood felt warm to the touch. There was no lock.

"Whatever we find inside, it belongs to all four of us," Eliza said, looking at her friends.

"We're not including Alice," Theresa said. "She's done nothing but complain and protest."

Eliza opened her mouth to retort, but Catherine stopped her with a hand to her arm. "She came inside with us even against her better judgment, which was very brave," Catherine said. "This trunk belongs to her, too."

Theresa rolled her eyes. "Fine."

Together, the three girls lifted the heavy lid of the trunk. It opened and fell back from their hands, slamming against the bottom half so loudly, that all three jumped. Holding her breath, Eliza peered inside.

"It's nothing but a pile of old books!" Theresa blurted.

Intrigued, Eliza reached in and took out the first hardcover tome. *"The Mystical Realm,"* she read from the spine.

Catherine put her candle aside and grabbed another. *"The Lunar Seasons,"* she read, her eyes bright with excitement.

Theresa removed the third. *"Rites, Sabbats, and Festivals."*

"I've never seen books like these," Eliza said, flipping through pages of diagrams and illustrations. Many of them had notes handwritten in the margins—arrows and measurements and sketches of planetary alignments. Quickly the girls removed each and every volume from the trunk, laying them in piles around their knees. Finally, Catherine reached inside and pulled out a heavy book that was bound in gray linen. When she opened the cover, Eliza saw that someone had drawn the same circular symbol on the inside. Catherine reached over and flipped to a random page. There was a list of ingredients down the center, followed by two paragraphs of directions.

"It's a recipe book," Theresa said, disappointed.

Catherine placed her palm reverently against the page, her middle finger just grazing the letters of the recipe's title. She looked up at the others with an excited expression in her eyes.

"'Potion for a Broken Heart,'" she read.

"Potion?" Eliza echoed, her brow furrowing.

"What does that mean?" Theresa asked.

"It means that this is not a recipe book," Catherine replied. "It's a book of spells."

CAMARADERIE

"Here's one I'd like to try," Theresa whispered, bending over the book that sat across the girls' laps in the center of Catherine's bed. "'The Swelling Tongue.' It says it will cause the tongue to expand, filling the mouth of any boy who tries to get fresh."

Eliza and Catherine giggled. "You wouldn't, really," Catherine said, her eyes dancing in the candlelight.

"Well, maybe with some boys," Theresa said. "But I'd never have to cast it on Harrison. He's a gentleman."

Eliza's happiness melted at the mention of Harrison, and her eyes flicked to the book he'd sent her earlier that evening. For a brief moment, she found herself mulling his intentions. But just as quickly, she put him out of her mind. What she was doing right now was far more interesting than anything a boy could offer.

The three girls were gathered closely together on Catherine's mattress, their backs against the wall, legs crossed in front of them.

Catherine held the book open over her lap, but it was so large that the front cover rested on Theresa's thigh and the back cover on Eliza's. The one candle they had lit sat on Catherine's desktop, casting shadows that shifted across the weathered pages.

"How old do you think it is?" Eliza asked, fingering the thick parchment as she turned the page.

"Older than us," Catherine said. "Probably even older than our parents."

"Look, a disorientation spell!" Eliza said, scanning the page closest to her.

"And on this side is a forgetfulness spell," Theresa put in. "Imagine what we could do with these. We could make old Britton forget all about giving us exams!"

Catherine laughed. "I'm not sure about that. You have to be careful with magic. The natural balance of things always has to be maintained."

Eliza and Theresa both stared at her.

Catherine blushed and looked down at the page, turning to the next. "I just heard that somewhere, I think."

Eliza's eyes narrowed. She had a feeling there was more to what Catherine had said than she was letting on.

"But what does it mean?" Theresa asked. "If we were to make Miss Britton forget to give us a literature exam, how would the natural balance, as you call it, be affected?"

"I'm not sure. It's just . . . I think what it means is, there are consequences to magic," Catherine replied, the color in her cheeks deepening. "For example, perhaps if Miss Britton forgot to give us an exam in literature, we would then be given an extra one in French. Something like that."

"Ugh. Then forget I said anything," Theresa said, sticking her tongue between her teeth. "I'd rather take one literature exam than two French."

"Agreed," Eliza and Catherine said in unison.

The three girls laughed, and Eliza sat back again, pulling her side of the book back onto her thigh. For the first time, she was feeling a real camaraderie with Theresa.

"Oh, look, Eliza. Here's one to brighten dull skin. Perhaps you should copy that one down," Theresa said, arching an eyebrow.

And just like that, any positive feelings Eliza had toward Theresa vanished.

"Thank you, Theresa. How very thoughtful. Maybe there's one in here for curing a permanently bad attitude," Eliza shot back.

Theresa glowered and opened her mouth to respond, but Catherine placed her hands on their wrists.

"Girls, please. I can't abide my two good friends fighting all the time," she said calmly. "No more insults."

Eliza gritted her teeth as she looked at Theresa. "Fine," she said.

"No more insults," Theresa agreed.

Catherine nodded and turned the page. "Thank you."

Eliza resolved to keep her promise and say nothing else against Theresa. At least, not tonight. But she knew that she would never understand how any rational person—Harrison and Catherine included—could ever tolerate Theresa Billings, much less love her.

THE BILLINGS LITERARY SOCIETY

The low-ceilinged Billings School library was as charmless inside as it looked from the outside. It gave the impression that it had been built off to the side of McKinley Hall as an afterthought, as if no one had imagined in the early days that a girls' school might be in need of an actual book collection. Although the library was architecturally bland and almost windowless, Eliza still managed to love it.

As she and Catherine slid into chairs beside Alice at one of the small wooden tables on Wednesday afternoon, she couldn't help but breathe in the room's musty, papery scent. Then Theresa dropped the heavy tomes from the chapel basement in the center of the table, chasing away the warm and cozy feeling.

"I cannot believe you brought those here," Alice whispered, glancing derisively at the ancient volumes. "Not only are those books an abomination against God, but if the headmistress catches you with them, you'll surely be expelled."

Alice stood up, turned her back on the other three girls, and sat down at the next table. She opened her history book, tugged her kid gloves from her fingers, and directed her attention to the page before her.

"How many times do I have to tell you, I can't be expelled?" Theresa hissed, leaning toward Alice's table to be closer to her ear. "Besides, these are your books as well."

"They are *not* my books." Alice sniffed. "I want nothing to do with them." She yanked her chair so close to her table, Eliza was sure she would crush her ribcage.

"Come on, Alice. It's all in good fun," Eliza said, removing her favorite hat—the blue one with white ribbon trim and a slight brim. She glanced surreptitiously around the library to make sure no one was listening in. A pair of girls sat nearby, taking notes from etiquette books. Clarissa was camped at a corner table, surrounded by huge books, chewing on the end of one of her golden braids as she concentrated. The elderly librarian was shelving books on the other side of the small room, seemingly unaware that there were any students present at all.

"Perhaps these books were hidden for a reason," Alice said. "Perhaps that box was buried because it was never meant to be found."

Theresa opened her mouth to speak, but Catherine interrupted. "Or maybe they were simply waiting for the right person to find them," she said, her eyes sparkling.

Eliza regarded her friend. Careful Catherine seemed quite ready to throw caution to the wind all of a sudden.

"I don't know about what's meant to be," Theresa said, opening to a page she had marked in one of the books. "All I know is, this whole thing sounds as though it could be the perfect antidote to this boring place."

"Haven't you people read the Bible?" Alice hissed under her breath from the next table. "'Thou shalt not suffer a witch to live?' Do you even realize what that means?"

"It's not as if we're going to be putting anyone under spells to do evil," Theresa whispered back. "It's like Eliza said: I'd just like to have a bit of fun."

"From what I've read, hell is no fun at all," Alice replied, looking at Theresa over her shoulder.

Theresa leveled her with a glare. "What about a potion to make a boy fall in love with you?" she asked, opening to another page and letting the book cover smack into the table's surface as a sort of exclamation point. "Does that sound like fun?"

Eliza and Catherine looked at Alice. Alice looked at the book. She bit her lip, twiddling her pen between her fingers. Then, abruptly, she lifted her chair, turned it around, and jostled in between Catherine and Eliza.

"Fine. Tell me more," Alice said.

Theresa grinned. Eliza hid a laugh behind her hand.

"It says here that if we can gather eleven strong women, we'll be able to summon the power of Mother Earth," Theresa said, running her finger across an open page. "That means we can cast spells, concoct potions. Basically, we'll have the power to do anything we want."

"Within reason, of course," Catherine said.

"Of course. Within reason," Theresa echoed, her gaze still focused on the books.

"I'm serious, Theresa," Catherine said, leaning toward the table. "Witchcraft is not something one should trifle with or use for selfish purposes."

"Look who's an expert all of a sudden," Theresa said snidely.

"It still feels wrong," Alice said, shaking her head, her auburn ringlets bouncing against her cheeks.

"Think of it as a club," Eliza suggested. "It's just a club of girls, getting together to read some strange books."

A thrill of excitement shot through Eliza's chest. A literary club actually sounded like a fantastic idea to her—one where real books were read, not just spell books. It would give the friends time to talk about things they might not otherwise have the opportunity to talk about, like books, politics, and the world at large. Things the properly demure ladies of Billings were normally forbidden to even think of.

Slowly, a new mission started to form in Eliza's mind, along with a list of qualities all members of the club should strive to possess: loyalty, intelligence, progressive thinking, industry, eloquence, and, without question, the ability to speak one's own mind.

"All right, then. A club sounds harmless enough," Alice said, looking around at the other girls. "Who would we invite?"

"We'll need seven more to complete the circle," Catherine said. "A coven needs eleven people."

"A coven?" Alice asked in an alarmed tone.

Catherine rolled her eyes. "A club, I mean."

From her bag, Eliza drew the empty journal her mother had given her and placed it on the table.

"I'll take notes," she said.

Alice reached around to her own bag for her fountain pen and then shook it to bring the ink into the point. As Eliza took the pen from Alice, she had to allow herself a private smile. Imagine what her mother would think if she knew what use her book was being put to.

Slowly, deliberately, Eliza wrote down the names of the four girls present: Elizabeth Williams, Catherine White, Theresa Billings, and Alice Ainsworth.

"All right. Who else, do you think?" she asked, looking up.

"Jane Barton, of course. She would never let it go if she weren't included," Theresa answered, leaning forward and resting her elbows on the table. "And Viola and Beatrice Hirsch."

"Isn't Bia a bit young?" Catherine asked.

"She's no younger than me," Alice pointed out.

"But she *seems* younger," Eliza said, thinking of the way Bia was always following Viola around, asking about her opinions.

"Yes, but Viola is one of my closest friends. She must be invited, and Bia must do anything Viola does," Theresa said flatly. "Besides, Bia can be quite sweet when she wants to be."

"All right, then. That's seven. We'll need four more," Eliza said, looking up from the page.

"Lavender," Catherine said, before Theresa could answer.

"Ugh! Lavender's awful," Theresa groused, crossing her arms over her chest. "She's so awkward and bland."

"But she's a good person to have on your side," Catherine replied. "Did you see the way she moved to protect us that night when Miss Almay caught us? She seems the type to lay down her life for her friends."

Eliza's heart thumped at the sentiment.

"Why are we talking about death?" Alice asked.

"Yes. Let's hope our club doesn't come to that," Eliza added. She reached up to her neck and rubbed the gold locket between her finger and thumb.

"All I'm saying is that I think she's loyal," Catherine replied in a soothing tone. "I'd like to invite her."

"I agree," Alice said. "She might not be my sort of person, but she's nice enough. Besides, she's my roommate, and I don't want to have to sneak around keeping secrets from her."

"All right, then," Eliza replied, writing down Lavender's name. "I nominate Marilyn DeMeers. She's worldly."

"Fine, but she'll have to leave that yippy dog of hers at home. And Marilyn won't come without Genevieve, so write her down too," Theresa directed, looking down her nose at the page. "How many is that?" she asked.

"Ten. We need one more," Catherine replied.

"What about Clarissa Pommer?" Eliza whispered, glancing sideways at Clarissa from across the room.

"Yes! Clarissa would be perfect," Catherine agreed.

Theresa wrinkled her nose in Clarissa's direction.

"But she's so . . . uppity," Theresa protested. "Who wants to be around someone who's not only smart but knows it and never stops telling you about it?"

"But that's just the thing about her," Eliza said, glancing at Clarissa. "She's smart. If we were ever to get into any trouble, it might be a blessing to have a quick thinker on our side."

"I think plenty quickly," Theresa replied.

"Not quickly enough to get us out of our punishments and back into the dance," Alice grumbled, sitting back in her chair.

Theresa shot her a withering glance.

"Besides, Clarissa has always been willing to cover for you," Catherine said. "Like the other night when we snuck out."

"Yes, but that's just because I pay her," Theresa muttered with a huff, crossing her arms atop the table.

"You do?" all three girls asked, speaking as one. Clarissa finally looked up, but only long enough to shush them.

Theresa tilted her head and lowered her voice even further. "All right, fine. Clarissa it is."

Eliza wrote down Clarissa's name, then turned the book around so the others could see it.

"It looks lonely," Alice said, sticking her bottom lip out slightly.

"She's right. It needs some kind of title," Catherine agreed, sliding her hand around the back of her neck to knead her muscles.

"Well, I can't exactly write 'Our Coven' across the top," Eliza whispered, placing the book down again and casting a look toward the librarian. "Imagine the inquiry if we misplaced it and one of the instructors found it."

"It's not a coven; it's a club," Alice said stubbornly.

"Oh, I've got it!" Eliza exclaimed. "The Billings Literary Society!"

Theresa snorted, sitting back hard in her chair. "Are *all* the Williamses bookworms?"

Eliza's face flushed hot. "What do you mean?"

"Your sister. The fabulous May," Theresa said, rolling her eyes.

Eliza's hand dropped down on the table with a *bang*. "What exactly is your quarrel with my sister?"

Theresa exchanged a glance with Catherine, whose cheeks flushed pink. "I have no quarrel with your sister," she said with a sniff. "She got exactly what she wanted, and I got exactly what I wanted . . . eventually."

"What does that mean?" Eliza demanded. "What did you both want?"

"Never mind that," Theresa said through her teeth. "What I was *trying* to say was that her first year here, May actually wanted to form some kind of novel-reading club. I wasn't a student here yet, obviously, but I overheard my parents and Miss Almay talking about it. My mother was in favor of it, but Miss Almay called it frivolous, and her word is law when it comes to student organizations."

Eliza's heart pounded shallowly in her chest. In all her letters, May had never mentioned a book club. She felt a sudden rush of pride, followed by a huge chasm of disappointment on her sister's behalf. Forming a club of that sort was so like the old May. If she had been so adamant about such things when she'd first come to Billings, how had she returned home so changed?

"The Billings Literary Society it is," Eliza said resolutely, writing the words in big, bold letters across the top of the page. "Miss Almay might not like it, but if she ever hears about it, we can defend ourselves by saying we're simply reading the great works in order to make our conversation more interesting for the boys."

"She'll love that," Alice said with a giggle.

"If only she knew what we're really reading," Catherine said, grinning as she opened the book of spells.

All four of the girls laughed then, earning another resounding *shhh* from Clarissa and a few of the other students in the room, as well as a stern glance from the librarian—which only made them laugh all the louder.

SILLY FAINTING FEMALE

That Saturday morning, Eliza and Catherine set out to the stationers in town, with Mrs. Hodge in tow as their chaperone, following behind at a respectful distance. Though they had told Mrs. Hodge they wanted letterhead on which to write their families, the stationery would in fact serve as invitations to the first official meeting of the Billings Literary Society.

"I love this time of year," Eliza said dreamily, tipping her face toward the sun and breathing in the fresh autumn air. For the first time since the term had begun, the awful humidity and heat had fallen away, leaving behind a pleasantly warm, clear day and a cool breeze.

"I could have sworn you'd told me summer was your favorite season," Catherine teased, swinging her small silk handbag by its cord as they turned up Main Street. "Actually, I believe the words you used were 'I want to die every year when summer turns to fall.'"

"I did say that, didn't I?" Eliza said, kicking a pebble with her sensible, brown walking shoes—her favorites of all she owned, for their comfort. "But there is something about those few days when you can feel summer melting into fall. There's a feeling of . . ."

"Possibility," Catherine finished.

Eliza looked at her and grinned. "Yes. That's it. Possibility."

Catherine nodded as she looked around at the leaves rustling in the trees. "Seasons don't change so drastically in Georgia. Every year when I arrive at Billings, all I can think about is that first snow."

Eliza's eyes widened. "There's no snow in Georgia?"

"No." Catherine laughed, shaking her head. "Not in southern Georgia, at least."

The girls stepped up onto the brand-new plank sidewalk together, heading toward the Easton Police Station and its austere brick façade. Catherine glanced back at their chaperone, then took Eliza's arm, leaning closer to her.

"There's something I wish to tell you, and I hope you will not judge me," she said quietly.

"I would never judge another without hearing all the facts," she assured her friend.

A pair of gentlemen tipped their hats to the girls as they strolled by. Eliza pretended not to notice their attentions.

"The reason I knew right away what the book of spells was . . . Well . . . my mother . . . She . . ."

Catherine hesitated, bringing a gloved hand to her face for a moment.

"Is your mother a witch?" Eliza gasped. The moment the words left her lips, she realized just how judgmental they sounded. She cleared her throat and ignored her pulse, which was now fluttering ferociously in her wrists. "I'm sorry. You were saying?"

Catherine paused in front of one of the two lampposts outside the police station. She glanced back at Mrs. Hodge again. Seeing them stop, the maid took the opportunity to rest on the bench in front of the Easton Feed Store.

"My mother has always been obsessed with youth and beauty," Catherine said, her blue eyes downcast. "She has spent much of her life in search of what you might call the fountain of youth. That one salve or elixir or . . . or potion that might keep her young."

"I see," Eliza said, even though she didn't quite see at all.

"This quest of hers has taken her to some . . . unsavory places," Catherine continued. "Including to the dens of some fairly notorious witches."

"I see," Eliza repeated. Suddenly her heart was in her throat. Until that moment, she had never truly considered the notion that magic was actually real. Her head felt light as she imagined the possibilities of such a thing . . . and the dangers.

"She brought me along on some of these visits, and I must say . . . I thought the whole practice was fascinating," Catherine said, speaking more quickly and freely now, as if she felt the hard part was over. "The things these women can do, the magics they're capable of producing . . . It's amazing."

Eliza glanced at Mrs. Hodge. She was eyeing the two girls

suspiciously. Eliza quickly looked away. "These potions, these spells in the books . . . It's all real?" she whispered.

"Oh, yes," Catherine said matter-of-factly. "I've seen things you would scarcely believe."

Eliza suddenly found she had to concentrate to breathe. Unbidden, the names of some of the spells flashed through her mind: the Love Spell, the Spell of Confusion, the Helen of Troy Spell, which made any girl irresistible to all men for the three nights of the full moon. Could these spells really work? And if they could, what did that mean for her . . . for Harrison . . . for Theresa? Could she ever use one to—

No, the answer came immediately. *Don't even think it, Eliza.*

"Eliza? Are you all right?" Catherine asked.

"I'm not sure. Is it very hot out?" Eliza asked. She touched her gloved fingertips to her forehead, and they came away damp. Breathless, she leaned back against the lamppost, fighting for focus.

"There's nothing to be afraid of, Eliza," Catherine said, reaching for her wrist. "Witchcraft is a wonderful thing, as long as it's used for good. And I don't think any of us intends to use it otherwise."

Mrs. Hodge appeared over Catherine's right shoulder, her expression one of sheer alarm. "Miss Williams! Are you unwell?" she asked.

"I think I need some . . . some water," Eliza managed.

Mrs. Hodge looked over her shoulder at the police station. "Stay here. Miss White, try to keep her cool. I'll be right back."

Then she turned, lifted her skirts, and scurried up the steps faster than Eliza would have thought possible.

"I'm so sorry, Eliza," Catherine said, holding on to her wrist with one hand and fanning Eliza's face with the other. "I didn't mean to upset you."

Eliza took several more deep breaths, but couldn't seem to calm her racing heart. Suddenly, her vision slipped out of focus.

"Eliza? Eliza!"

A pair of strong arms caught her as she went down. Eliza's eyes fluttered open, and she found herself nestled in the firm grasp of Harrison Knox.

She looked directly into his dark blue eyes and felt faint all over again.

"Miss Williams! Are you all right?" he asked.

Somehow Eliza found the strength to straighten up. She pressed her palm into the cool lamppost behind her again and cleared her throat. Before long, her mind felt solid once more and she was able to collect her thoughts. She looked up at Harrison and saw that Jonathan was with him as well, hovering with Catherine just over Harrison's shoulder with a look of pure concern.

"Here. Come sit on the stairs," Jonathan said, gesturing at the stone steps of the station.

"No. No, thank you. I'm fine," Eliza replied, cursing herself silently for being so feeble.

"Are you sure you're all right?" Harrison asked, taking her hand and looking deeply into her eyes, as if he was trying to see inside her body for himself and make sure all was well.

The tenderness and concern in that glance made Eliza want to lean into him and beg him to take her home. But something moved in the corner of her vision, and she turned her head. Mrs. Hodge was on her way down the stairs with a tin mug of water. When she saw the boys, Mrs. Hodge paused, as if startled. Then her jaw set with determination and she hustled toward Eliza even faster.

Eliza glanced at Catherine, panicked. But Catherine was staring at Eliza's and Harrison's hands, which were still touching. As Theresa's best friend, Catherine was surely obliged to tell her about such things. Blushing furiously, Eliza quickly withdrew her fingers.

"Here, Miss Williams," Mrs. Hodge said, handing the mug of water to Eliza and helping cup her fingers around it. "Drink slowly."

Eliza sipped the cool water as Mrs. Hodge shot Harrison an admonishing look. He took a step back.

"Mr. Knox, Mr. Thackery, thank you for your assistance," Mrs. Hodge said stiffly. "You may go now."

"Of course," Harrison said quickly.

"Feel better, Miss Williams!" Jonathan called out as the two boys started down the sidewalk again.

Before Eliza could say anything, Mrs. Hodge swooped in, checking her pulse, feeling her forehead, and ushering her to the nearest bench. As she sat, her eyes trained on Harrison's retreating form, Eliza felt ill all over again—but for reasons having nothing to do with her fainting.

WITCHES

The following evening, just before midnight, Eliza sat in the basement of the Billings Chapel along with Alice, freezing in her whisper-thin white nightgown. Alice shivered next to her, though Eliza was certain it was more out of fear than from the cold, for her gown was made of flannel. Catherine and Theresa walked over to join Eliza and Alice on the floor.

"Well, what do we think of our temple?" Theresa asked, tucking the skirt of her own white nightgown underneath her and looking around in a self-satisfied way.

"Must we call it that?" Alice asked, shivering. "It sounds so . . . *satanic.*"

"Covens meet in temples. That's what the spell book says," Catherine replied.

Eliza, Catherine, Theresa, and Alice had spent the past hour transforming the plain white room into a colorful, candlelit cavern.

Catherine and Eliza had purchased dozens of candles at the general store in town yesterday, and the candles were set into holders and candelabras of various heights that stood around the periphery of the room. Alice and Catherine had gathered all the scarves the four girls owned, and Eliza had swiped a hammer and nails from the toolshed behind McKinley Hall. Now the purples, golds, reds, greens, pinks, and blues of the scarves hung about the room, forming a cozy setting. Theresa had also managed to collect dozens of strings of cheap glass beads, which she had strung from the ceiling. In the candlelight, the beads twinkled like stars, giving the basement an ethereal feel. The coziness of it all had chased out Eliza's remaining nerves about the evening. She couldn't wait for the other girls to arrive.

"I simply don't feel right about this," Alice said, her teeth chattering. "Couldn't we have found another place to hold our meetings? This is God's house."

Theresa sighed, straightening the lace cuffs of her nightgown. "It's not his house. It's his basement."

Eliza couldn't help laughing, and Catherine joined in as well.

"Do you think anyone will come?" Alice asked, ignoring their laughter.

"I hope they will," Theresa said. "My hand still hurts from addressing all those invitations last night."

Theresa had insisted on writing out all the invitations herself, claiming that her handwriting was the most formal. Then Eliza and Catherine had been granted the distinct honor of shoving the envelopes under the girls' doors that morning.

"I'm sure they'll come," Eliza said, lifting her chin. She reached up to rub the gold locket between her finger and thumb. "How could anyone not be intrigued by a midnight meeting at a chapel?"

"Intrigued? I'd be terrified," Alice replied. "I still am. I'll wager only half of them come here."

"Yes, but which half?" Catherine joked.

Just then, the ceiling above them creaked and moaned. Alice grabbed Eliza's arm, tense with fear. Whispered voices wafted down from above.

"They're here," Eliza whispered.

"This is where it all begins," Catherine added, her skin glowing with excitement as she looked up at the ceiling.

The girls stood, holding their breath and clutching hands, waiting for the first of their friends to appear. Before long, Lavender arrived at the bottom of the stairs. She had a look of pure suspicion on her brow, until she caught sight of Eliza and Catherine. Then her usual just-plain-serious look returned to her face. She stepped into the room, the scalloped hem of her white nightgown grazing her ankles, and was quickly followed by Marilyn and Genevieve—Eliza was pleased to see that Marilyn had left Petit Peu behind, but Genevieve had her ever-present bag full of sweets—and Viola and Bia, who were clutching each other's arms with both hands, as if afraid the other might blow away. Jane was right behind them, her brown hair hanging loose down her back. The moment she saw Theresa, she rushed forward and kissed her. Then each of the girls soundlessly joined the circle, as if they realized that was where they were meant to be. Viola and Bia looked around fretfully, but the others simply seemed excited. Eliza could tell that Jane was biting down on her tongue to keep from asking questions. Only Clarissa had yet to arrive.

The moments ticked by, and Eliza's heartbeat slowed to a dull, disappointed thud. Clarissa was not coming. And without Clarissa, they would not have eleven members.

This thought had just flitted through her mind when another set of footsteps sounded hurriedly through the office above. Moments later, Clarissa alighted on the basement floor, breathless. She wore a high-necked gown, and her golden blond hair was tied back in two girlish braids, as always. Giving the room a cursory, appraising glance, she clucked her tongue and looked at Theresa.

"This does not look like a proper setting for a literary society," she announced, breaking the silence.

"Why are we all wearing our white nightgowns, Theresa?" Jane blurted, as if Clarissa's declaration had released her from some vow of silence.

"If it was five degrees cooler outside, we could have caught our deaths," Lavender pointed out. "Look at Bia. She's practically blue."

"And I've torn the hem on mine," Viola whined, tugging the skirt of her white cotton gown.

"And we have all risked expulsion again," Marilyn pointed out. "I do not wish to be sent back to France so soon, and neither does Genevieve."

"Ladies, ladies, please. Everything is going to be fine," Theresa said, stepping forward. "We are not here to form a literary society."

The seven new girls glanced around the circle in confusion. "But that's what the invitation says," Clarissa pointed out, removing the card from the pocket of her nightgown and holding it out helpfully.

"We know," Eliza said patiently. "But that was just a ruse, in case any of the teachers found them."

"Then why are we here?" Lavender asked, crossing her arms over her chest.

Eliza glanced around at Catherine, Theresa, and Alice for courage. "We're going to form a coven," she said simply.

Clarissa laughed through her nose. A few of the other girls gasped.

"You're joking," Marilyn said, reaching for Genevieve's hand. "You are making a joke."

"No. This is not a joke," Eliza said firmly.

Instantly the smile fell from Clarissa's face, and she began to chew on her hair. Both Viola's and Bia's faces turned ashen. Marilyn frowned thoughtfully as Genevieve plucked a chocolate from her bag and popped it into her mouth.

"You wish to make us . . . witches?" Genevieve asked, her mouth full.

"We wish to try," Eliza said. A few of the girls glanced toward the door. Clearly they were all going to need some convincing—the quicker, the better. "There's nothing to be afraid of."

"Really? Then why does Alice look about ready to burst into tears?" Clarissa pointed out, removing her braid from her lips for the moment.

Eliza glanced at Theresa, but for once the girl was mute. Why was she suddenly so unwilling to speak up? Eliza took a deep breath and rounded her shoulders, stepping into the center of the room.

"We—Catherine, Theresa, Alice, and I—found this stack of old books down here the other night, and there are all these spells and potions and enchantments in them," she said in a rush, gesturing at the trunk. She looked each girl in the eye as she talked, feeling as though it might reassure them. "It might be a lot of bunk, but we thought it could be fun to try. To see if it's really real."

"Why didn't you just do it yourselves?" Clarissa asked, moving toward the trunk and peeking at the books inside. "Why make all of us traipse out here in the dead of night?"

"We need eleven women," Catherine said.

"We chose you out of all the girls at Billings to join us," Theresa finally chimed in.

Bia, for the first time, stopped staring at the door. Lavender straightened up slightly.

Clever, Eliza thought. *Make them feel special, make this feel exclusive, and they'll be more likely to stay.*

"If you think it's safe, Theresa, that's all I need to hear," Jane said.

"What about you, Alice?" Clarissa said. "You haven't said a word."

Alice coughed, covering her hand with her fist. She was still trembling slightly, but having the attention focused on her seemed to bring back some of her spirit. "There are spells in the book for making a boy fall in love with you, spells for beauty, spells to make you more graceful. What if . . . what if they actually work?"

"If what you say is true, I would like to try this," Genevieve said eagerly, reaching for another chocolate. "I would like to try this very much."

"We have to perform a ritual," Catherine said, gathering up a set of purple candles.

"A ritual?" Bia said, backing away. "Like a sacrifice? We're not going to kill a bunny, are we? Oh, Viola, please don't let them kill a bunny."

"We're not going to kill a bunny, Bia," Viola said. Then she looked up at Catherine as she accepted her candle. "Right?"

"We're not going to kill anything," Eliza assured them, touching the locket at the base of her neck. "We're simply going to light these candles and recite a few lines together."

Once everyone had their candles in hand, Catherine looked at Eliza and nodded. "Eliza. You'll do the honors?"

Eliza's knees quaked beneath her as she picked up the nearest candle at the end of the candelabra on the floor and lit her own wick with its flame. Then she went around the circle and lit the other girls' wicks. Suddenly the uncertainty of it all was excruciating. What if something went wrong? What if something happened to her? Or to one of the other girls?

By the time she reached Alice, her right hand was trembling, and she had to use her left hand to brace it. Finally, she took her place in the circle between Alice and Catherine, looking around at the faces of their chosen ones. Lavender's serious expression had not changed. Bia looked as if she was about to faint, but Viola seemed resolute. Jane swallowed over and over again, her eyes transfixed on Theresa, while Clarissa continually scanned the room, as if she was making mental notes. Marilyn and Genevieve simply appeared intrigued.

"Here's what we're going to recite," Theresa said, her voice confident and clear. "'We come together to form this blessed circle, pure of heart, free of mind. From this night on we are bonded, we are sisters. We swear to honor this bond above all else. Blood to blood, ashes to ashes, sister to sister, we make this sacred vow.'"

Eliza clutched her candle as the group tentatively began to recite. Most of them spoke clearly and slowly, their voices mingling in the dark. Only Bia seemed to be whispering. Her eyes were closed as she furtively rushed through the words, as if she feared to speak and yet at the same time feared to stop speaking the words.

"Blood to blood, ashes to ashes, sister to sister," Eliza said, holding her breath and looking around the room in anticipation. "We make this sacred vow."

There was a brief moment of total silence, during which Eliza was certain they were all on a fool's errand—that nothing could possibly come of this. And then a whipping wind tore through the windowless chamber. Bia screamed. Alice grabbed Eliza's arm and buried her face in her shoulder. A few of the other girls gasped as every last one of the candles flickered out. The tiny room was plunged into complete darkness, and without the light of the candles, it seemed even colder than before. Just as quickly as it came, the wind died, leaving behind an unnatural stillness.

Terror flooded Eliza's veins.

"I told you I told you I told you," Alice whimpered into Eliza's nightgown. Somewhere in the darkness, someone wept.

"Bia! Bia, are you all right?" Viola's voice was strained with panic.

"God has come to drag us all to hell," Alice whispered furtively. "We're going to burn for this, Eliza. We're going to—"

Suddenly, Eliza's candle flickered to life. Then, one by one, tiny pinpricks of light illuminated the room once again. With each flame, a new face glowed. Alice's tear-streaked cheeks. Theresa's pale skin. Viola and Lavender on the floor next to Bia, who was just coming around. Jane and Clarissa huddled near the door. Marilyn and Genevieve standing just where they'd been. Catherine seemed not to have moved a muscle in all the mayhem.

Eliza looked around in wonder and saw her sentiment reflected in the eyes of her friends. None of the other candles along the walls had been relit. There were but eleven flames in the room.

"It worked," Catherine said breathlessly. "We're witches."

BASIC SPELLS

"What do we do now?" Alice said tremulously, gathering the folds of her nightgown in her hands.

"I think we should try a spell," Eliza said. She handed her candle to Catherine and plucked the book of spells off the top of the trunk, opening it to a page near the front. "There are some basic ones in here that seem simple enough."

"We'll just try something small. Something harmless. Here. Give it to me." Theresa reached for the book, but Eliza held onto it. Theresa tugged once, then looked at Eliza with an expression of shock. Apparently no one had ever failed to yield to her before.

"Let's all sit," Eliza said flatly.

Her heart pounded, but she held her ground. It was as if reciting the initiation rite had imbued her with more strength than she'd had before. Theresa rolled her eyes, let go of the book, and sat down on the floor. Then all the girls sat as well, tucking the skirts of their nightgowns beneath them.

"All right, let's see," Eliza said, running her finger down the list of basic spells. Her gaze fell on something that seemed perfect. "Here's one for you, Viola. To mend a torn seam."

"Really?" Viola asked, her eyebrows raised.

"That's what we're going to use magic for?" Clarissa said. "Something we could do with a needle and thread?"

"Let her try it," Lavender said forcefully.

Clarissa lifted her shoulders and let them fall.

"Fine. Here's what you do, Viola," Eliza said, squinting down at the page. "Hold your right palm over the tear and say, 'Resarcio.'"

Viola glanced at Theresa and bit her lip, but did as she was told. Her hand fluttered a bit as she smoothed the torn part of her gown on the floor. She placed her palm over the long, ragged edge, then closed her eyes and said the spell.

"Resarcio."

She said the word at a whisper, opened her eyes, and looked. Everyone in the circle leaned in. The seam was still torn.

"Nothing happened," Viola said with a pout.

Eliza felt a swoop of disappointment.

"Try it again," Catherine instructed calmly. "This time, stare at the back of your hand and really concentrate. Say the spell loudly and clearly. Believe that it will work."

Marilyn and Genevieve both eyed Catherine with interest, as if they were seeing her for the first time. Eliza was impressed as well. Catherine really sounded as if she knew what she was talking about.

Viola held her hand over the tear. She closed her eyes again, then remembered Catherine's instructions and quickly snapped them open. She stared at the back of her hand and this time said the spell in a loud voice. An odd snapping sound filled the small room. Eliza flinched. When Viola lifted her hand, the gash in the cotton had vanished. The nightgown was as good as new.

"It worked!" Bia said breathlessly.

"What else can we do? What else?" Jane blurted, clapping her hands.

Suddenly the room was filled with giggles and twitters. Genevieve pulled out her box of chocolates and passed it around. Eliza looked at Catherine, a grin lighting her face. "You did it." Catherine blushed.

"What about this one? To change the color of a frock?" Theresa said, tugging the book off Eliza's lap while she was distracted. "Alice? What do you say? Would you like a pink nightgown instead of white?"

Alice looked down at her flannel uncertainly. "Will it hurt?"

"Oh, please," Theresa said. She held a flat hand out toward Alice, leaning past Eliza and Catherine. "Hubeo pink!"

Another snapping sound. Suddenly a spot of color appeared at the center of Alice's nightgown. Alice squealed and grasped Catherine's arm, her legs bouncing up and down beneath her.

"Get it off! Get it off!"

Eliza watched in amazement as the spot swirled and grew and swirled and grew. Clarissa got up, walked over to Alice, and touched the spot where the color had sprung to life, her brow knit with curiosity.

"It's warm," she said, looking at Eliza. "Very warm."

"Make it stop!" Alice whined, squeezing her eyes shut as the color seeped across her chest and down her arms, then finally swirled to the floor-length hem. She peeked from the corner of her left eye, then squeezed it shut, holding her breath until she turned beet red. "Is it over?"

"Look!" Eliza told her.

Alice opened just one eye to a sliver, then the other. She gazed down at herself, and suddenly both eyes widened in wonder. "It's pink!"

Just like that, every one of the girls was on her feet, gathering around Theresa for a better look at the book of spells.

"Here's one for reviving a dying plant!" Lavender exclaimed.

"This one polishes silver," Jane said, spinning the silver bracelet on her wrist.

"Is there anything about getting rid of freckles?" Genevieve asked, leaning so close from behind that she almost folded Theresa in half.

"I have always dreamt of having raven hair," Marilyn said, gazing into space.

Viola reached out to touch Marilyn's blond locks. "But your hair works so well with your coloring."

"*Vraiment*? I do not think so," Marilyn said, touching her hair as well.

"Why not just dye it?" Jane suggested.

Marilyn shook her head. "Oh, no, no, no. That would be far too *gauche*." She looked at Theresa. "Is there anything for changing hair the way you changed her dress?" she said, gesturing at Alice.

"Patience, patience," Theresa said, clearly enjoying her place at the center of attention. "We'll get to everything in time." She looked over at Eliza and Catherine and smiled giddily.

"This is unbelievable," Eliza said to Catherine in awe. "We're witches."

"Yes," Catherine said. "We certainly are."

ETIQUETTE

"Now, girls, in your role as ladies of society, you will rarely be serving tea yourselves, but you must know the proper technique so that you may instruct and correct your servants if need be."

It was a stiflingly warm Tuesday afternoon as Miss Almay strolled around the parlor, which had been set with four round tables, each seating four girls. Gathered at the table nearest the door were Theresa, Eliza, Alice, and Catherine. Lavender, Marilyn, Jane, and Viola hovered around them. For the moment the latter girls were the servers, while the former were the guests. Marilyn had set Petit Peu on a small pillow near the door, where he was now curled up and snoring quite loudly. Helen stood in the corner, watching the girls' every move.

"Always serve the tea from behind on the left side," Miss Almay instructed, gesturing with her folded bifocals. Petit Peu let out a snort, and she cast a disapproving look in his direction. "The vast majority of people are right-handed, and you do not wish to accidentally bump someone's arm with the tea kettle as you serve."

Theresa waited until Miss Almay's back was turned, then nudged Eliza with her elbow. She trained her eyes on Eliza's salad fork and narrowed them into slits. "Levitas."

Eliza's heart nearly stopped as the fork twitched, then lifted from the lace tablecloth, floating three inches off the surface of the table. Her eyes widened and she glanced over at Alice, who lifted her lace-gloved hand to her chest.

"Fantastic," Eliza whispered to Theresa, her pulse racing with the intoxicating mixture of wonder and fear. It wasn't every day that she saw tableware floating about as if suspended by invisible puppet strings.

Theresa smirked. She lifted one finger and twirled it slowly in the air. Instantly, the fork began to spin lazily as well.

"You've been practicing, Theresa," Catherine whispered proudly.

"I've always been a quick study," Theresa said with an immodest grin. "I think we should try some of the potions next. I've already gotten Jane, Viola, and Bia to start collecting some of the ingredients we'll need from the herb garden."

"What? Without talking to us about it first?" Eliza whispered.

Theresa rolled her eyes. "I'm talking to you about it *now*."

"I think it's a fine idea," Catherine said happily.

"I want to try," Alice whispered. She looked down at her own silverware. "Levitas!"

Her spoon jumped off the table, then slammed right down again.

Luckily, Petit Peu barked in his sleep at the same moment, so the noise was muffled. Miss Almay paused in her circuit of the room, her back to Eliza's table, and then kept walking.

Alice leaned back in her chair and pouted. "It didn't work," she said, jutting out her bottom lip and glaring at the offending spoon.

"It's just like I told Viola, Alice. You have to concentrate," Catherine advised, laying a comforting hand on her wrist. "Try again."

Alice took a breath, leaned forward again, and narrowed her eyes just as Theresa had.

"Levitas," she whispered.

Both her knife and spoon floated up, clinking softly together in the air. Alice hid a squeal behind her hand, keeping her gaze squarely on the silverware. Catherine giggled, while Eliza's heart swelled. If this was what witchcraft was about—making the most boring class of all seem tolerable—then it was the best discovery she'd ever made.

Then Miss Almay started to turn, and Eliza smacked her hand over Theresa's fork, slamming it back in place. There was a loud clattering of silverware and china as Alice did the same. Petit Peu awakened with a start and let out a few short barks before readjusting his position and promptly starting to snore again. Behind Eliza, Marilyn and Jane just barely covered their laughter with polite coughs.

"Is there a problem, girls?" Miss Almay asked, staring down her nose at Eliza and her friends.

"No, Miss Almay," Theresa replied sweetly, her hands folded in her lap. "No problem at all."

"Fine, then. I'd appreciate no further interruption, Miss Williams," Miss Almay said. "Unless you'd like me to contact your mother and let her know how very much you are *not* living up to May's high standards."

Eliza's skin burned with anger. "No, ma'am."

"Good. We'll continue." Miss Almay turned and started pacing along the west wall. Eliza concentrated on the hem of the headmistress's dark gray skirt and narrowed her eyes.

"Levitas," she whispered.

Suddenly Miss Almay's skirt flew up, revealing the many old-fashioned petticoats underneath. The headmistress let out a very unladylike shriek as she whirled around, attempting to tamp it down. All the girls in the room dissolved into laughter.

"What was that?" Miss Almay demanded as soon as her clothes were set to rights.

"Did you not feel that gust of wind, Headmistress?" Catherine said, arching her brows. Eliza scarcely dared to breathe.

"Perhaps we should close the windows," Alice offered, standing as if to help.

"Sit, Miss Ainsworth," Miss Almay snapped, the color high in her cheeks. "Helen!" she shouted, snapping her fingers. "Close these windows."

Helen rushed forward from her place near the door and did as she was told. As soon as the large windows were shut, the room became stiflingly hot.

"Servers! Kindly pour the tea!" Miss Almay ordered. Then, clearly flustered, she quickly sat in a wing-backed chair near the front of the room and fanned her face with her hand.

"Thanks for that, Eliza," Viola whispered, stepping forward to serve Eliza's tea from the left side. "I'm already starting to perspire, and this is a new blouse."

"I'm sorry," Eliza replied under her breath. "But she deserved it."

As Viola poured out her tea, Eliza glanced up to find Helen staring right at her. Eliza's heart skipped a startled beat, but she forced herself to hold the servant's gaze. Helen's hazel eyes narrowed. It took all of Eliza's determination to keep from being the first to break eye contact, but the longer the two girls stared at each other, the quicker her blood rushed through her ears.

Suddenly Miss Almay stirred, and Eliza's gaze flicked to the headmistress. She scolded herself silently for losing the challenge to the maid, but her stomach flip-flopped when she saw that Miss Almay was looking from Helen to Eliza and back again, as if she realized what was going on between them.

"Miss Williams," Miss Almay said suddenly. "See me in my office after class."

Eliza's heart sunk. Theresa snorted a laugh.

"You too, Miss Billings," Miss Almay said.

Both girls slumped down in their chairs, suddenly forgetting about etiquette entirely.

DUE RESPECT

A cold trickle of sweat raced down the back of Eliza's broiling-hot neck. Miss Almay had been pacing behind her and Theresa for at least five minutes, ominously silent. As each moment passed, Eliza had grown warmer and warmer, and at this point, she was actually fantasizing about tearing her dress off and diving into a pool of ice water.

Theresa sat perfectly still in the next chair, staring straight ahead at the horridly gothic portrait of the dark-haired headmistress herself, which hung behind the wide, ornately carved desk. From it, the visage of Miss Almay glared down at them, the crags of her bony face shadowed, the bend of her nose accusatory. With one Almay before her and one seething behind, Eliza felt as if she was being stalked by a pair of identical fiends.

If Miss Almay was attempting to intimidate her, it was working.

Suddenly, the pacing stopped. There was a prolonged moment of silence, and then Miss Almay brought her hands down on the backs of the girls' chairs with a *bang*. Eliza jumped.

"Yesterday I caught Clarissa Pommer and Jane Barton coming out of the general store in town, toting several small bottles of oils and a jar of imported figs," the headmistress stated, leaning down so that her face hovered just between the two girls. "And when I returned from town, I spied Viola and Bia Hirsch gathering wildflowers out on the meadow."

Eliza dared not move a muscle, but she slid her gaze toward Theresa. Apparently the girl had assigned more errands than she'd admitted to. Theresa shook her head so slightly, the move was almost imperceptible. The headmistress stood up straight again and strode around her desk until she was standing right in front of her own image. She laced her fingers together at her waist and stared down at Eliza and Theresa.

"I *know* you ladies are up to something," she said vehemently. "Tell me what it is."

Eliza felt as if her heart was pounding inside her mouth, filling her cheeks and choking off her air supply. She was going to be sick or finally faint dead away. Miss Almay knew. She knew. Eliza reached up to tug at the gold chain holding her locket in place, feeling suddenly as if it was trying to choke her.

"If I may speak, Miss Almay?" Theresa said, in her most falsely sweet voice.

"Of course, Miss Billings," Miss Almay replied. "It is why I've brought you here, after all."

"Well, with all due respect, of course, Miss Almay," Theresa began.

Eliza closed her eyes.

"If you would like an explanation on the activities of Clarissa, Jane, Viola, and Bia, then why are they not here?" Theresa asked, lifting her chin. "Why question the two of us?"

Miss Almay's eyes narrowed. "Because, Miss Billings, I am not a fool," she snapped. "Those girls look up to the two of you. You seem to have a power over them that is . . . almost unnatural."

At this, Eliza's throat completely closed over. She tried to hold back a cough, but found she simply could not do it. She covered her mouth with her fist and doubled over in her chair, her lungs racked.

"Eliza! Are you all right?" Theresa asked with false concern.

Miss Almay snapped her fingers at the office door. Instantly Mrs. Hodge appeared and raced to pour out a cup of water at the sideboard beneath the window.

"I'm fine, I'm fine," Eliza choked out, waving away the proffered water. "It's just a tickle."

Mrs. Hodge placed the glass of water atop Miss Almay's desk. The moment she stepped back, Eliza grabbed it and gulped it down, biding her time. Not until she replaced the empty glass on the desk again did Miss Almay speak.

"Ever since your stunt at the welcome, Miss Billings, lateness has been in fashion," she said. "And you, Miss Williams, seem to have inspired an influx of patrons to our library."

Eliza stared at the woman. It was hard to believe that as head of a school, she saw heightened interest in books as a bad thing.

"And I know you two were behind that late-night jaunt to Easton," she continued. "I saw the two of you wait for the others to return to Crenshaw before you brought up the rear. Why would you do that unless you were the ringleaders?"

Eliza glanced at Theresa out of the corner of her eye, annoyed. Of *that*, she was falsely accused.

"I am certain that whatever is going on with those girls, the two of you are responsible," Miss Almay said. "Rest assured, I will put a stop to it."

Eliza stared up at her and a sudden hatred surged through her heart so strongly it shocked her. This was the woman who had squelched May's spirit and sent her back to Eliza a changed, meek girl. And now here she was, accusing Eliza and Theresa of manipulating their friends, with no real evidence to support the claim.

"We are responsible for no one other than ourselves, Miss Almay," Eliza said firmly. "I respectfully suggest that if you wish to learn more about those girls and their actions, you ask them."

Theresa looked at Eliza, stunned. Miss Almay simply froze. She was so still, Eliza couldn't even tell if she was breathing. Her pupils dilated with anger so that her eyes looked almost black. For a moment it looked as though she was going to reach out and strike Eliza. But then she moved to the door and opened it. "That will be all, girls," she said.

Eliza and Theresa scrambled to their feet and were out the door so fast, they didn't even think to bid the headmistress good day. They were mere steps into the hall when the heavy oak door slammed behind them.

"What was that?" Theresa asked Eliza as they scurried toward the main hallway. She sounded impressed. "I've never seen you so—"

"So like you?" Eliza shot back.

Theresa blinked. "You say it as if it's a bad thing."

"Good or bad, I had to get us out of there somehow," Eliza replied.

Theresa leaned back against the wall, crossed her arms over her chest, and looked Eliza up and down. "I may have underestimated you, Eliza Williams."

Eliza felt a surprising flutter of pride over Theresa's approval.

"Well, Theresa Billings," she said, lifting her chin. "You may not have noticed before now, but I am not my sister."

SPELL OF SILENCE

The following night, at the stroke of midnight, Eliza found herself in the basement of Billings Chapel once again, but this time the mood was decidedly lighter than it had been on Sunday. Laughter and conversation filled the chamber, and candles flickered warmly over the decorated walls. Eliza and Catherine paged through the book of spells, waiting for Theresa, who was the only member of the coven yet to arrive. Eliza laughed as Alice skipped by, eating one of the pastries Genevieve had procured in town for the meeting. Powdered sugar covered her chin, and she had woven a wreath of fresh flowers into her hair.

"You suddenly seem very keen on being here," Eliza said, stopping Alice in her tracks.

Alice tilted her head quizzically, her auburn curls grazing her shoulders. "Why wouldn't I be?" she asked without a trace of irony.

Eliza and Catherine exchanged an amused glance.

"No longer afraid of repercussions from above?" Catherine asked, holding the book open in her lap.

"Oh. That," Alice said. She took a step closer to them and lowered her voice. "I figure that if God disapproved of what we were doing, he would have smote us all down the moment we said the incantation that made us witches. But so far, we're all fine. So I have to believe he approves!"

With that, she skipped away.

"It must be nice living in Alice's world," Eliza mused.

"I wouldn't mind paying a visit," Catherine agreed. "But I don't think I'd want it to be a lengthy one." She looked down at the page she'd just turned to. "Ugh. Look at this."

Eliza looked down at the page, and a shudder went through her. In the center was a grotesque illustration of a bare skull with roses sticking out of its eyes. Across the top, in elaborate script, were the words LIFE OUT OF DEATH SPELL. She slammed the book closed, almost flattening Catherine's fingers.

"We won't be needing that," she said, standing. "Perhaps we should get this meeting started." She spoke loudly so the other girls could hear her over their conversation and pastry munching. "Theresa will be here soon. There's no harm in deciding on a new spell to cast before she gets here."

She took the book from Catherine and placed it on the pedestal she and Lavender had found in the chapel's storage closet earlier that evening. The other girls gathered around as Eliza took the position of authority.

Viola clasped her hands beneath her chin. "Are we going to make the Easton boys fall in love with us?"

Everyone laughed.

"A lofty goal, but I think we can come up with something better," Theresa said, appearing suddenly at the bottom of the stairs. She had her hair swept up dramatically to one side, where it fell in curls along her left cheek. Her dress was jade green with a tight bodice, and she wore a black shawl with beads dangling from its ends in strands of varying length. She crossed the room and stood next to Eliza, practically pushing her out of the way. "I think I can take it from here, Eliza."

"That's all right, Theresa. I was just about to begin," Eliza said, pressing the side of her foot against the side of Theresa's, trying to regain some ground.

"I can flip through this book just as well as anyone and find us a spell," Theresa said blithely, turning the pages. "What do we want to do? Give all the adults on campus laryngitis? Make it rain for three days? Learn how to make someone faint on cue?"

"Oh, I don't like that one," Bia said fretfully from her spot near the door, next to her sister.

Eliza watched the titles on the pages as Theresa hurriedly skimmed through them. Suddenly something caught her eye and she slammed her hand down on the book, stopping the incessant flipping.

"Eliza!" Theresa scolded.

"Let's do this one," Eliza said. "This one will get us exactly what we need."

"Boys?" Alice asked.

Giggles ensued. Catherine rolled her eyes, but smiled.

"Freedom," Eliza corrected, her eyes gleaming as she looked out at the other girls. "Although the company of boys could be a welcome side effect," she added to appease her romance-hungry friends. Alice, Viola, Bia, and Genevieve squealed happily. A picture of Harrison flitted through Eliza's own mind as well, but she shoved it aside quickly.

"What is it?" Catherine asked, stepping up to better see the page.

"It's called the Spell of Silence," Eliza said. Her eyes flicked over the page. "It says that if we cast it successfully, no one but us will be able to hear a sound we make. We'll be able to shout, slam doors, laugh, scream . . . and Miss Almay will be none the wiser."

"So we can sneak out and visit the boys!" Alice cried happily, clasping her hands together under her chin.

"For what are we waiting?" Genevieve pushed the last of her cream puff into her mouth, dusted sugar from her fingers, and chewed. "Tell us what we are to do."

"Wait," Theresa snapped. "There are hundreds of spells in here that we could try. I don't see why Eliza has the last word."

Eliza's cheeks burned indignantly. "Fine. Then let's take a vote."

Theresa opened her mouth as if to retort, but Clarissa interrupted her. "All in favor of Eliza's spell, say 'aye,'" she said, flipping one of her braids over her shoulder.

"Aye!" the shouts filled the room. Only Theresa abstained, although Jane's "aye" was slightly less adamant than the others, and she made sure not to look at Theresa as she cast her vote.

"Spell of Silence it is!" Eliza said triumphantly. She retook her spot at the center of the podium, bumping Theresa out of the way. "Everyone kindly form the circle."

Theresa's lips were set in a thin, angry line as she took her spot between Eliza and Jane. It was all Eliza could do to keep from sticking her tongue out at the girl. But she had gotten what she deserved for trying to take over so rudely, and after being more than fifteen minutes late, no less.

"Please take one another's hands," Eliza instructed. She reached for Theresa's and Catherine's hands. Theresa did not clasp her fingers in return, but left them flat. Alice swung Catherine's and Clarissa's hands in anticipation, swiveling her hips as well so that her voluminous skirts swished back and forth.

"I'll recite the spell once," Eliza said, "then we'll all recite it together: 'Wherever we go, wherever we might, let us walk in silence as the night,'" she intoned.

"That's it?" Clarissa blurted.

"Sometimes the simplest spells are the most powerful," Catherine informed her.

"At least it's easy to remember," Jane said.

"Shall we get this over with?" Theresa snipped.

The girls nodded and spoke as one. "Wherever we go, wherever we might, let us walk in silence as the night."

The strange wind picked up again, and Eliza's grip on her friends' hands tightened. Even Theresa's fingers now curled around hers. The wind sent chills all up and down Eliza's arms. For a moment she thought of Catherine's warning about upsetting the natural balance of the world. But when she glanced over at her friend, Catherine seemed perfectly at ease.

Eliza breathed out and told herself it would be all right. If Catherine—the one among them who knew more of magic than the rest—was unconcerned, so should she be. A minute later, the wind stopped. This time, the candles held strong and the light prevailed, but Eliza herself wobbled on her feet. Her vision prickled over, but the sensation quickly passed. Jane staggered forward slightly, but after a few breaths, seemed fine. As Eliza looked around, she could tell that each of the girls had felt the momentary dizziness. Was it a side effect of the spell?

Another thump of apprehension vibrated through Eliza's chest, but she forced herself not to consider it. They were fine. Everyone was fine.

"Well? What do we do now?" Alice asked finally.

Eliza smiled, deciding to put her concerns aside and embrace the fun. "Let's go see if it worked!"

GIRLS' NIGHT

"Who's going first?" Eliza asked, peeking around the corner into the first-floor hallway. The door to Miss Almay's room stood a few feet away. It was closed, but a shaft of light shone through the crack at the bottom, indicating that the headmistress was, indeed, inside and awake.

"Not so much the fearless leader now, eh, Eliza?" Theresa said, smoothing the front of her green dress as she stepped away from the corner. "You scaredy-cats stay here. I'll be right back."

"Theresa! Wait!" Catherine whispered, trying to grab for her skirt.

But Theresa just walked right up to Miss Almay's door and knocked three times. Loudly. For a long moment Eliza couldn't move or breathe or even think. All she could see in her mind's eye was Miss Almay whipping the door open, her face purple with fury.

"Hello!?" Theresa shouted. "Anybody home?"

Then she turned, looked at Eliza and Catherine—the only two brave enough to peer around the corner—and raised her palms.

"We did it!" she said giddily. "Come on, girls! You try!"

Eliza's heart was still pounding as she pulled Catherine out into the hall by both arms. She started to whistle a jaunty tune as she stomped past the headmistress's room. Gathering her courage, Catherine hummed the tune as well, knocking her fist against the wall to keep the beat. When the two of them arrived at the far end of the hall without incident, they both collapsed on the floor, laughing with relief and a heady feeling of power. They had really done it.

"This is too fun!" Catherine cried, slinging her arm around Eliza's shoulders.

"What now?" Viola asked.

"Let's go over to the boys' dormitories!" Alice cried.

"Not tonight," Catherine said, stepping forward.

"What?" Alice lamented. "But Eliza, you said—"

"She's right," Eliza put in. "Tonight should be about us. Let's go outside and have some fun."

"Part of being a witch is about communing with nature," Catherine added, taking Alice's other hand. "I say we go out and celebrate with Mother Earth."

Alice let out a disconsolate moan. "But boys are far more exciting than boring old Mother Earth."

"Oh, come along, you," Theresa said, rolling her eyes. "We'll take some of the exercise equipment out of the shed and play in the moonlight."

"I don't know why we can't celebrate just as well with the boys," Alice pouted.

"Because this is not about the boys," Eliza said. "This is about us."

The eleven girls, led by Eliza, Theresa, and Catherine, marched
down the hallway as loudly as they could possibly manage, talking at
the top of their voices and stomping their feet all the way. Outside,
Catherine opened the unlocked equipment shed, and Alice and Bia
were the first inside, ransacking the shelves and hooks and emerging
with armfuls of hoops. Clarissa went in after them and pulled out the
badminton racquets and birdies, while Catherine and Eliza extracted
a pair of bicycles with wide handlebars.

"Shall we race?" Eliza challenged her friend with a grin.

Catherine opened her mouth to respond, but Theresa came over
and took the handlebars right out of her grasp.

"I'll race you," she announced. Then she straddled the bicycle
and took off after Bia, Viola, and Jane, who shrieked as they chased
the hoops down the slight grassy hill in front of Crenshaw House.
Eliza's heart dropped in response to Theresa's rudeness, and Catherine
looked stunned.

"What was that?" Eliza asked.

Catherine recovered herself. She rubbed her palms together and
shrugged. "That's Theresa. She wants what she wants."

"Come on, Williams! Are you going to race me or not?" Theresa
shouted back.

Eliza looked at Catherine uncertainly.

"Go ahead," Catherine said. "I'll take the next turn."

"Are you sure?" Eliza asked, even as she straddled the bike.

"Yes. Please. Just . . . beat her," she said with a laugh. "She'll be
insufferable if you don't."

Eliza took off after Theresa, letting the wind whip through her hair and blow away her irritation and surprise over the way Theresa had treated Catherine—her supposed best friend. Theresa had ridden all the way down the hill and was now racing along the tree line, and Eliza pumped her legs to catch up. Lavender, Genevieve, and Marilyn chased after them, running and chanting the Spell of Silence over and over again like a triumphant mantra. Petit Peu brought up the rear, leaping about merrily at the chance to stretch his little legs.

"You can't catch me!" Theresa shouted over her shoulder, bending low over the handlebars.

"Watch me!" Eliza retorted. She leaned into the pedals as the tires bumped over rocks and tree roots and skidded on dusty dirt patches. Soon she had brought herself even with Theresa, and just before they hit the walkway to the McKinley building, Eliza burst ahead.

"I win!" she shouted, skidding to a stop.

Theresa slid to a halt a few feet ahead of her. Eliza heard her mutter a curse under her breath, but when she turned around, her expression was perfectly placid. "That's twice now you've beat me at a race, Eliza. You're so athletic, you're practically a boy." With that, she rode back past Eliza, giving her a condescending grin as she slipped by. Eliza was left with her jaw hanging open over the insult.

"Do not listen to her," Marilyn whispered to Eliza, coming up alongside her with Petit Peu in her arms. She scratched the little dog's head and bumped Eliza with her elbow. Together they watched Theresa as she hopped down from the bike and walked it back up the hill, toward the spot where the rest of the girls played badminton and cheered one another on. "You are prettier than half the girls in Paris."

Eliza laughed as she dismounted, then slung one arm around Marilyn's slim waist. "And you are lovely for saying that."

They walked together up the hill with Lavender and Genevieve trailing behind. Up ahead, Clarissa let out a screech as the birdie sailed wide of her racquet. Then, as if from nowhere, Eliza heard a voice whisper in her ear.

"Turn back."

Eliza whipped around suddenly, loosening herself from Marilyn's grasp. There was no one behind her. No one anywhere in sight.

"Eliza? What is it? What is wrong?" Marilyn asked, following Eliza's startled gaze.

Eliza swallowed a terrified lump in her throat and turned around again. "Nothing. It was nothing."

But then, she saw something move in one of the Crenshaw windows. Her blood stopped cold. The movement had come from the window all the way at the far end of the first floor—the very same window in which she had noticed something flicker during the carriage ride from the train. This time, however, the blonde watching her didn't duck away. Instead, she stayed and stared, her eyes as blank as stones.

It was Helen Jennings, the maid, who undoubtedly had seen everything.

HER VERY NATURE

"Do you think she's tattled on us yet?" Theresa asked, running to catch up with Catherine and Eliza as they walked into the Prescott dining hall the next morning. She glared at Helen, who stood with Mrs. Hodge near the wall behind Miss Almay's table, at the head-mistress's beck and call as always. Helen had her eyes trained on her feet. "Look at her, so smug. Doesn't she know I could have her fired right now if I wanted to?"

"You wouldn't," Eliza protested.

"Wouldn't I? I'll wager she *has* told," Theresa continued. "She has that look about her. Anything to please the headmistress. Probably went to Miss Almay with her hand out, looking for some kind of reward."

"Theresa, please," Catherine said as she pulled out a chair at their assigned table and seated herself.

"Helen seems like a nice girl," Eliza said, sitting as well. "Perhaps she's said nothing."

Theresa laughed derisively. "She's a servant, Eliza," she said, opening her napkin with a snap and folding it in her lap. "They're always looking to make an extra buck."

Eliza cast an appalled look at Theresa. One of the servers rushed forward to fill their water glasses. As soon as the girl had scurried away again, Eliza spoke.

"Theresa. How can you lump all of the serving class together?" Eliza asked. "Everyone is different."

"It's not as if I'm saying it's her fault," Theresa replied, rolling her eyes. "It's simply in her very nature."

Eliza forced herself to keep her tongue. This was neither the time nor the place to debate matters of class. Soon Alice, Viola, and Bia had filled the other three seats at their table. Viola kept her hands folded in her lap. Bia's every movement was a flinch, and she knocked her silverware from the table more than once. Alice had nary a conjecture about what the boys might be doing right then, and Catherine kept glancing up at the headmistress as if waiting for her to bring down the hatchet on all of them.

By the time the dishes were cleared, Eliza's stomach was so knotted, she'd hardly been able to choke anything down. She reached up and rubbed her gold locket between her thumb and forefinger.

"If she's already told, then why has the headmistress yet to say anything?" Viola said finally, looking up as the waitress whisked her dish away.

"I don't understand it either," Catherine whispered. "This is torture."

"Perhaps that's what this is meant to be," Eliza mused, glancing sidelong at the headmistress. "Miss Almay's own personal style of torment."

She was just reaching for her water glass when her eyes caught Helen's from across the room. Helen was staring right at her. Eliza felt the force of it right down to her toes. Why did it seem that Helen was always watching her?

Suddenly the maid stepped away from the wall, leaned down, and whispered something in the headmistress's ear.

"Oh, no," Eliza said, placing her glass back down so hastily that half the water spilled over the rim. "Don't look, but I think she's telling her right now."

Alice whimpered quietly, looking up at the head table, as everyone else held their breath. Slowly Miss Almay placed her spoon on the table and rose from her chair. As she did so, Helen backed up to her spot near the wall, casting an unreadable glance at Eliza.

"Ladies, if I may have your attention," Miss Almay said, casting a dour look at the room.

Instantly every conversation in the room came to a halt. Eliza felt her heartbeat pounding behind her very eyes. This was it. This was the end of her short tenure at the Billings School for Girls. Would any other respectable school have her once she was expelled? Would her mother even let her back into their home?

"As you all know, many of our students were put on probation on the first night of the term," the headmistress said, her eyes sliding over those tables which were home to the offending girls, all of whose faces had drained of blood and now appeared pale and waxy. "At that time I revoked their welcome dance privileges and wrote out chores and punishments for each of them. But due to their recent ameliorated behavior, I have been forced to reconsider my decision."

Eliza glanced at Catherine across the table. Confusion filled her friend's eyes. "Because of their superb conduct over the past week, I have decided to allow these girls to attend the dance after all," Miss Almay announced.

A shriek of delight emanated from the depths of Alice's lungs, and all the girls laughed happily. Eliza was so baffled, she was not yet able to feel relieved. Why hadn't Helen told? She looked at the maid, but the girl's gaze was once again fixed squarely on the floor.

"Do not make me regret my decision!" Miss Almay announced loudly enough to be heard over the hubbub. But still the girls gasped and chattered and began to plan their dresses and hair. Eliza smiled slowly and turned to Theresa with muted glee.

"Well. So much for Helen's debased nature," she said, raising her eyebrows.

Theresa's grin dropped from her face. "No one likes a know-it-all, Eliza."

But Eliza was unaffected by the slight. All she could think about was the dance, and whether she'd get a chance to take a turn with Harrison Knox.

THE HISTORY OF HELEN

"Oh, oh! What about this one? The Smitten Potion?" Alice giggled and pointed at the open page in front of her. "If a boy and a girl drink from the same draught, it's guaranteed to make them smitten for twenty-four hours. I think we have all the ingredients for it too!"

Eliza glanced at Catherine in the three-way mirror at the dressing table they were sharing in the parlor. Three such tables had been added to the room for the night so the girls could all get ready for the dance together.

"I suppose we should have expected this," Eliza joked. "There will probably be more spells cast tonight than any other night of the year."

Catherine smiled slightly. "So long as no one overdoes it. There's a fine line between good spells and bad."

"And what do you think that line is?" Eliza asked, genuinely curious.

"Anything that alters someone's mind or soul, anything that goes against the natural order of things," Catherine replied, reaching for her powder compact. "I admit, it's a fuzzy line. I suppose everyone has to define it for themselves," she added, glancing over at Alice.

Like the rest of the girls, Alice had already changed into her dress for the dance, a peacock blue frock with a low neckline, of which Miss Almay would certainly disapprove, and a full skirt that accentuated her tiny waist. She was now seated on a parlor chair with the book of spells open across her lap and Viola and Marilyn leaning in from either side to better see the pages. Theresa stood nearby, tugging on her black gloves and admiring herself in a full-length mirror, while the other coven members helped one another with makeup and hair.

"Lavender, hold still," Jane instructed from a settee in the corner. "It's one of the basic spells. I'm sure it won't hurt. And you don't want that blemish on your chin distracting boys from your lovely eyes."

Lavender blushed. "You think I have lovely eyes?"

"Of course you do!" Bia told her, looking up from her compact mirror. "With all those tiny gold flecks? I wish I had tiny gold flecks."

"All right, then," Lavender said, lifting her chin a bit higher. "Go ahead."

Jane raised her hand and held it an inch from Lavender's chin. Lavender squeezed her eyes closed but stayed completely still.

"Clarus!" Jane said.

The telltale snapping sound filled the room. Lavender's eyes popped open as Jane and Bia clapped their hands.

"It's gone!" Bia said, handing over her mirror.

Lavender's jaw dropped as she inspected her face, turning it from left to right. "Thank you, Jane!"

The two girls hugged, and Eliza smiled. It was nice to see her friends growing closer—to see the way magic could bring them all together.

"Clarissa!" Theresa said suddenly, looking up at the door. "*What* are you wearing?"

Everyone turned to stare. Clarissa's dress looked like something out of a prairie girl's nightmare. It was green and purple gingham with frayed lace trim and a high neckline. Her braids had been pinned to the back of her head in a coil, making her appear almost like a scary old maid out of a children's book.

"It's the best one I have," Clarissa lamented, her arms drooping at her sides. Eliza had never known Clarissa to be vain, so she knew right away that the frock was truly bothering her.

"Well. We can fix that, can't we, girls?" Eliza said, standing.

"Yes, we certainly can," Genevieve said, laying aside her finger sandwich and standing up.

All the other girls gathered around Clarissa as Catherine stood up to close the double doors leading to the front hall—an act that was strictly forbidden but necessary for the moment.

"What color dress would you *like* to have, Clarissa?" Eliza asked.

"I've always loved dark pink roses," Clarissa said. "My grandmother grows them in her garden."

"Pink rose it is." Catherine held out her hand toward Clarissa's dress. "Hubeo deep rose."

Instantly, a swirl of color appeared in the center of Clarissa's stomach. Just as Alice's nightgown had changed that first night, Clarissa's dress transformed into a lovely solid pink.

"It's beautiful!" Clarissa exclaimed, giving a twirl.

"Not so fast!" Viola said. "We must do something about that neckline." She held her hand out and bit her lip. "Collar exposé!"

With a snap, the fabric around Clarissa's neck tore free and fell to the ground, leaving her collarbone exposed. Clarissa's hands flew to her neck.

"I've never worn anything so revealing," she protested with a blush.

"Trust me. I know fashion, and this is au courant," Viola replied, taking her hand in a reassuring way. "What do you think, girls? Shall we fix the skirt next?"

"*Absolument!*" Marilyn said, clapping her hands.

Soon all the girls were comparing ideas, holding out their palms, and making adjustments. Scraps of fabric fell to the floor. The lace trim shot right into the fireplace. A set of ribbons lifted off Alice's dressing table and flew over to adorn Clarissa's bodice, and another set wove through her hair. When Eliza and her friends finally stepped back, Clarissa looked as if she'd stepped out of a magazine. Her hair was done up in a curly, chic updo with blond tendrils around her face. Her skirt was slim around the hips with a slight flare at the ankle, and the rose color was perfectly complemented by the dark purple velvet ribbon trim.

"The boys are going to fall over themselves to dance with you," Eliza assured her.

Slowly Clarissa turned and looked into one of the mirrors. She touched her hair carefully with her fingertips, her mouth open in awe. "Thank you, girls! Thank you so much!"

Eliza hugged her as the others congratulated themselves over a job well done.

"Come on! Let's get to work on that potion for wandering hands!" Jane suggested, grabbing Alice's wrist.

"What does this one do, exactly?" Clarissa asked, carefully lifting her new skirt as she followed them to the far wall.

"It will give boils to any boy whose hands wander too far," Alice said mischievously.

"Oh. I like the sound of that!" Lavender put in. They all gathered around the coffee table where Alice had already laid out the small tubs and satchels of herbs, petals, and roots they had been collecting around campus over the past few days.

"It looks as though we have everything," Alice said. "Dandelion, mushroom, poison oak . . . But we need someone with gloves to handle it."

"I'll do it," Theresa offered, holding up her gloved fingers.

Theresa's dress was of a modern style, with sleeves that opened wide over her shoulders, exposing the sides of her arms, before the fabric came together again just above her elbow. The bodice was white, with a black bolero-style vest, and the skirt was made of several layers of black and white fabric draped one atop the other. She looked like a *Harper's Bazaar* illustration come to life, and Eliza noticed more than one of the other girls eyeing her enviously.

"But what about the Smitten Potion?" Genevieve asked as Theresa got to work, measuring out the ingredients into a glass bowl. "I thought that sounded interesting."

"Turns out, it only lasts for twenty-four hours," Alice said dismissively.

"Good riddance, then. I have no interest in twenty-four hours," Genevieve said with a sniff, turning toward the mirror on the east wall to add a purple feather to her hair. "What I need is a potion that will win a husband for me forever!"

Eliza laughed as she and Catherine returned to their vanity table.

"See that? That's where I would draw the line," Catherine said. "You can't make a boy fall in love with you for all eternity."

Suddenly, the double doors opened.

"Shhhh!" Alice said, slamming the book and tucking it behind her.

Eliza turned, expecting to see the headmistress hovering at the door with a severe expression on her face. Instead, Helen hovered in the doorway, carrying a tray laden with a glass pitcher of water and a set of glasses.

"Hello, Helen," Eliza said in a welcoming voice, even as her heart fluttered with nervousness. After having caught Helen watching her so many times, she felt constantly on edge around the maid. "How are you this evening?"

Helen placed the tray on the side table near the door and walked up to Eliza and Catherine.

"Well, thank you," she said quietly, looking Eliza directly in the eye.

"We haven't had a chance to properly thank you for keeping us out of trouble," Catherine said, turning in her chair to face Helen. "You could have told on us, but you didn't. We're all very grateful."

"You're welcome, miss," Helen said tonelessly.

Eliza wasn't sure what to make of the girl's complete lack of personality or inflection.

"Here. Would you help me fasten my necklace?" she asked, hoping to get the girl to warm up a bit. She sat before the vanity, placed her compact down, and lifted the gold locket from the table. Helen reached for it, but hesitated when she saw the pendant. Her skin looked almost gray.

"What? What is it?" Eliza asked, alarmed.

Helen blinked, tearing her eyes from the etching in the pendant's surface. "It's nothing, miss." She took the clasp and worked it in one try. "It's beautiful, Miss Williams," she added politely. "Yours as well, Miss White."

Catherine touched the gold fleur-de-lis that dangled from a simple chain around her neck. "My mother gave it to me," she said, smiling. "And please, Helen, I must have told you a hundred times in the past, you can call me Catherine."

"And me Eliza," Eliza added. "We're all the same age, aren't we?" She turned to look up at Helen. "How old are you?" she asked when the other girl didn't answer.

"Seventeen, miss," Helen replied. Her eyes flicked to Eliza's locket again, but just as quickly flicked back to her face.

"Then you are our senior and should certainly call us by our first names," Catherine said warmly.

Helen seemed about to respond when Theresa interrupted from across the room. "Well, I look stunning tonight, if I do say so myself," she announced turning this way and that in front of the full-length mirror. "I'm going to have a tough time keeping Harrison's hands from wandering."

"Would you like some of . . . what we were making?" Alice asked, glancing warily at Helen.

"No, thank you." Theresa smirked, then looked across the room at Eliza. "I think I'll take my chances."

This brazen statement was met with gales of laughter. Eliza, however, saw Catherine glance sympathetically at her. Eliza immediately looked down at the surface of the table, pretending to be preoccupied with the many colors of rouge laid out before her. Did Catherine suspect something? Did she know how Eliza felt about Harrison?

But you feel nothing, remember? she told herself. *He's just another boy, and he's engaged.*

She took a deep breath and held it, driving out the awful feelings of disappointment and guilt. In the reflection of the mirror, she saw Alice slip the book of spells out from hiding again, and a few of the girls bent over its pages, whispering now so that Helen wouldn't hear.

Avoiding Catherine's eyes, Eliza smiled brightly at Helen. "So tell us about yourself, Helen," she said, patting the stool next to her chair, opposite Catherine. "How did you come to be at Billings?"

Helen glanced around warily at the girls before taking the offered seat. She tucked her ankles and laced her fingers together in her lap.

"I used to live here, Miss Wil—I mean, Miss Eliza," Helen said. "When it was an orphanage."

Eliza felt the color rising in her cheeks. "Oh, my . . . well, then . . . your parents are not with you?"

"They were both taken by the measles. As well as my little brother, when he was just a baby," Helen replied matter-of-factly.

"That's horrible, Helen. I'm so sorry," Eliza said.

"There's no need to pity me," Helen said, meeting Eliza's gaze. "If there's one thing I can't abide, it's that. I was the lucky one. When the Billings family bought this house to turn it into a dormitory, Mr. and Mrs. Billings were kind enough to take me in and give me room, board, and wages. I owe a world of debt to them."

"What was this place like when it was an orphanage?" Catherine asked, looking around at the plate glass windows, the scrolling wall sconces, the gleaming floors.

"Nowhere near as nice as this," Helen said. "This room was used as our classroom, though not many learned a thing in here. It was loud and crowded, and there were too many young ones running around."

Eliza gazed across the busy, bustling chamber—at the gloves and evening bags strewn about, the fine jewelry being exchanged and borrowed, the rouge and lipstick being applied—unable to imagine the life Helen had experienced here.

"Here, Miss Eliza," Helen said suddenly, lifting something off the dressing table. "Don't forget these."

In the palm of her hand were Eliza's garnet earrings. Eliza smiled gratefully and fastened them in her earlobes.

"My mother always says that if I keep daydreaming, I'm going to miss out on my real life," Eliza said with a laugh. "She says May didn't get engaged by sitting around thinking." She looked at her reflection wistfully, imagining May seated right in the very same place the year prior. Had she been excited to see George at the welcoming dance? Had they already had some kind of understanding then, or was it just a new flirtation like the one she'd thought she had with Harrison Knox?

Instantly, Eliza's gaze flicked to Theresa, who was busy checking her hair.

Stop thinking about him, she reminded herself. *Stop, stop, stop.*

"You look beautiful, Eliza," Catherine said, startling her.

"She's right," Helen added. "I'm sure your dance card will be fuller than anyone's tonight."

Eliza laughed under her breath. "You don't have to humor me, you two," she said, dropping her gold compact into her evening bag. "I know I'll never be a true beauty like my sister."

"May?" Catherine's eyes widened in surprise. "Oh, you're far more beautiful than May."

Eliza was incredulous. "No one is more beautiful than May."

Helen shook her head. "Miss Catherine is right." She reached over and plucked a satin ribbon from the dressing table, running it through her fingers. "Your sister . . . Miss Williams's beauty is expected," she said, frowning thoughtfully. "Yours, Miss Eliza, is far more exotic . . . unique."

The blush rose through Eliza's chest, up her neck, and into her face. She gazed at her reflection in the mirror, wondering if it could possibly be true. The shape of her eyes, their deep green color, her gleaming brown hair . . . she supposed these features *were* rather exotic next to May's blue eyes and blond hair.

Eliza glanced at Helen again. She was gazing, her head tilted, at Alice and Viola in the reflection of the mirror as the two of them practiced waltz steps in the center of the floor. The silk ribbon still slipped through her fingers methodically, over and over again. Eliza was clearly not the only daydreamer in the room. Perhaps she had misread Helen from the beginning. Perhaps the maid wasn't always staring at Eliza, but merely daydreaming.

"You should come along to the dance," Eliza offered.

"Oh, yes! I'm sure one of the girls has a dress you could borrow," Catherine agreed enthusiastically.

Helen's tilted head snapped upright, and she blinked down at the ribbon in her hands. "Oh, no." She quickly replaced the ribbon and stood, smoothing the front of her plain gray skirt. "Thank you, but the headmistress would never allow it."

"Perhaps there's a way we could convince her," Eliza said pointedly, looking at Catherine.

Catherine smiled, immediately understanding Eliza's meaning.

"No," Helen said again, more firmly this time. Eliza could have sworn the maid glanced at her necklace once again. "No, thank you, Miss Williams. Please don't."

Eliza's face fell as she looked at Helen. "But you don't understand. We may be able to—"

"No," Helen snapped, taking a step back.

Stunned, Eliza was about to ask her what was wrong, but at that moment the headmistress walked into the room, her evening dress of old-fashioned black crepe nearly filling the doorway. Alice slammed her book shut and shoved it under her seat, perching on top of it. The room became so suddenly and deathly silent, Eliza was certain the headmistress was going to suspect something.

Quickly she stepped forward and threw her arms wide to block the view of the parlor. "Good evening, Headmistress Almay!" she said gaily. "My, how lovely you look."

Miss Almay glared down her nose at Eliza's sapphire blue dress. "As do you, Miss Williams." Eliza could tell it pained her to say the words.

Eliza reached for Helen's hand, intending to ask the headmistress if the girl could come along to the dance, but her fingers caught only air. When she glanced around, Helen was nowhere to be seen.

"Well, ladies," Miss Almay said, lifting her chin to look past Eliza's shoulders. "Shall we?"

Alice clapped gleefully. Eliza looked at Catherine, a sizzle of antici-pation rushing right through her, pushing all thoughts of Helen out of her mind. The men of Easton Academy awaited!

COMPLIMENTS

The dance was held in the solarium of Mitchell Hall on the Easton Academy campus. The marble floors had been freshly waxed, and gleaming floor-to-ceiling windows looked out over the gorgeous green vistas of eastern Connecticut. The sun was just starting to set behind the trees, dyeing the sky outside a romantic shade of pink, as Eliza and her friends entered the hall. A string quartet played in the corner, and tuxedoed waiters proffered refreshments in crystal glasses.

As soon as Eliza stepped through the door, her eyes met Harrison's. It was as if he'd been waiting for her all night long. But then Theresa emerged from the throng of girls and greeted him with a kiss on the cheek, forcing Eliza to face the awful truth that Harrison belonged to another.

"Come, Eliza," Catherine said, slipping her arm through her friend's. "Let's go get some punch and watch Alice flirt."

Eliza squeezed Catherine's arm. The two girls helped themselves to raspberry ice punch from the tray of a passing waiter and, along with Lavender, spent the first half hour of the dance people watching, giggling, and wondering whether Miss Almay would take a turn on the floor with Headmaster Crowe of Easton.

"Theresa and Harrison make a handsome couple, don't they?" Catherine said, eyeing Eliza in a knowing way.

Eliza blinked and blushed. She'd been caught staring.

"I don't think so," Lavender said baldly. "She's very severe and dark, and he's so boyish and blond. I don't think they go together at all."

Eliza pushed away from the wall and, feeling suddenly light-hearted, bestowed a quick kiss on Lavender's soft cheek. "I knew I liked you, Lavender Lewis-Tarrington!"

Lavender touched her cheek with her gloved hand and laughed uninhibitedly for the first time since Eliza had met her. Grinning, Eliza turned around and, not caring for propriety or decorum at the moment, grabbed the arm of the first boy she could catch hold of, which turned out to be Jonathan Thackery.

"Well, Miss Williams!" he said, his eyebrows raised. "You look lovely this evening."

"Thank you," Eliza said. "Do you fancy a turn around the floor?"

Jonathan laid his crystal cup of punch aside and offered his arm. "We may as well start practicing. I'm sure we'll be expected to dance together all night at the wedding."

"How very conscientious of you, Mr. Thackery," Catherine joked.

"I'm nothing if not conscientious," he replied, teasing in return. "But don't go anywhere, Miss White. You're next."

Catherine laughed as Jonathan squired Eliza to the center of the floor. They danced a waltz together, followed by a quickstep. Before long, Jeff Whittaker cut in, then a dark-haired boy who introduced himself as Cooper Coolidge, which, Eliza thought, was an unfortunately alliterative name. As she danced, Eliza managed to forget all about Harrison Knox. She was truly having a good time. She didn't even look for him over the shoulders of her many partners. Not more than once or twice, anyway.

And then, just as a new waltz was beginning, a hand came down on Christopher Renaud's shoulder. It belonged to Harrison. He glanced quickly at Eliza, giving her a private smile that she felt all the way down to her toes.

"Chris, my friend, do you mind if I cut in?" he asked.

"Not at all," Christopher replied. He stepped away from Eliza and bowed his head. "It's been a pleasure."

Eliza barely managed a nod. Harrison's closeness made her feel heady, and her skin, already warm from dancing, was now blazing hot.

He held his arms out to her and Eliza stepped into them, feeling weightless as his hand touched her waist, as his fingers curled around hers. He had a clean yet musky scent. As they started across the floor she felt that if he didn't hold her up, she might actually faint from the giddy dizziness of it all.

"That's a lovely locket, Miss Williams," he said in a formal tone.

"Thank you," Eliza said. "I'm glad you like it."

"It's quite unique," he said, looking deeply into her eyes. "Much like its owner."

Eliza blushed and looked away. "I've been meaning to thank you for the book," she said quietly.

"I hope you're enjoying it."

"Oh, tremendously," Eliza said, adding playfully, "You know how I feel about tragedy."

"I do at that," Harrison replied. They both smiled, dancing in silence for a few moments. "Tell me, Miss Williams," he said finally. "Are you having a good time, dancing with all the men of Easton?"

Eliza looked up at him through her lashes, detecting an edge to his voice. "I've been having a fine time, thank you," she replied. "Are you enjoying your many turns with Theresa?"

Harrison's grip on her tightened. "It's been quite pleasurable, thank you."

Eliza gulped back a knot of envy, which in the next moment hardened in her stomach in the form of guilt. Why should she be envious? He and Theresa were engaged.

"But it would have been far more pleasurable if I could have been dancing with you," he whispered, bringing his lips close to her ear.

Eliza's heart skipped a beat and her foot came down atop his. The two of them tripped together sideways, bumping right into Alice and Jeff.

"My, my. Aren't we graceful?" Alice joked before turning away.

Eliza dropped Harrison's hand and took a step back, her face burning as she stared at the floor. But to Eliza's surprise, he grabbed it back and pressed his thumb lightly into her palm. She looked up into his eyes.

"Eliza, I . . ."

She swallowed hard and glanced around. Miss Almay was talking to a pair of instructors near the windows, but her gaze was cast sidelong at Eliza. Theresa stood near one of the tables with Jane and Viola, and all of them were staring right at her and Harrison—staring and judging.

"Mr. Knox, we mustn't—," she began.

"Eliza, I just wish we could go someplace and talk," he said quietly. "Ever since that first night . . . you're all I can think about."

Eliza's heart expanded like a flower in the sun. But then she saw something move out of the corner of her eyes: Theresa, her arms crossed over her chest, was making her way toward them.

At that moment, the sound of a crystal goblet crashing against the floor cut through the room.

"Oh, my—! What . . . what's happening?"

Everyone turned to see Cooper Coolidge, shards of broken glass at his feet, backing away from Marilyn DeMeers. He held his hands up, his eyes wide with horror. Eliza covered her mouth in surprise. Several nasty, yellow boils had popped up on Cooper's palms.

Girls pressed themselves to the walls as one of the Easton teachers lurched forward to escort a whimpering Cooper from the room. Marilyn, however, simply stood by, a superior smirk on her face. Eliza saw her tuck a small bottle into her evening bag. It seemed Cooper had gotten a bit fresh for Marilyn's tastes and she'd slipped the boil potion into his drink.

Once the door shut behind Cooper, the room erupted in speculative conversation. Theresa grabbed Catherine by the hands and let out a whooping laugh.

"What was that?" Harrison said, stunned.

A useful distraction, Eliza thought, resolving to thank Marilyn for saving her from Theresa's wrath.

Headmistress Almay clapped her hands. "Students! This is no time for gossip! Mr. Coolidge will be fine. Let's get on with our evening!" she shouted.

"We should keep dancing," Eliza said. She stepped back into Harrison's arms, but made sure to keep a good, respectable distance this time.

"But about . . . what I said?" Harrison asked.

Eliza pressed her lips together for a moment, her heart at war with her conscience. She hadn't come to Billings to meet a boy. And she certainly hadn't come to Billings to steal a boy who was betrothed to another. But somehow she couldn't stop herself from looking deep into his eyes and saying, "We will find a way."

THE WEATHER

"I am going to marry Jeffrey Whittaker!" Alice announced, jogging to catch up with Eliza and Catherine, who were walking arm in arm on their way back to Crenshaw House. Marilyn and Genevieve were several paces behind, going over the events of the night in rapid French, while Jane, Lavender, and Clarissa had clumped together for some sort of intense conversation peppered with random giggles. Only Theresa walked along untouched by any of the other girls, her arms wrapped tightly around herself, her skirts whipping about her legs as she went.

"Mrs. Jeffrey Whittaker!" Alice gushed. "Doesn't it have such a dignified air to it? 'May I present Mr. and Mrs. Jeffrey Whittaker?' Oh, I just *adore* the way it sounds."

"Do you love him, then, Alice?" Bia asked, her wide eyes innocent as she walked alongside her sister.

"You know, Bia, I think I do!" Alice replied enthusiastically. "Even if I don't, I know that I *can*. Especially if it means being called Mrs. Jeffrey Whittaker!"

The other girls laughed as Alice executed a wide-armed twirl under the stars.

"Alice Ainsworth! If you continue to conduct yourself in such a silly manner, no man will ever ask you to be his wife," Miss Almay scolded from behind.

"Oh, larynx infectus," Theresa muttered under her breath, holding a hand out at her side, palm toward Miss Almay.

A snapping sound filled the air. Miss Almay and Mrs. Hodge paused, looking up at the sky.

"Was that thunder?" Mrs. Hodge asked.

Miss Almay opened her mouth to reply, but all that came out was a croak. She lifted her hand to her throat, eyes bulging in surprise. "I can't talk!" she whispered.

Eliza gaped at Theresa, who kept on walking as if nothing had happened. The other girls all looked around, stunned, unable to believe Theresa's daring. Alice glanced at Eliza uncertainly.

"It's all right," Eliza whispered to her as Mrs. Hodge attempted to look down Miss Almay's throat, holding a lantern over the headmistress's open mouth. The girls kept walking, putting more distance between themselves and their chaperones. "Just carry on."

"Okay . . . well . . . what about you, Eliza?" Alice asked, glancing over her shoulder at the older women. "Did you fall in love tonight?"

Eliza's skin tingled even as her chest went hollow. Catherine's grip on her arm tightened, and she cleared her throat. Eliza automatically touched her locket, remembering how Harrison had complimented it.

"No, Alice, I can't say that I did," she answered.

I believe I fell in love the day we arrived at Billings.

"What were you and Harrison talking about?" Theresa interjected, her voice a bit louder than necessary.

Eliza's heart thumped. She exchanged a glance with Catherine. "We didn't actually talk much," she replied. "It was just one dance, after all."

"Yes, but we all saw you talking. You must have been discussing *something*," Theresa said. "What was it?"

Eliza's tongue felt like a brick in her suddenly dry mouth. Theresa had just rendered Miss Almay speechless in front of everyone, simply for insulting Alice. Imagine what she might do if she discovered Eliza's true feelings for Harrison?

"The weather," Catherine replied suddenly. "They talked about the weather."

Eliza's eyebrows came together in confusion as she looked at her friend.

"You told me after the two of you danced, remember?" Catherine laughed lightly. "You see? The conversation was so dull, she doesn't even recall."

"He kept saying how fine the day was," Eliza lied, casting a glance at Theresa's narrowed eyes. "How perfectly fine the weather had been ever since we'd arrived. I could scarcely get him to say anything else." She tilted her head to better see Theresa past Catherine's frame. "You must have used up all his good conversation, Theresa."

For a long moment, Theresa said nothing. But then her mouth curved into a wry grin. "Perhaps."

As the group grew closer to Crenshaw House, Bia and Viola raced ahead, their laughter wafting back to the other girls through the balmy air. Theresa and Alice exchanged a mischievous look, then suddenly both gave chase, holding their skirts up away from their ankles. The other girls all shouted encouragement while Miss Almay grabbed Mrs. Hodge.

"Girls! Girls!" Mrs. Hodge shouted on Miss Almay's behalf, speed-walking past Eliza and Catherine. "That is no way for young ladies to behave!" She huffed over to the door where the four offenders now waited.

"Thank you for that, Catherine," Eliza said quietly once the two girls were alone. "I don't know what happened. I must be overtired. I couldn't even form a thought, which must have made me look very . . . and I didn't mean—"

"Anytime, Eliza," Catherine replied with a warm smile, stopping Eliza's rambling excuses. "Anytime."

BEST FRIENDS

All throughout services at Billings Chapel on Sunday morning, Eliza felt the pull of the temple beneath her feet. She could tell that the other girls did, too. Giggles were hidden behind hands, whispers abounded, knees jiggled impatiently, and Miss Almay grew more and more tense as the minutes ticked on. By the time the final prayers were said, Eliza felt as though she were practically suffocating.

"Oh, my!" she exclaimed as she stepped outside, unbuttoning her lace-trimmed jacket to let the air in. "I thought I was going to expire in there."

"What a gorgeous day," Catherine said, tilting her head back to look up at the sun. "Let's all go for a bike ride." She looked at Theresa and Alice. "We could even ride over to the Easton campus if you like."

"I can imagine how you might think that would appeal to me, Cat, but I already have plans," Alice said blithely, swinging her satin bag by her side. "I'm going into town with Jeff Whittaker!"

"You are?" Eliza asked, her eyes wide. "How ever did you get permission?"

"I telephoned my mother last night, and she spoke to Miss Almay," Alice said, lifting one shoulder. "My parents did send me here to meet my future husband, after all. And once they heard what the Whittaker family is worth, they gave their approval posthaste!" Then her face screwed up in consternation. "Although we're to be escorted by Mrs. Hodge, of course."

"Well, then, what about you, Theresa? A bicycle ride?" Catherine asked.

"I am going to go back to my room to catch up on my correspondence," Theresa replied. "Why don't you come with me, Catherine?"

Catherine hesitated. She looked at Eliza, then back at Theresa. Eliza suddenly felt a nervous niggling in her heart on her friend's behalf. Clearly Theresa was testing Catherine.

"Thank you, Theresa, but I'd really rather stay outside in the sunshine," Catherine said finally.

Theresa glowered for a moment, but quickly put on a fake smile. "All right, then. Enjoy your . . . *exercise*," she said, pronouncing the final word as if it tasted sour on her tongue. Then she walked off toward Crenshaw House alone, her head held high.

"Are you all right?" Eliza asked, stepping closer to Catherine as they watched Theresa stride away.

"I'm fine. Sooner or later Theresa Billings is going to have to learn how to take no for an answer," Catherine said wryly.

Eliza laughed. Then the two of them set off at a sprint for the equipment shed.

"Slow down, girls!" Mrs. Hodge called after them. "You'll twist your ankles in those shoes!"

But Eliza and Catherine paid her warnings no mind. Within minutes they had mounted their bikes and tossed their Sunday best jackets, hats, and bags on the grass outside the shed.

"Where shall we go?" Eliza asked.

"To Easton, of course," Catherine responded.

"I thought that was just a suggestion for Alice's benefit," Eliza replied, her pulse already racing at the thought of a potential chance meeting with Harrison.

"And yours," Catherine said.

Eliza avoided her friend's gaze, instead setting her sights on the spire of the Easton chapel and the other side of the valley. The two girls took off down the grassy hill, bumping along the uneven terrain until they reached the trodden dirt path that ran along the tree line. Eliza slowed her pace to let Catherine fall in alongside her. "Where do you think you would have gone to school, if not here?" Catherine asked as they neared the back of Gwendolyn Hall.

"There's a day school in Boston called Brighton," Eliza replied, glancing toward the center of the Easton campus. A pack of boys was playing baseball, but they were too far away to identify. "It offers a better curriculum, actually—more focused on academics than on polite behavior. But my mother thought Easton men would make more suitable husbands."

Catherine smirked. "I see."

"What about you?" Eliza asked, swerving a bit to avoid a large rock on the pathway.

"Oh, my mother used to tutor me," Catherine replied. She gazed off into the distance, toward the quad. "I suppose I'd still be sitting in our parlor going over the classics with her."

"Your mother taught you the classics?" Eliza asked, feeling a twinge of envy. "I can't even imagine my mother reading, let alone with me."

"It's not as cozy as it might sound," Catherine replied with a trace of bitterness. "Or rather, you might say it's a bit *too* cozy. Stifling, even."

Eliza suddenly imagined Catherine's mom as a stern type who never let her daughter play outdoors or leave the family property. Unless, of course, she was taking her to New Orleans in search of witch doctors.

"Parents can be strange creatures," Catherine mused, as if reading Eliza's mind.

"Yes, they can be," Eliza agreed.

There was a sudden crack of the bat, and shouts of "Run!" and "Get it!" came from the boys on the quad. Eliza hit the brakes and placed her feet on the ground, lifting her hand over her eyes to better see the game. Her heart skipped when she realized it was Harrison running for the ball. His cap flew off his head as he raced into the outfield, while Cooper Coolidge—clearly recovered from his spontaneous boil outbreak—rounded the bases at a sprint.

"He's not going to make it," Eliza said under her breath.

Then, suddenly, Harrison flung himself forward, making a heroic dive for the ball. Eliza gasped, and her hands flew up to cover her mouth. Harrison slammed into the grass with his arms outstretched, his glove reaching . . . but the ball landed two feet from his grasp.

Half the boys on the quad groaned, while the other half cheered. Cooper rounded third and headed for home, jumping with both feet on whatever it was the boys were using as home plate.

Eliza's spirits sunk. "He missed it."

Catherine eyed her with a discerning glint in her eyes. "But you missed nothing," she teased.

Eliza blushed and looked back out at the quad. Harrison was just getting up and dusting himself off. He grabbed the ball and, head hanging, loped back toward his friends.

"A valiant effort, m'boy!" Jonathan Thackery greeted him with a slap on his back.

"He likes you, you know," Catherine said.

Eliza's head snapped up. "What?"

"He does," Catherine said firmly. "I saw it in the way he held you that day in town. And the way he looked at you at the dance last night. That boy is completely smitten." She paused and smiled. "You didn't feed him any of Alice's potions, did you?"

"I wouldn't dare." Eliza took a breath and swallowed hard, her heart pounding. She knew it was wrong, and she knew that she risked everything by admitting it, but suddenly the words itched the tip of her tongue. "I think I'm in love with him." She hazarded a glance at her friend.

"I thought as much," Catherine said.

"Yet you haven't told Theresa?" Eliza asked.

Catherine squinted into the sun. "What good would it do?" She placed her hand over Eliza's on the handlebar. "Besides, I would never betray your trust, Eliza."

Eliza gazed out at the Easton Academy campus, watching as Harrison tagged a player out. Harrison's friends slapped his back, congratulating his effort as they left the field and headed for the plate.

"I feel awful," she said. "Falling for an engaged man. I fear it makes me a horrid person."

"You're not. You can't control who you fall in love with, Eliza," Catherine said, giving her friend's hand a squeeze before releasing it. "For what it's worth, I think you should follow your heart."

Eliza looked at her, surprised. "But Theresa's your best friend."

"She is," Catherine said with a nod. "But so are you."

Eliza's heart warmed inside of her. No one had ever called her a best friend before. "And you're mine," Eliza said, meaning it.

Catherine grinned in response. "Then as your best friend, I should tell you that I don't think Theresa is truly in love with Harrison. I'm not even sure her heart would be broken should anything, or anyone, come between them. It might even be good for her. It might help her realize her true feelings now, before it's too late."

"What makes you think she doesn't love him?" Eliza asked, scarcely willing to let herself believe it—to believe that Harrison might actually one day be free.

Catherine looked down at her hands, kneading her fingers. "I've not told you this before, because I didn't think it was my place, but now . . . there's something you should know. About Theresa and May."

Eliza blinked. She felt as if the sun had suddenly shifted on her, throwing off her entire view of the world. "Theresa and *May*?"

"Yes, well, I know you've noticed that May doesn't exactly hold a fond place in Theresa's heart," Catherine said.

"I've noticed," Eliza said.

"Well, there *is* a reason for that. The thing is . . . Theresa was in love with George Thackery," Catherine said.

Eliza felt suddenly dizzy. "Theresa and George?"

"Yes. For years," Catherine said, looking out across the Easton campus. "She was completely heartbroken when he proposed to May. Heartbroken and furious. She went after Harrison soon after, telling herself and everyone who would listen that he was the better catch anyway. Harrison was so stunned and taken in by her that I think he just went along with it. I don't even know if he realized what was happening until he was so embroiled in that situation, it was too late to veer off course."

Eliza was at a complete loss for words. May had stolen Theresa's love out from under her? No wonder Theresa had detested Eliza from the moment she'd learned her last name.

But still—it wasn't Eliza's fault that George had fallen for May. The whole thing was so unfair, so petty. And to think Harrison might be tied to this person for life—this person who didn't even care about him.

Eliza looked up to find Harrison at bat. "How could she play with his heart that way?" she asked, toying with her locket. "I understand that she was heartbroken, but why involve someone else? She altered his whole life just to suit her whim."

"That's Theresa," Catherine said. "But that's also why I'm telling you."

Eliza nodded. There were so many thoughts swirling in her mind, she couldn't make heads or tails of them all. The only thing she knew for sure was that Harrison shouldn't be manipulated by Theresa Billings.

"Well, what are you going to do?" Catherine asked.

Eliza narrowed her eyes as Harrison pulled back to take a swing. "I'm going to . . . race you back to Billings," she said.

And before her words could even sink into Catherine's mind, she'd turned around and started back along the path.

"No fair, Eliza Williams!" Catherine shouted after her.

But Eliza just laughed, feeling the wind in her hair, not even looking back when she heard the telltale crack of the bat.

GOOD MEMORIES

"Eliza! Help me!"

Eliza woke with a start, her heart pounding in her throat. She clutched her blankets to her chest in terror and looked at Catherine's bed. It was empty.

"Eliza! Eliza! Where are you?"

Eliza flung the covers aside and raced for the door. Sleep still clung to her eyes, blurring her vision.

"Help! Help me!"

Eliza threw the door open and stepped into the woods. The dark branches tangled and wove overhead, blocking out the sky and stars. The earth beneath Eliza's feet was soft and wet, as if it had been recently soaked by a good rain. Mud seeped between her bare toes and coated her skin, and the piney scent of wet evergreen needles was all around her.

"Help! Eliza! Help!"

Eliza crashed through the underbrush ahead of her. Her pulse raced with fear, heating her from the inside as she shoved aside brambles and branches and tripped over fallen limbs. Catherine was out here somewhere, and Eliza had to find her. She had to find her now.

"Catherine! Where are you?"

"Eliza! I'm here! Please hurry!"

The voice seemed to be coming from somewhere in the dense trees to Eliza's right. She turned and shoved her way through the bushes. Sticks and jagged rocks cut into the bare soles of her feet, but she forged on. There was no visible path, no clear route to take, but she was headed toward Catherine now. She was certain of it.

"Eliza! Where are you? Help me!"

Eliza paused. Now the voice was coming from behind her. She turned around, and a branch snapped against her face. She felt blood trickling down her cheek, but ignored the pain and doubled back the way she'd come.

"Catherine! I'm coming! Just hold on! Please, hold on!"

Eliza stumbled. She threw her hands out just in time to keep from breaking her forehead open on a jagged stone. When she pushed herself up, her breath caught in an inaudible scream. It wasn't a jagged stone at all, but a bone. A human bone, broken and jutting at an angle from the ground.

"Eliza!"

Tearing her eyes from the awful sight in front of her, Eliza looked up. There was a clearing in the woods dead ahead. A clearing that hadn't been there just moments ago. And there was Catherine, clad in her white nightgown, one arm held by Theresa Billings, the other by Helen Jennings. The two girls were shoving Catherine toward a gaping hole in the ground, their teeth gritted in concentrated effort.

"Catherine!" Eliza screamed, and the scream seemed to pierce her own heart.

She shoved herself off the ground and took a step forward, but the earth fell from under her feet and her toes came down atop a bare skull. She stopped in her tracks as the mud and gunk and fallen leaves melted away before her, leaving nothing but a broken, battered terrain of human bones. Empty eye sockets stared up at her. Jagged teeth caked with grime, finger bones, toe bones, shattered ribs—they all seemed to point up at her like a ghastly, accusatory jury.

"Eliza! Help!" Catherine screamed.

Theresa and Helen had Catherine right at the edge of the hole now—a hole that seemed to extend down, down, down forever.

"Theresa! Helen! No! Stop! Stop, please!" Eliza begged.

Catherine struggled, but Theresa and Helen were too strong for her. Eliza tried to take another step, cringing as her bare sole came down on a broken skull. The skull turned to ash beneath her foot, and she fell face-first against bony terrain.

"Please. Please help me," Catherine begged.

Eliza stared at her, tears of desperation filling her eyes. Even if she could get up, even if she could traverse the perilous landscape, the hole still separated her from Catherine. Eliza looked left and right, trying to discern a bridge, a felled tree, a rope, any means of crossing it, but there was none. There was nothing she could do but stay where she was and watch. Watch and beg for her friend's life.

"Theresa," she whispered. "Helen. Please."

Helen looked up at Eliza then, peered directly into her eyes, and spoke ever so calmly.

"This is all your fault, Eliza. You should have turned back."

Eliza's blood went cold in her veins as Helen and Theresa flung Catherine over the edge. Her friend's scream echoed against the never-ending walls of the hole, ricocheting back to Eliza like a reproach.

"No!" Eliza screamed.

She sat up straight in her bed, her nightgown soaked through with sweat. In the bed across from her was Catherine, her eyes wide with fright.

"Eliza? Are you all right?" Catherine asked.

Gasping for breath, Eliza pressed her hands into the mattress beneath her, touched her blankets, touched the cold wall beside her bed. She had to assure herself that she was there, that this was real, that Catherine was alive.

"I just . . . I had a nightmare," Eliza replied, the awful images racing back into her head and swirling all around her. She reached back and lifted her hair from her neck. It was so wet, she might have just emerged from the ocean.

Catherine sat up a bit more. "Do you want to talk about it?" she asked.

Eliza looked at her friend, but all she could see was terror—the terror Catherine had felt in her dream. The pleading way she had looked at Eliza just before she'd been tossed to her doom. Eliza's heart pounded desperately, and she had to look away.

"No. Thank you, Catherine," Eliza said, trying to blink the images from her mind.

"Try to get some sleep, then," Catherine said. "Just lie back and think about a happy memory. You'll be fine."

Eliza settled back, grimacing as her body hit the sweaty sheets. Catherine quickly dozed off again, but Eliza knew she was done with sleep for the night. She feared that if she closed her eyes, her friend would not be there when she opened them again.

FRIENDS AND ENEMIES

Eliza closed her journal with a sigh on Monday afternoon. It was no use trying to make sense of her thoughts about the coven and the awful nightmare she'd had the night before. She'd pushed them from her mind as best she could. She got up to pace at the parlor windows. The roofs and spires of the Easton Academy campus were just visible behind the trees, and suddenly her heart was full of nothing but Harrison Knox.

She'd had her moments of distraction, like that morning's impromptu fashion show after Theresa had received a trunk of new dresses from her father. But now the girls were in the midst of their free time, and while everyone else was occupied with studies or music or sewing or spells, Eliza could not stop thinking about Harrison, wondering how and where they would meet. Wondering if he was thinking of her, too.

"Eliza Williams, would you please stop that incessant pacing?"

Clarissa demanded, letting her hand fall across her French text. "I'm trying to write out this translation, and I can't concentrate with you walking back and forth like a caged animal."

"I'm sorry, Clarissa," Eliza replied. She turned reluctantly away from the windows and looked toward the far side of the room, where Catherine was reading the coven's divination book, which she'd tucked inside a history text, and Theresa was scribbling out more of her correspondence. Eliza was desperate to get Catherine alone, but she couldn't do so without enduring questions from Theresa.

Catherine lazily turned the page, and Eliza was hit with an idea. Perhaps a bit of magic could be useful here. Having long since memorized the list of basic spells, she had a few dozen tricks at her fingertips. She held out her hand discretely at her side, palm toward Catherine's books.

"Gravity potens," she whispered.

Both the divination and history texts flew out of Catherine's hands and hit the floor. A few of the girls gasped at the noise, and Catherine looked up, startled, right into Eliza's eyes.

"Catherine!" Theresa said, hand to her heart. "You just made me scribble all over this note!"

Eliza tilted her head toward the door, silently beckoning Catherine to follow her. She walked out past Helen Jennings, who was stationed near the door, and endeavored to ignore the girl's steady stare. From the foyer, Eliza glanced back inside, hoping Catherine had understood her.

Catherine hesitated, then spoke. "I'm sorry, Theresa. I must have dozed off for a moment there." She got up to gather the books. "I think I'll go upstairs for a bit and lie down."

"And I suppose I'll just start this all over again," Theresa groused, crumbling up her letter.

Catherine hastened out of the room to join Eliza. She took her roommate's arm and tugged her toward the front door of Crenshaw House, as far away from the parlor as they could get.

"What is going on?" Catherine asked. "You scared me half to death!"

Eliza felt a chill at Catherine's mention of death, but shoved it out of her mind. It had been only a dream.

"I'm sorry, it's just . . . this is sheer torture," Eliza replied, leaning back against the thick door.

Catherine took a deep breath and hugged her books to her chest. "What is?"

"It's Harrison," Eliza whispered, glancing back toward the parlor. "I've never felt this way before, Catherine. It's as if my heart is trying to tear my chest open and run off to him."

Catherine stuck out her tongue. "That's disgusting."

Eliza walked to the staircase and slumped against the banister in a way that would earn her a slap on the wrist if Miss Almay were to see her. "What do I do? I have to see him soon, or I'm going to go mad."

Suddenly, Catherine's blue eyes brightened. "Oh! We could try scrying for him."

"What's scrying?" Eliza asked, standing up straight.

"Basically, it's a magical way to find out where any person is at a given moment," Catherine replied.

"So I could know where Harrison is right now?" Eliza said.

"Exactly," Catherine confirmed, grasping Eliza's hand excitedly. "I think I have everything upstairs in our room."

"Then what are we waiting for?"

Eliza and Catherine raced upstairs hand in hand. Once the door of their room was closed safely behind them, Catherine crouched on her knees next to her bed. She tugged out the long, flat box with the gold clasp that Eliza had seen her hide there on her first day.

"What's in there?" Eliza asked, her curiosity piqued.

"A few things I brought from home," Catherine replied. She laid the box on her bed and undid the clasp. "Can you fill the wash basin?"

Eliza used the pitcher full of cold water to fill up the ceramic bowl. Catherine, meanwhile, opened the case and began to carefully pick over its contents. Eliza was startled to see that the box was full of items mentioned in their books on witchcraft. There were several jars full of spices and herbs, a couple of white candles, a few crystals, some velvet pouches full of substances Eliza couldn't see, and a few colorful sticks, which appeared to be made of crystal.

"What is all this?" Eliza asked.

"Some things I picked up on travels with my mother," Catherine replied. "It's all quite basic stuff, but you need a specific crystal for scrying."

"Is it this one?" Eliza asked, lifting one of the sticks. It was bright yellow in color, with uneven edges, as if made by hundreds of tiny jagged rocks fused together.

"No. That's sulfur," Catherine replied. "You're supposed to be able to make a spark by holding it and reciting a simple spell, but I've never gotten it to work."

"That could come in handy on our midnight jaunts," Eliza joked. "No candles needed."

Catherine laughed. "If only we could get it to do what it's supposed to do."

She gently took the sulfur stick from Eliza's hand and replaced it in the box. "Ah. Here it is." She turned and grinned at Eliza, holding a black ribbon attached to a long, multifaceted purple crystal. "Let's scry for your beau."

Eliza reached up to finger her gold locket, her heart pounding with excitement at the idea of Harrison as her beau. But then a picture of Theresa appeared in her mind's eye, and her chest flooded with guilt. She was consumed by the awful, sour, heavy sensation she felt whenever she allowed herself to recall that Theresa and Harrison were engaged—even if they'd become so under dubious circumstances. For a moment she thought to stop Catherine, even reaching for her arm. But then she remembered Catherine's belief that Theresa did not love him, and the moment passed.

Catherine grabbed a jar full of what looked like tiny blue pebbles and approached the filled wash basin.

"Do you have anything of Harrison's?" Catherine asked.

Eliza shook her head, feeling a twist of longing in her gut. "No."

Catherine's lips twisted up in thought. "What about something he's touched?"

Eliza immediately thought of the book Harrison had gifted her, but she'd lied to Catherine about its sender. She shoved aside another pang of guilt.

"My glove!" Eliza said, remembering. She turned and yanked open the top drawer of her bureau, then took out the left glove she had worn the night of the dance. "He held my hand when I was wearing this."

Her skin tingled at the recollection, and she ran her thumb over the palm of the glove.

"Perfect," Catherine said, snatching it out of her hand. She tied the crystal's black ribbon around one of the fingers of the glove, then laid the whole thing aside on their dressing table. "Now, you'll need to dump the pebbles into the water. Concentrate on an image of Harrison as you do so."

"All right."

Eliza took the jar of pebbles and removed the lid. Holding the jar over the washbasin, she closed her eyes and concentrated. In her mind's eye she saw Harrison just as he was on that first day, playing out on the quad with his friends. Then she saw him in the basement of Gwendolyn Hall—his open, frank, interested expression as she spoke to him about *The Jungle*. Then at the dance in his formal wear, his hair combed back from his handsome face, his whisper in her ear . . . She felt a thrill go through her, and she overturned the jar. The tiny pebbles raced into the water with several tiny *plop*s.

"What now?" Eliza asked breathlessly, opening her eyes.

"Hold the crystal over the water," Catherine said, handing the small bundle—ribbon, glove, and pendant—to Eliza.

Letting the crystal drop from her palm, Eliza dangled it above the basin. She caught a glimpse of herself in the mirror and suddenly felt very silly. Here she was, nearly a grown woman, hoping some trinkets and a bowl of water and rocks would lead her to her true love. Catherine, however, wore a look of serious concentration and determination, so Eliza wiped the smile off her face.

"Repeat after me," Catherine said. "Spirits from the other side, let your wisdom be my guide, show me the place where this person hides."

Eliza reached out and took Catherine's hand in her own.

"Say it with me," she said. "I know it will work better if you do."

"Okay," Catherine replied with a smile, as if flattered.

The two girls held hands, closed their eyes, and recited the incantation.

"Spirits from the other side, let your wisdom be my guide, show me the place where this person hides."

A light breeze blew Eliza's hair from her face, and her breath caught. She felt suddenly dizzy, and she wrenched her eyes open in an attempt to steady herself. As she watched, the crystal began to spin above the bowl of its own accord. Eliza clung to Catherine to get her bearings. After a moment, she was able to focus on the miraculous things happening before her.

The crystal spun in a wider and wider circle, and the water in the bowl began to ripple.

"Are they . . . are the pebbles moving?" Eliza gasped, leaning closer as the blue stones at the bottom of the bowl began to jiggle and jerk.

Catherine nodded, her lips pressed together giddily as she held tightly to Eliza's hand. "It's really working!"

Then, ever so suddenly, the pebbles arranged themselves at the base of the bowl, the water stopped rippling, and the crystal hung straight. Its tip pointed down at the water like an arrow. Eliza's heart was in her throat. She could scarcely believe what she'd just seen.

"I don't understand," Catherine said. "What does this mean?"

Eliza bent closer to the water, narrowing her eyes as she began to detect a shape among the pebbles. An image came to her: three thick, winding limbs attached close to the base of a trunk—heavy branches, laden with leaves, hanging almost to the ground. "Is that . . . ? Yes! It is! It looks just like the old elm!"

Catherine grabbed the sides of the bowl with both hands and stared. "You're right!"

"Do you think Harrison's out there right now?" Eliza asked, barely able to believe what she was saying.

Catherine snatched the crystal from Eliza's hand and tossed it in the long box, then threw the whole thing back under her bed. The two girls clasped hands and ran down the hallway, nearly flattening Lavender, who was on her way to her room. They laughed as they tripped down the stairs and out the front door, then raced around the back of Crenshaw House to the garden that had been the site of one of their first punishments. Eliza sprinted to the tree, expecting to see Harrison's blond hair gleaming in the sunlight.

But he wasn't there.

"I suppose it was too good to be true," Eliza said, her shoulders slumping.

"The spirits would not have led us to the wrong place." Catherine strode forward, ducking beneath one of the lower-hanging branches. Eliza watched her, amused. Did she think she was going to find Harrison hanging from the limbs?

"Eliza!" Catherine said, her word but a gasp. "Come quickly!"

Startled, Eliza rushed forward and ducked down. Catherine was holding a piece of white parchment in her shaking hand. "I found this tucked into one of the knots in the trunk."

"Well?" Eliza prompted. "Open it!"

"But it's for you." Catherine held the paper out to Eliza.

Holding her breath, Eliza took the parchment. Inside she found a short note, written in familiar, masculine handwriting. She read it out loud to Catherine.

Eliza,

Would you do me the honor of meeting me this evening in the woods just south of Billings Chapel? I'll be waiting for you at midnight.

Yours,
Harrison Knox

The word *yours* brought a warm blush to Eliza's cheeks.

"Thank you, Catherine. I never would have found this without you." She stepped toward her friend. "There's something I should tell you. That book? The one I received our second day here? It wasn't from my father. It was from Harrison. I'm sorry I lied."

"I understand," Catherine replied. "How could you have known to trust me back then?" She reached for Eliza's hand and squeezed it. "But I hope you know you can trust me now."

Eliza grinned. "I trust you above anyone, Catherine White."

She was just about to fold the note and tuck it away in the pocket of her skirt when she caught a glimpse through the thick leaves of some-one rapidly approaching. She froze.

"Miss Eliza?"

Eliza's heart dropped. "Helen? Is that you?"

Helen ducked under the low branches and stood next to Eliza, her hands folded in front of her skirt. She glanced at Catherine, then at the piece of parchment trembling in Eliza's hand. Her face went ashen, and she took a step back.

"Mr. Harrison Knox sent word through one of the Easton servants that he had left something for you at the tree," Helen said. "I was to give you the message. How did you know it was—"

She stopped abruptly as Eliza and Catherine exchanged a look.

"Oh. I see," she said, her tone shifting completely.

Eliza felt as if she had been kicked in the chest. What, exactly, did Helen see?

"Aren't Harrison Knox and Theresa Billings betrothed?" Helen asked.

Eliza's skin burned. She opened her mouth to speak, but Catherine stepped up and touched her arm, stopping her. "Our affairs are none of your concern, Helen," she said. "You've delivered your message. Kindly leave us."

Helen's face hardened as she dipped into a quick curtsy. "Yes, Miss White."

Then she ducked under the branches and was gone.

Suddenly Eliza's breath was coming at an alarming rate. She looked at the ground and fought to calm it, pressing one hand against the comforting strength of a thick tree limb.

"Are you all right, Eliza?" Catherine asked.

"You needn't have spoken to her that way," Eliza replied, bringing Harrison's note to her chest. "I think you've upset her."

"Well, as much as I like the girl, she has no right to judge you," Catherine replied, supporting Eliza with an arm around her back. "No one does."

Eliza took a deep breath in through her nose and blew it out through her mouth. "You don't think she'll tell Theresa, do you?" Eliza asked, looking off in the direction in which Helen had disappeared.

"I don't know. She didn't tell on us before, but who knows if her discretion or her loyalty to the Billings family will win out?"

Eliza nodded and rolled her shoulders back, trying to appear collected, but that look in Helen's eyes had unnerved her. She had a feeling that Helen Jennings was not a good person to have as an enemy. And she hoped the young maid hadn't just become one.

A BLESSING

Eliza's hands fidgeted with the folds of the skirt on her favorite navy blue dress, the one with the buttons all up the side of the sleeves and the wide boatneck collar that showed off her gold locket perfectly. Harrison was going to love it. If he ever got a chance to see her in it.

"Here's a good one!" Theresa announced from behind the podium at the center of the temple. "The Genius Spell."

It was Theresa who had called this last-minute meeting of the coven, then announced to the others that they were going to go through the book of spells, page by page, and make a list of the next ten spells they would try. The other members of the coven were all gathered around in a circle, seated in rickety wooden chairs they had lugged down from the storage closet. Marilyn yawned, which caused Genevieve to yawn as well. Jane, Bia, and Viola were focused on Theresa, but Clarissa looked bored as she gazed up at the ceiling, and

Lavender and Catherine were both working on literature homework at Eliza's side.

"It will make you all-knowing for twelve hours," Theresa continued. "I'd say that's long enough to take a history exam, no?"

"Oh, I like that one!" Jane announced, raising her hand.

"But that's cheating!" Clarissa protested, dropping her booted feet to the floor and leaning forward. "We can't use that."

"Maybe you can't, but I will," Viola said with a sniff, tugging on the lace cuffs of her sleeves. "Just because you're a genius every day doesn't mean we shouldn't have the chance to experience it for ourselves." She raised her head, sitting up perfectly straight on her chair.

"All in favor of the Genius Spell?" Theresa asked.

Everyone but Catherine, Eliza, and Clarissa raised their hands. Theresa surveyed the room and made a quick note. Eliza glanced quickly at her delicate gold watch, and her heart lurched. It was already eleven forty-five. In fifteen minutes, Harrison would be standing out in the woods, waiting for her. She reached into her pocket for his note, intending to check it again to make sure she was right about the time, but her fingers felt nothing but fabric. Her heart skipped a beat and she dug deeper, but there was nothing there. Her pocket was empty. The note was gone.

Instantly, Eliza looked up at Theresa. Theresa was gazing right at her, a smirk on her face. The entire room seemed to darken as Eliza felt a bull's-eye form on her chest. Had Theresa found the note? Did she know? Was that why she'd called this impromptu meeting?

Guilt pressed in on Eliza from all sides. She was, after all, planning a clandestine meeting with another girl's fiancé. Whatever her bond with Harrison, his engagement to Theresa was a fact. Maybe she shouldn't be doing this. Maybe she had let herself get caught up in the romance of it too quickly.

"All right, then, the Genius Spell is on our list with a vote of eight yeses and three nos," Theresa announced.

She made a final tick on her notes, then looked back at Eliza. "I notice you haven't voted yes once, Eliza," she said perkily. "What are you waiting for? Are you in the mood for something more creative? Because the next one will apparently make a painting come to life."

The other girls giggled, and Eliza shifted in her seat. She felt warm all over—conspicuous. "I suppose I just haven't found any of the spells worthwhile."

"Oh, really? And here I thought you were being sullen just because this was my idea," Theresa said, turning fully to face her. "No one likes a spoilsport, Eliza."

Jane gasped, and Viola whispered something to her behind her hand. All eyes darted between Eliza and Theresa. Eliza sat up straight, her guilt slowly beginning to ebb. "I'm not being a spoilsport. I just think there are better things we could be doing with our time."

Like meeting Harrison, she thought. Catherine closed her book and glanced at her two friends warily.

"What is it with you Williams girls?" Theresa said, throwing a hand up and letting it slap down on the podium. "Why do you think the entire world must revolve around what you think?"

Eliza's face burned as the girls all gaped at her. This was the last straw. She had to get out of this basement and away from this awful girl, and she had to do it now. Across the room, Bia whispered to Viola, and suddenly a plan came to Eliza.

"I'm sorry, Theresa," she said, making her voice all breathy, the way Bia's always sounded just before she went faint. "I don't believe the world must revolve around me. I'm just . . . I'm having a hard time concentrating tonight."

"Are you?" Theresa asked, with what seemed to be false surprise.

"Yes. In fact, I'm not feeling very well," Eliza stated. "I'm feeling a bit . . . dizzy."

"Oh, no!" Bia jumped up, suddenly wide awake, and crouched down in front of Eliza's chair, taking her hand. "Don't faint, Eliza!"

"Take some deep breaths," Marilyn added helpfully, getting up to stand next to her chair.

"She's not going to faint," Theresa said, stepping away from the podium. Her red skirt swished around her ankles, making a gratingly raspy noise.

"Yes, she is! Dizziness always precedes fainting," Bia said over her shoulder. "I should know."

"She's right. Bia faints more than anyone else I know," Lavender stated.

Suddenly all the girls were on their feet and gathering around Eliza.

"You should get some fresh air, Eliza," Catherine said, laying her books aside, obviously catching on to Eliza's plan. "Everyone step back and give her some room to breathe."

"Yes, I think I'll just go back to Crenshaw House and lie down," Eliza said as Catherine pretended to help her to the door. "The walk might do me some good."

"You shouldn't go alone," Theresa said, dipping down to retrieve her leather carryall. "I'll come with you."

Eliza's heart skipped a panicked beat and she looked at Catherine. "I'll go with her," Catherine blurted right away. "You have your votes to tend to."

"Thank you, Catherine," Eliza said, sounding as weak as she could. Before Theresa could reply, Catherine and Eliza had started up the winding staircase toward the empty pastor's office up above.

"Let's talk about this moving painting spell," Clarissa said down below. "Do the subjects come to life as three-dimensional beings or two-dimensional pictures?"

Eliza and Catherine closed the door behind them at the top of the stairs and laughed. The windows of the chaplain's office rattled in the strong wind that had been blowing all evening.

"Thank you!" Eliza said, drawing her friend into a hug.

"I'll hide up here for a few minutes, then come back saying I've delivered you to the front door of Crenshaw," Catherine replied, her eyes bright.

Eliza gave her friend one last hug before she went. "Thank you, Catherine, truly. I couldn't be doing this without you."

"You're welcome," Catherine replied. "Now go! I'll see you back at our room, and you can tell me all about it."

As she raced through the chapel and out into the moonlit night, Eliza knew that of all the blessings she had in her life, Catherine White was one of the greatest.

IRREDEEMABLE

It wasn't until Eliza had crossed into the woods just south of the chapel that she realized she had no idea where she was going. A rumble of thunder sounded in the distance, and Eliza looked up anxiously at the sky. How far into the woods would Harrison be waiting? Would he be directly to the south, or somewhat east or west of the chapel entrance? Would she make it to him before the storm broke? She paused a few feet along one of the dirt paths that crisscrossed the woods and took a breath. The trees and bushes were being tossed by the wind, rustling and crackling, making it difficult to focus. Her heart rate was already accelerated with the anticipation of seeing Harrison. She had to calm down. She had to think.

What would Catherine do?

The answer came to her in an instant. *Scry.* But could she do it on her own? Another rumble of thunder sounded so close, it made Eliza flinch. The truth was, she didn't have much choice. Alone she was.

Closing her eyes and ignoring the sliver of fear that ran down her spine, Eliza concentrated on a mental picture of Harrison. She didn't have the pebbles or the water, the crystal or the glove, but she had an intense desire within her, and she hoped that would be enough. At the last moment, she decided to change the words slightly, hoping the specificity might help.

"Spirits from the other side, let your wisdom be my guide, take me to the place where Harrison hides."

Suddenly raindrops started to drop all around her, drizzling onto her shoulders and back. Eliza felt the dizziness that seemed to accompany more complicated spell-casting, and she leaned a hand against the nearest tree until it passed. She tilted her face toward the sky, letting the raindrops cool her and bring her back to herself. Once she felt steady again, Eliza opened her eyes, unsure of what to expect. A sudden wind hit her from behind, tossing her hair in front of her face and tripping her forward.

Eliza gripped the tree and hesitated. Was this just more wind brought by the storm, or was this something else? She closed her eyes and concentrated. The wind whipped at her from behind, so hard she could barely keep her grasp on the tree bark. When she looked around again, she saw that the underbrush was being flattened in the opposite direction. That was the wind from the storm. This wind, the wind at her back, was something else entirely. This wind was leading her to Harrison.

Biting her lip in excitement, Eliza followed the breeze. Soon she came to a fork in the path, and suddenly the wind shifted. Her hair blew across her face to the right, tickling her cheekbones and making her giggle. The rain, meanwhile, grew harder and more persistent, pounding on the leaves and branches above. Luckily the branches and leaves protected Eliza from the worst of the deluge. As she took the designated pathway, she was still relatively dry. Only a few drops here and there were visible on her dress.

Eliza walked a few paces and came to a large boulder, tall, white, and wide. When she came around the side of the boulder, she found Harrison Knox seated on a long, flat outcropping of the rock. He scrambled to his feet, and immediately the wind died down.

Eliza's heart pounded. Magic was becoming rather useful in her life.

"I wasn't sure if you'd come," Harrison said. "Especially in this weather."

He stepped forward and took her hand. He was dressed in a suit of brown tweed, a green-and-blue tie loosely knotted around his throat. The color combination somehow made him appear boyish—innocent. His blond hair was slightly wet from the rain, making it appear darker than usual.

"Of course I came." The smile on her face was so broad, it ached.

"Eliza . . . I can't stop thinking about you," Harrison said earnestly.

The pitter-patter of the rain on the leaves above abated slightly, but another rumble of thunder sounded.

Eliza closed her eyes, letting his words wash over her. "Nor I, you," she said, looking up at him again.

His handsome face broke into a grin.

"But what about Theresa?" she forced herself to ask. She didn't want to, but she had to know how Harrison felt about his betrothed.

Harrison's smile fell away. He dropped her hand and turned his back on her. It was the longest moment of Eliza's life.

"I care for Theresa. I do," Harrison said passionately, facing her again. "We've known each other all our lives, and I don't wish to hurt her."

Eliza's heart panged miserably in her chest. Perhaps she should have waited just a few minutes longer to ask the question. Perhaps she should have allowed herself just a couple of moments to bask in the bliss of Harrison's attention before causing it all to crumble away.

"But you should know, Eliza, our engagement . . . it's not real," Harrison said. He stepped forward again, and this time he took both her hands in both of his.

"It's not?" she asked, confused but hopeful.

"I have to admit, last summer when it became clear to everyone that Theresa Billings had turned her attentions to me . . . I was very flattered," Harrison said. "All the fellows coveted her. They were all jealous. Of me."

Eliza swallowed hard.

"I got swept up in it," he said, lifting his shoulders. "Suddenly everyone was asking me when we'd be engaged, where we'd make our home together, where we'd honeymoon, and it just seemed like . . . that was what I was supposed to do. If Theresa Billings loves you . . . you love her back."

Eliza looked at the ground. Tears blurred her vision.

"But Eliza . . ." Slowly he drew her fingers up. Her breath caught as he tentatively, sweetly, brought them to his lips. "Eliza," he said again. "I *don't* love her. I realize that now. I could never feel about her the way I feel about you."

"And how is that?" Eliza said, feeling weightless.

Harrison swallowed hard, his eyes searching Eliza's. "I feel . . . I feel . . ."

With his right hand he gently cupped the back of Eliza's neck. He was going to kiss her. She could see it in his eyes. As his lips edged closer to hers, she realized that all she wanted in the world was for him to kiss her. Her eyes fluttered closed and she tilted her head back, aching for the feel of his lips against hers.

And then they heard a shout. Harrison backed away, his eyes scanning the dark trees around them.

"What was that?" he asked.

There was another shout, and this time, Eliza recognized Catherine's voice. A gust of wind whirled through the trees, drowning out the next words, but Eliza could have sworn she heard Theresa respond. Her heart flew into her throat as a flash of lightning was followed quickly by a clap of thunder.

"Someone's out there," Harrison said, reaching for her protectively. "Come. I'll take you back to Crenshaw."

"No," Eliza replied. Harrison looked at her, his face creased with confusion. "I mean . . . no, thank you, Harrison. I can find my own way back. If you're caught on the Billings campus—"

"What is that to me when your safety is on the line?" Harrison said, placing his arm around her waist.

Eliza glanced over her shoulder as another shout was whisked away by the wind. Theresa and Catherine were out there right now, arguing, and she knew it most likely had something to do with her. She had to go to them. She had to stop this.

I'm sorry about this, Harrison, she thought. Then she placed her hand flat behind him, palm facing his back.

"Domicilus," she whispered.

Instantly, Harrison released her and walked off, his eyes unfocused as if he was in a daze. He was headed for his own dorm on the Easton campus, just as the spell intended. Eliza bit her lip as his foot slipped on some wet leaves, but he righted himself and kept walking. She only hoped he would get there safely and not encounter anyone along the way.

"Stop it, Theresa!" Catherine's voice shouted, closer than ever this time. "Let's go back! Just come back with me!"

"Leave me alone!" Theresa responded. "You're no friend to me, Catherine!"

Once again, the rain picked up, this time breaching the protective canopy of the trees and soaking Eliza through. She blinked the water off her lashes, hitched up her skirt, and ran toward the arguing voices, only hoping there was something she could do to help.

BROKEN

"I know they're out here somewhere, and I know that *you* helped them!" Theresa screamed as Eliza emerged from the tree line into a small clearing.

Catherine and Theresa stood on the far side of a ravine that cut right through the trees. Theresa's dress was soaked, the heavy fabric clinging to her skin. She whirled on Catherine, her dark hair matted to her face and neck. Eliza blinked, feeling an odd sense of déjà vu, but the memory was gone as quickly as it had come.

Theresa went on, "How could you do this to me? You're supposed to be my best friend!"

"I *am* your best friend, Theresa," Catherine replied, holding both hands above her eyes, shielding them from the rain. A flash of yellow peeked out between her fingers—the sulfur stick.

Neither of the girls had noticed her yet, and Eliza found herself frozen with uncertainty. Should she say something? Do something?

Or should she simply slink back into the woods as if she'd never been here? Suddenly her locket felt warm against her skin. She could have sworn it was actually pulsating, as if it was somehow reflecting the tenor of Theresa and Catherine's argument.

But how could that be?

"But you don't love Harrison," Catherine continued. "We both know you don't."

"I'm not talking about Harrison right now," Theresa replied, bending at the waist. "I'm talking about Eliza Williams! You like her better than me, don't you? That's why you're helping her sneak around with *my* fiancé!"

A bolt of lightning lit the night, and Catherine's eyes suddenly flicked to Eliza. Theresa turned around and instantly, Eliza began to sway on her feet, improvising a plan. She unfocused her eyes and looked from Theresa to Catherine and back again.

"Catherine? Theresa? Is that you?" Eliza said weakly.

Theresa whirled around and her jaw dropped. "What are *you* doing here?"

"Where am I? Is this the way to Crenshaw?" Eliza squeaked.

Theresa's eyes narrowed. "Oh, so you're lost, are you?" she demanded, stalking to the very edge of the ravine that separated her from Eliza. "What happened? Did Harrison desert you? Or did he never arrive? Perhaps he suddenly remembered that he was engaged to be married!"

Eliza gulped, her face burning even as it was pelted by cold rain. Part of her wanted to keep up the charade, out of both pride and self-preservation, but as she looked at Catherine, standing there with her shoulders slumped as if exhausted, she decided enough was enough. She stood up straight, rounded her shoulders, and tried to ignore the sick, nervous feeling in her gut.

"How did you find out?" Eliza asked.

"I found his little love note!" Theresa said, whipping the paper from her pocket and holding it out. "Here's some advice, Eliza Williams. If you're going to try to steal someone's beau, take better care of your correspondence."

Eliza's face stung at the sight of the cherished note clasped in Theresa's fingers, turning to pulp in the rain.

"That's one thing I can say for your sister," Theresa said, tearing the note up into tiny bits. "When she stole George Thackery away from me, she was much more covert about it."

The wet scraps of paper fluttered down around her feet. Eliza felt as if she could scream, but instead, she took a deep breath.

"Harrison didn't desert me," she said loudly, clearly. "He was there, but I sent him back with a spell when I heard you two fighting."

Theresa paled. "So you admit it! You admit carrying on an affair with my future husband."

"Theresa," Catherine said impatiently.

"We've done nothing improper," Eliza replied firmly.

"Nothing but plan a secret midnight rendezvous," Theresa shot back. She took a step forward, and the unstable edge of the ravine crumbled beneath her toes. Eliza's heart swooped. The gash in the ground was at least ten feet deep.

"Be careful," Eliza warned her.

"Oh, you're the one who should be careful," Theresa replied, her eyes narrowed. "Do you even realize what I could do to you?" Eliza's heart turned cold, remembering the spell Theresa had cast so cavalierly on Miss Almay. Her gaze flicked to Theresa's raised hand. Was the girl about to use some new spell she had up her sleeve?

Suddenly it all came back to her in a rush. The dream—the awful dream about Catherine's death. They had been in the woods, in front of a hole just like this one. Eliza's throat seized with fear. "Theresa, please!" she croaked. "Step away from the ravine."

"You think you've won? You think you've stolen my Harrison?" Theresa continued. "Well, from this moment on, you're going to want to watch your back, Eliza Williams."

"Theresa!" Catherine shouted. "Stop it!"

"And you, Catherine White!" Theresa spat, whirling on her. "You are no longer my friend! Both of you stay far, far away from me from now on!" Theresa started to stalk past Catherine, but Catherine reached for her as she went by.

"Theresa, stop! Please!" Catherine said, throwing her arm out.

The moment she did, the sulfur stick suddenly let out a huge spark. Theresa shouted and jumped back in surprise as the spark hit a thick tree limb directly above Catherine's head. Instantly, the branch severed, the cracking noise so loud, it drowned out the wind and rain. Eliza looked up as the branch began to fall. Her heart flew into her mouth.

"Catherine! Watch out!"

Catherine looked up, her eyes wide with fright. Theresa grabbed for her, but it was too late. The limb came crashing down. Catherine's body crumbled like a rag doll's, and she tumbled backward into the chasm.

DEAD

"No!" Eliza shouted.

She collapsed at the edge of the ravine; Theresa did the same on the other side, like a mirror image. They stared wordlessly into the chasm.

Catherine lay at the bottom, rain pelting her broken body. Her gray dress was so soaked, it looked black. Her dark hair fanned out around her head in wet clumps. Her ice blue eyes were wide, her mouth frozen open. It was almost as if she was trying to call out to her friends, but the unnatural bend in her neck meant she would never speak again.

"Theresa! There you are!" Alice came tromping up behind Eliza, her light blue dress clinging to her body. "I sent everyone home like you asked me to. Did you find Catherine?" She stopped next to Eliza. "What are you doing here, Eliza? Why are you staring down into that—" Alice looked over the edge of the ravine and screamed. "Catherine! Oh my . . . Is she . . . ?"

"She's dead," Eliza said. She could barely choke out the words. Her mouth felt as if it was full of cotton. Her dream, at least part of it, had just come true before her eyes. The locket weighed heavy around her neck, cold as a stone in winter.

"She can't be dead!" Alice wailed. "She simply can't be!" She turned around and got on her hands and knees, backing herself toward the edge of the ravine. Eliza stared at her for a moment in catatonic wonder. Demure, girly Alice on her hands and knees in the mud. But then she realized what her friend was doing, and she sprang to her feet.

"Alice! No!"

But it was too late. Alice was already lowering herself down into the chasm. She clung for a moment to a tree root that stuck out of the dirt wall, then let herself fall the last couple of feet. As soon as she recovered herself at the bottom, she got up, wiped off her hands, and began trying to remove the tree limb from across Catherine's chest.

"It's too heavy! I need help!" Alice called up to them. "Theresa! Eliza! Come help me!"

Eliza's and Theresa's eyes met across the ravine, and suddenly it was as if the life had been breathed back into the both of them. Eliza slid forward and lowered herself exactly as Alice had. A branch caught her ankle and left a deep scratch in her skin, but she barely even noticed. She slid the last few feet, her fingers clinging to the dirt wall to slow her descent, and fell to her knees at the bottom of the ravine. Theresa alit on the other side, and all three girls grasped the branch, with Alice at the center.

"On the count of three," Theresa instructed. "One, two, three."

Eliza braced her feet against the slick, muddy ground and dug in, pulling with all her might. Theresa let out a grunt as the branch finally freed itself. The three girls stumbled backward and dropped the limb at Catherine's feet. Eliza climbed over the branches and twigs and leaves and fell to her knees once again, this time at her friend's side. The back of Catherine's head lay atop a jagged rock. It was covered in blood and matted hair. Next to her on the ground was the bright yellow sulfur stick, its tip singed to a dingy black. She looked into Catherine's wide-open, lifeless eyes, and finally the tears came.

"What happened?" Alice cried, taking up Catherine's lifeless hand. "What happened to her?"

Eliza looked up at Theresa, her vision blurred.

"She fell," Theresa said, her voice high and breathless. "She was trying a spell and it went wrong and the branch snapped. She fell. She fell, and there was nothing we could do."

"Poor Catherine," Alice said, kneading the girl's hand within her own as tears sluiced down her cheeks. "Poor Catherine."

"We have to fix this," Eliza said, wiping the back of her grimy hand across her nose. She looked at Theresa. "We have to fix this."

Theresa stared back, her jaw working, and Eliza knew that she understood. This was no accident. This was their fault. Catherine never would have been out in these woods on this night if it hadn't been for their own selfishness, their stupid feud.

"She's right," Theresa said, shoving her soaking wet hair behind her ears.

"Fix it?" Alice wailed throatily. "Catherine's dead, Eliza! There's no fixing this! She's dead!"

"All right, Alice, that's enough," Theresa snapped.

Alice's mouth hung agape as she gasped over and over again, struggling for breath through her surprise and grief. "That's enough? Theresa, she's dead!"

"I understand that she's dead," Theresa said, hovering over all of them. "The question is, what are we going to do about it?"

Eliza's head whipped around as she looked up at Theresa. Suddenly an image flitted through her mind: a drawing of a skull with roses growing out of its empty eye sockets. The Life Out of Death Spell. The page that had so frightened Eliza that night in the temple.

"What are you talking about? There's nothing you can do about death!" Alice cried, scrambling to her feet. The light blue skirt of her dress was covered in mud and muck, with evergreen needles and bits of rotted leaves clinging to the wet fabric. "The Lord has chosen to take her and—"

"The Lord didn't choose anything!" Eliza shouted vehemently, rising to her feet. She grabbed the sulfur stick and shoved it into the pocket of her skirt. "He would never have taken her. She was too good, too kind, too . . . loyal. She—"

"Eliza's right, Alice," Theresa interrupted. "She was only sixteen years old. This was not her time. If there's something we can do about it, I say we do it."

"We have to move her. We need to get her back to the temple," Eliza said, needing to have a task to focus on. To have a plan. To have something to think about other than Catherine's gaping eyes, the unnatural twist of her neck.

"No. We need to go for help," Alice said, shaking her head as tears streamed down her face.

"I'll get under her arms, you get her feet," Theresa instructed Eliza.

Alice tripped backward a few steps to get out of Theresa's way. "No. You can't do this. No."

"Alice. You're either helping us, or you're not," Eliza said tersely. Alice just continued to sob, covering her face with her dirty hands. Eliza's heart was suddenly hardened against the girl. How dare she try to stop Eliza from saving her best friend?

"We'll lift again on three?" Eliza said. Theresa nodded determinedly.

Alice let out a wail as Catherine's body rose off the ground. Eliza started backing toward the sloping portion of the ravine, the way down which Theresa had come.

"No! Wait!" Alice shouted.

Automatically, almost against her will, Eliza stopped. Alice stepped forward and, her hand shaking violently, reached out and placed her thumb and forefinger over Catherine's eyelids. Turning her face away, her own visage screwed up in grief, Alice drew Catherine's lids down over her eyes.

"God bless you, Catherine," she whispered. Then she took a deep breath and looked at Eliza, her chin lifted, her eyes shining. "Now go."

CREATIVITY

Eliza tried not to think about the gruesome load she was carrying as she and Theresa struggled down the dark, winding stairs to the temple, the wooden steps groaning ominously beneath their weight. She tried not to think about where Catherine's soul might be right then, whether her friend was watching them. Tried not to think about how things had gotten to this horrible point. How, if Eliza hadn't been so selfish, they would both be asleep in their room right now.

Instead, she thought about the next day, when Catherine would be back with them. When their power had brought her back. The power they never would have realized they had, if not for Catherine.

"We'll lay her in the center of the circle," Theresa said. Perspiration covered her face, but she hadn't complained once, nor had she asked to stop.

"Wait!" Alice cried.

She gathered a few of the softer scarves and tapestries and laid

THE BOOK OF SPELLS

them out reverently on the floor. Arm muscles straining, Eliza waited until Alice was satisfied with the bed she had fashioned. Then she and Theresa moved forward and laid their friend's body down carefully, her blood-matted hair coming to rest on Alice's mink jacket, which she'd folded for that purpose. Eliza felt a pang of gratitude.

"What do we do?" Eliza asked as Theresa made a move for the book.

"We can't just do it now," Theresa replied, flipping quickly through the pages. "There are special supplies. And we'll need the entire coven."

"What?" Eliza asked, devastated. "But I thought—"

"Special supplies?" Alice interrupted. "You're not . . . you girls aren't actually planning to . . . to bring her back?"

"Why do you think we carried her all the way back here?" Theresa demanded.

"I thought we were just bringing her out of the woods," Alice said, her bottom lip trembling. It seemed she was unable to face reality. "Bringing her home."

Theresa slapped a thick page down. "Here it is. The Life Out of Death Spell."

Eliza rushed over to peer over Theresa's shoulder. A shudder went through her at the sight of the awful skull, and she wrapped her arms around herself as the cold air of the chapel started to slither around her wet limbs. She averted her eyes from the drawing and concentrated instead on the words, clinging to them like a mantra.

Life Out of Death. Life Out of Death.

"No. We can't do this," Alice said, backing toward the stairs. "It's unnatural."

"What's unnatural is a sixteen-year-old girl falling to her death in the middle of the night in the woods because of a stick of sulfur," Eliza replied, glancing up from the list of instructions for the spell.

"I can't be a part of this," Alice said, shaking her head. "I have to go."

Then she turned on her heels and raced up the stairs, her tiny feet making scrambling sounds until the door had slammed behind her. The sound echoed down the stairs, and Eliza shivered, feeling suddenly closed in, closed off, buried alive.

"And so we are down to two," Theresa said wryly.

Eliza took a deep breath and tried to ignore the foreboding feeling that swirled through her.

"Three," she corrected, glancing at Catherine.

She looked so peaceful now that she was inside and out of the mud. The branch that had fallen on her had left not a scratch on her face. From the right angle, she looked as if she was merely sleeping peacefully—as long as one didn't get a glimpse of the awful wound on the back of her head.

"Right. Three," Theresa replied. She pointed to the list of ingredients needed for the spell. "We're going to need some time to gather these things. The spell can be done anywhere up to forty-eight hours after the subject's death. We need to move fast."

"But we have classes tomorrow," Eliza said, pacing away from the pedestal and toward the wall. "How are we going to explain Catherine's absence?"

Theresa bit her lip. Eliza had never seen her look so uncertain, and suddenly she felt an odd connection to Theresa. They were in this together now. Together—for Catherine.

"We could tell them she received an urgent message from her parents. That a coach came in the middle of the night to take her home."

Eliza leaned one hand against the cold clay wall and nearly froze. She pushed herself away again, pacing the periphery of the room to try to warm herself from the inside.

"It won't work. All messages have to go through Miss Almay."

She thought of the Spell of Silence. "Is there anything in that book we can use? Something that will make them think they see her, even though she's not there?"

Theresa shook her head and flipped a few pages, frustrated. "Nothing. And believe me, I know. I read through the entire thing earlier tonight, remember?"

"I do," Eliza said, her heart twisting in agony. Tonight she had been sitting just there on the right side of the room with Catherine. If she concentrated hard enough, she could see her friend bent over the book across her lap, studying for an exam she would never take.

"Wait a minute," Eliza said, a rush of realization running through her. "What if we made up a spell on our own?"

"Can we do that?" Theresa asked.

"Why not? We can word it like the Spell of Silence, but make it so that none of the adults miss her." She walked over to the book and flipped to the beginning, where the more basic spells were written. "Wherever we go, wherever we might, let us walk in silence as the night," she read, contemplating the words.

Eliza stared at the wall, rhymes floating through her mind. Perhaps something about keeping adults in the dark? Or making them forget Catherine ever existed? But then how would they explain who she was when she came back? Unless they made the spell last for only forty-eight hours . . .

"What about something like . . . 'Wherever we go, wherever we breathe, let others see Catherine where she might usually be'?" Theresa said, walking around to the front of the pedestal.

Eliza blinked. "Theresa, that's amazing. We should write it down," she said, picking up the pen on the pedestal. "In case it works and we need it again."

Theresa flipped to the center of the book, where the spells ended and the blank pages began. Eliza handed over the pen.

"Here, you should do it," she said. "It's your spell."

"All right," Theresa said, the pen hovering over the blank page. "But what shall I call it?"

Eliza's brow knit. "How about the Presence in Mind Spell?"

Theresa nodded. "I like that."

She wrote the title across the top of the page in large letters, then scrawled the words beneath, separating the lines as if the spell was a stanza of poetry. Finally she placed the pen down and, much to Eliza's surprise, took Eliza's hand. "Come. We'll say it together."

"No. Wait," Eliza said, gazing down at the body of their fallen friend. "We should hold Catherine's hands too."

Theresa shuddered. "You can't be serious."

"I am," Eliza said. "The spell will be stronger if we're connected to her."

"Why? How do you know?" Theresa asked her.

"I just feel it. We must be connected to her when we say it," Eliza replied. She walked over and knelt next to Catherine, trying not to look at her face. "What are you so skittish about, Theresa Billings? You carried her all the way back here."

"All right, all right." Theresa knelt next to the body as well and took Catherine's left hand in hers. Eliza held Catherine's right hand, which was now as cold as ice, then reached across her torso for Theresa's hand. They looked into each other's eyes and nodded.

"Wherever we go, wherever we breathe, let others see Catherine where she might usually be."

The dizziness wasn't as nauseating this time, but Eliza wasn't sure what that meant. Was she getting stronger—more resilient? Or was the spell not strong enough? She opened her eyes, and a pathetic flutter of wind tossed the pages of the book, lifting Eliza's hair briefly from her shoulders.

"Do you think it worked?" Eliza asked, still holding hands.

Theresa gazed down at Catherine's serene face. "We'll just have to wait and see."

"Theresa," Eliza said tentatively, feeling a flutter of nervousness in her stomach. "I think I . . . the other night I . . . I dreamt about this."

Theresa's face snapped up. "Dreamt about what?"

"About Catherine dying. The dream, it was . . . it wasn't exactly as it happened tonight, but she died the same way. In the woods, falling into a deep hole." Eliza saw no reason to tell the other girl that in her dream, Theresa and Helen had pushed Catherine to her death. She knew it would only anger and upset her.

"Are you saying that you saw the future?" Theresa asked.

"I don't know. I didn't think so at the time, of course, but now . . ."

Theresa sighed and looked down at Catherine's body. "A month ago, I never would have thought something like that was possible, but I'd believe it now."

"But that means . . . that means I could have stopped this," Eliza said, her eyes filling with tears. "If only I'd told her about the dream, she might have thought twice about following you into the woods. She might have been more careful."

"There's no way you could have realized, Eliza," Theresa said with surprising force. "Besides, she would have followed me anyway. That's Catherine. Always trying to protect everyone."

"But I—"

"Eliza," Theresa cut her off, squeezing her hand. "What's done is done. And by tomorrow, it won't matter any longer," she assured Eliza, looking her firmly in the eye. "Tomorrow night, we'll bring Catherine back."

AGREED

"What are we doing here? Why are you two acting so mysterious?" Clarissa asked, sitting on Theresa's brocade settee in her single room.

The chamber was larger than any of the rooms the other girls shared—large enough for the entire coven to gather comfortably—with two huge windows that looked out across the darkened campus. Lightning flashed in the distance, illuminating the underbelly of the gray clouds and casting odd shadows over the trees and buildings. Theresa closed the door quietly and stood next to Eliza. The two girls had washed and changed their clothes, then gone from room to room, waking the others and telling them to come up to Theresa's. But Eliza could still feel the rain on her skin, the grime under her fingernails, the weight of Catherine's body straining her arms. The seven girls gazed back at them, each clad in nightclothes. Only Alice was not among them. She had refused to come.

"And where are Catherine and Alice?" Clarissa added.

"Girls, we've brought you here to tell you some disturbing news," Eliza began. Her heart felt as if it was made of pins and needles, jabbing outward at her chest with each breath.

"What is it?" Bia asked from the edge of Theresa's bed, the color draining from her face. She reached for Viola's hand and drew it into her lap.

Eliza looked at Theresa for help—something she had never thought she would do. Theresa cleared her throat and rested her hand on the back of her desk chair.

"After she walked Eliza home earlier tonight, Catherine took a path through the woods on her way back to the chapel," Theresa began, as thunder clapped outside the window. "She got lost and she . . . she fell."

Viola gasped, covering her mouth with her free hand.

Lavender pushed herself away from the closet door. "Is she all right?"

"No," Theresa said, tears suddenly filling her eyes. "Catherine is dead."

Bia stifled a scream and hid her face against Viola's shoulder. The other girls gasped and covered their mouths, looking around as if someone else might explain this away. Marilyn gripped Genevieve's hand and stepped forward.

"Where is she? You have telephoned the police? You have told Miss Almay?" Marilyn asked.

"No. No one knows but us," Eliza said, her own tears spilling over onto her cheeks. "Us and Alice, who's back in her room."

"What happened?" Clarissa asked, sitting forward. "I don't understand? Who would wander in the woods alone on a night like this?"

Eliza and Theresa exchanged a glance.

"She had a sulfur stick and was trying a spell to make it light," Eliza said, withdrawing the stick from her pocket.

"But why didn't she return to the temple first? Why didn't she wait for us to go with her?" Clarissa demanded. "Why would she go into the woods alone?"

"We don't know why. She just did," Theresa snapped.

Clarissa blinked and sat down again. Lavender wrapped her arms around the girl's back in a comforting way.

"I'm sorry, Clarissa," Theresa said, rubbing her brow. "I'm just exhausted. I can't believe this is happening."

"Why haven't you told anyone, Theresa?" Jane asked, her bottom lip trembling as she looked up at Theresa.

"Because," Eliza said, "we're going to bring her back."

"What?" Viola, Genevieve, and Marilyn said at once. Bia's sobs grew louder as she clung to her sister's side.

"There's a spell—the Life Out of Death Spell," Theresa explained. "We've already laid Catherine in the temple so that we can use the spell on her and bring her back."

"But we're going to need all your help," Eliza added, trying to look each one of them in the eye. "The entire coven needs to be present for the spell, and we're going to need to spend the day tomorrow gathering all the ingredients."

"And if we succeed, if we can do this spell properly, we can make her alive again?" Marilyn asked hopefully.

"But this is impossible," Genevieve said. "No one can bring someone back from the dead."

"It's not impossible," Theresa replied firmly. "Two weeks ago
would you have thought it possible to change the color of someone's
dress at whim? To give a boy boils? To take someone's voice? No. If we
can do all that, we can do this, too."

"We have to do it," Eliza said, her heart feeling heavy. "We must, at
the very least, try."

"I'm willing," Clarissa said, standing.

"Me, too," Lavender added, rising next to her.

"If it will bring Catherine back, I'll do it, too," Viola said. "Bia?"

Bia nodded mutely, sniffling against Viola's shoulder.

"Jane?" Theresa said.

"I'll be there," Jane said resolutely.

"Marilyn? Genevieve?" Eliza prompted.

The two girls looked at each other, communicating silently the way
only lifelong friends can.

"We will do it," they said in unison, facing Eliza.

"Then we are agreed," Eliza said, stepping forward so that the group
formed a true circle around the still seated Viola and Bia. "Tomorrow
night, we all gather at the temple to bring Catherine back."

She reached for Clarissa's hand, then Theresa's. Theresa hesitated
but a moment, then clasped Eliza's fingers. Suddenly, her locket felt
warm against her skin. Slowly all the girls grasped one another's hands,
and Eliza felt as if she could sense their strength coursing through her.
With her friends, her sisters, her coven, anything was possible.

ROLL CALL

The next morning, ten girls walked from breakfast to McKinley Hall together in a state of solemn silence. Lavender and Viola supported Bia between them, and every now and then Bia would sniffle and hold a handkerchief to her face, but otherwise, there was no sound from them. All ten of them had suffered nervously through morning services and their meal, waiting for Miss Almay to ask where Miss White was, to demand an explanation, but Miss Almay had been too distracted by a heated conversation with one of the teachers to acknowledge any of the students.

Yet now would come the real test of the Presence in Mind Spell. They were about to attend classes.

Jane pulled out the list of ingredients Theresa had jotted down for the Life Out of Death Spell. "We can gather most of this in the garden and the fields," she whispered. "But what about the fig oil? That can only be purchased in a store."

"And I hardly think the general store in Easton carries it," Marilyn added.

Eliza turned around and everyone stopped. "We cannot talk about this now. After lunch we'll meet under the elm tree. But right now there are too many ears."

She slid her gaze from the left, where Miss Almay was talking animatedly with Helen and Mrs. Hodge, to the right, where two of their teachers were about to mount the stairs to McKinley Hall. The other girls nodded or hung their heads. Eliza looked at Theresa, and together they walked inside.

Most of the girls slipped into the French classroom, while Genevieve and Marilyn bid them good luck and headed to conversational English, a course established for all the foreign students, of which there was a grand total of four. Eliza was heartsick as she sank into her usual chair. She tried not to look at the empty seat to her right, but she couldn't help it. Catherine should have been there, but instead she lay all alone in the chapel basement.

She's gone and it's my fault, Eliza thought. *And if we are caught right now, that will be my fault as well.*

"It's going to be all right," Theresa said as she sat down at Eliza's right.

Eliza felt a grateful pang for Theresa's confidence. Not once had they mentioned their argument of the night before, and the word *Harrison* hadn't been uttered between them. Eliza felt as if they had some sort of unspoken agreement to focus only on Catherine. Today, and for the next few hours, nothing else mattered.

Then Miss Tinsley walked into the room, and Eliza clutched her desktop. The Presence in Mind Spell had to work. It simply had to.

"*Bonjour, classe!*" she intoned.

"*Bonjour, Mademoiselle Tinsley,*" the girls replied, less than enthusiastically.

Just then, the door opened again and in walked Helen Jennings with a tea tray. She set it down on the teacher's desk and went about pouring out a cup for Miss Tinsley. As she did, her eyes darted around the room and paused when she saw Catherine's empty seat.

Eliza's stomach sank through her toes. Helen saw that Catherine wasn't there.

"*Veuillez repondre quand je dis votre nom!*" Miss Tinsley picked up her class roster and looked up at the room as Helen replaced the teapot on the tray. "Alice Ainsworth."

"*Presente,*" Alice replied, sounding ill.

Helen stepped back against the wall and hovered there, waiting. But for what? Why didn't she just go? Eliza clutched the desk harder.

"Jane Barton," Miss Tinsley read.

"*Oui, mademoiselle,*" Jane said weakly.

"Theresa Billings," Miss Tinsley said, looking right at Theresa.

"*Presente, mademoiselle,*" Theresa said rather loudly.

As the teacher read through the rest of the list, Eliza held her breath. She was last in alphabetical order, with Catherine right before her. There was a stillness in the room that she could hardly stand, and it felt as if all the oxygen had been removed, leaving behind a thick, wet cloud that choked her senses. She couldn't stop staring at Helen, willing her to just leave. But Helen stayed where she was and stared silently back.

"Clarissa Pommer?" Miss Tinsley said.

"*Presente, mademoiselle,*" Clarissa said.

Eliza's stomach clenched. This was it. This was the moment of truth. Miss Tinsley looked at her class list. She looked up at the empty chair next to Eliza. A huge lump formed in Eliza's throat. Her hand shot out and caught Theresa's, which was there waiting for her.

"Catherine White?"

No one moved. No one breathed. No one said a word. There was a moment of complete suspended time, in which Eliza felt as if the whole world was about to implode around her. Helen's glare hardened as she seemed to stare right through Eliza's chest. Then, as if drawn by some invisible string, Miss Tinsley's gaze slid to Eliza.

"Eliza Williams," she read.

"*Presente, mademoiselle,*" Eliza said, her voice a mere whisper.

"*Bon! Toute la classe est presente!*" Miss Tinsley said, turning and dropping her roster on her desk. Finally, finally, Helen turned and left the room. Eliza could have cheered as she watched her go. She felt somehow as if she had won a standoff with the maid. As if she had just proven something—but of course, that wasn't possible. Helen could have no idea what had just gone on; she was completely in the dark. Wasn't she?

"*Attention, étudiantes!*" Miss Tinsley said, clapping her hands sharply. "*Répétez, s'il vous plaît!*"

Eliza looked at Theresa as the instructor began her daily routine of call and response.

Then, suddenly, Eliza's heart fluttered with pride. Their spell had worked. They had cast a huge spell, just the two of them, and it had worked. Perhaps this was why the dizziness hadn't been as debilitating as usual when they'd cast their spell. Maybe it meant they were growing accustomed to it, growing more powerful.

When she looked at Theresa again, she saw her feelings reflected in her friend's eyes. If the two of them could accomplish something of this magnitude alone together, they stood a chance of raising the dead.

PATH TO DAMNATION

"Here. We need a full cup of rosemary," Alice said, kneeling on her gardening pad in Crenshaw's herb garden that afternoon. She yanked up a few bunches of the fragrant, spindly herb and tossed them in Eliza's basket. "That should do it."

Eliza knelt down next to her friend and glanced tentatively at her profile. Alice continued working, the brim of her wide straw hat shading her pale skin from the sun. Eliza wanted to ask why Alice was helping with their plan even though she had been steadfastly against it last night.

"I hope Jane and Lavender are able to get the fig oil in town," she said instead.

"I'm sure they will," Alice said, tugging out a weed and tossing it toward the side of the garden. "Theresa set them on the task, and Theresa always seems to get whatever she wants."

"Even the eye of newt?" Eliza said.

Alice didn't respond. She simply went on with her work.

"What will we tell Miss Almay if she comes out for a stroll on the grounds?" Eliza asked. She pushed herself up and walked over to the bushes near the house to gather some lavender.

"We'll tell her we're weeding," Alice said flatly, tossing another dandelion off onto the grass. "What's another white lie, after all?"

Eliza paused and turned back toward her friend. "Alice, I can't tell you how much I appreciate your help in all this. I know how you must feel, and I'm so very sorry this has happened, but I honestly think this is going to work. Everything is going to be all right. I promise."

"I keep thinking about that first night," Alice said, still refusing to make eye contact. She moved methodically—trowel in the dirt, dig, yank out the weed, throw it—the same pattern over and over again. "How you convinced me to go into the chapel. How you told me you'd never let any harm come to anyone you loved." Finally, she stopped digging and stared right into Eliza's eyes. "Perhaps you should think about keeping your promises to yourself from now on. Because from what I can tell, Catherine is dead, and the rest of us are doomed to eternal damnation."

Eliza's jaw dropped open, the wind knocked right out of her. Tears of confusion, regret, and anger filled her eyes. She was just opening her mouth to speak when Alice turned away from her, and a pair of well-worn leather shoes appeared in her line of vision.

"Miss Eliza?"

Eliza looked up and shaded her eyes with her hands. The sun lit

Helen Jennings from behind. Quickly she placed the twig, laden with lavender leaves, into her basket.

"Yes, Helen?" she said, wiping her dirty hand on her apron. Her voice cracked, and she saw Helen's brow knit with concern. This surprised her, given their previous encounter.

"Is everything all right, miss?" Helen asked.

The tiny hairs on the back of Eliza's neck stood on end. "Everything's fine, Helen," she said firmly, looking the girl in the eye as she fiddled with her locket. Helen's expression hardened. She glanced at Alice, who was still intent on her work, then held out her hand. Tucked into the cup of Helen's palm was a small folded note. Eliza's heart skipped a beat, and she quickly took it and squirreled it away in the pocket of her dress.

"I came to see if the two of you wanted a refreshment from the kitchen." Helen glanced past Eliza at her wicker basket, which was half full of herbs. "Lavender, rosemary, and ginger root, I see." Then she looked Eliza in the eye and arched her brows. "Are you making a potpourri?"

Eliza swallowed hard. "Yes. We thought they might make a nice gift for our parents on parents' weekend."

"How thoughtful of you," Helen said flatly.

Feeling completely flustered, but not entirely sure why, Eliza took a deep breath. "We don't need any refreshments, thank you. Right, Alice?" she said, gazing directly into Helen's eyes.

"No, thank you, Helen," Alice replied.

"All right, then," Helen said.

She gave Eliza one last knowing look before she turned and walked away slowly, carefully avoiding the vegetable plants as she went. Eliza stood and watched Helen until she had gone inside the house and closed the door behind her, but even then she had this awful, prickly feeling that she was being watched.

Helen Jennings knew more than she was letting on. And the thought frightened Eliza to her core.

FUNERAL PARTY

That night, the girls gathered in Eliza's room and quickly performed the Spell of Silence so they could sneak out to the chapel. Everyone was dressed in dark tones—black, gray, navy blue—as if attending a funeral instead of an awakening.

"When will we be leaving, Eliza?" Genevieve asked. "I would like for this to be finished."

Anxiety was etched on all her friends' faces. All but Alice's, who sat at the foot of Eliza's bed and had drawn the hood of her black cape over her face so that only the very tip of her nose could be seen.

"We'll go as soon as Theresa arrives," Eliza replied. "Don't worry, Genevieve. This will all be over soon."

The door to Eliza's room suddenly opened and Theresa entered. Eliza felt a thump of foreboding and guilt the moment she saw her. The note Helen had delivered earlier had been from Harrison—a request for her to meet him again tonight. Eliza hadn't felt comfortable sending her refusal through Helen, so she knew that Harrison was going to be standing in the woods tonight, waiting for a girl who would never come.

"You really should knock, Theresa," Lavender said. "For all we knew, you could have been the headmistress."

"Thank you for that lesson in etiquette, Lavender," Theresa said sarcastically.

Theresa had dressed in a royal purple frock, the most festive of the bunch. The book of spells was clutched against her chest, and she glanced around the room until her gaze came to rest on Eliza.

"We have a problem," she said, keeping her voice low.

Every single girl turned to look at Eliza. All except Alice.

"What is it?" Eliza said.

Theresa opened the book as she walked to Eliza. "The instructions are quite clear. This spell will not work without all eleven members of the coven present to recite it."

"What?" Jane exclaimed, stepping forward.

All around there were questions and whispers and panicked twitters. Eliza took the book and scanned the page. Theresa was right. The instructions referred to "eleven voices raised" and "twenty-two" crossed arms. The numbers were there over and over again. Her heart sunk into her toes and disappointment descended over the room.

"Well, we'll just have to try it with ten," she said, trying to sound firm.

"I don't think so," Theresa said.

"She's right," Marilyn spoke up, for once without Petit Peu in her arms. "What if something goes awry because we do not have enough power? This is Catherine's life we are talking about."

The other girls murmured their assent. Eliza couldn't help wondering if some of them were grateful for an excuse to not perform the spell.

"We need an eleventh," she heard herself say.

"Where are we going to get someone new now?" Viola whined, fidgeting her black-gloved hands. "Not to mention someone who won't run screaming when we tell them what we're about to do."

An idea flitted through Eliza's mind. It made her feel sick to her stomach, but what other choice did she have? Catherine's life hung in the balance.

"I know someone," Eliza said.

"You do? Who?" Theresa asked.

"I'd rather not say until I know that she is willing," Eliza told her. "All of you go to the chapel and wait for me there. If I haven't arrived within an hour, you can return."

As the girls grumbled and whispered and gathered their things, Theresa latched on to Eliza's arm tightly.

"We can't wait much longer to do this," Theresa said through her teeth. "Those forty-eight hours are wasting away."

"I know," Eliza said, lifting her chin. "I just need a little time. Trust me. I will bring our eleventh."

THE ELEVENTH

Eliza waited until her friends had walked out into the night. From her large window overlooking the Crenshaw House entry, she saw the lights of their candles and lanterns bounce merrily through the darkness, as if unaware that anything could be wrong in the world.

She snuck out of her room and closed the door quietly behind her. Crenshaw House was dark and perfectly still. She took a moment to get her bearings in the wide hallway before tiptoeing down the runner carpet and onto the wide oak stairs. Her fingers lightly brushed the polished banister as she scurried down the steps. The first floor was deserted, but she could see a shaft of light beneath the door to the kitchen. Cringing at every creak in the old floor, Eliza moved slowly and cautiously toward the light, her ear tilted toward the ceiling to catch any noise, any sign of life, from Miss Almay's room. Just outside the latchless kitchen door, she paused. Whoever was inside was humming, and the tune was low and mournful, like a funeral dirge. A chill of fear raced through Eliza and she stood for a moment, her hand on the door, her breathing shallow and raspy.

Thinking of Catherine, Eliza screwed up her courage and pushed the door open on its hinges.

Helen sat at the table, her back to Eliza, her blond braid down the back of her blue shawl. She was polishing silver methodically as she hummed.

"I delivered your message to Harrison Knox, Miss Eliza," Helen said.

Eliza nearly collapsed. How did Helen know she was standing there? She hadn't made a sound. And what message was she talking about?

Helen turned around slowly. "He won't be waiting for you. I let him know you couldn't be there, as you were to be otherwise occupied."

Eliza's mind swam as Helen blithely returned to her work. She took a tentative step into the room and was surprised when her weakened knees held her.

"What . . . how did you . . . ? Did you read his message to me? How did you know I couldn't go to him?"

Helen simply arched one eyebrow as she rubbed a serving fork with her rag.

"What do you know?" Eliza asked, walking boldly over and standing next to Helen's chair. Her skin pulsated with uncertainty and fear, but she wasn't going to let Helen see that. "How much do you know?"

The polishing continued, as did the awful tune.

"How did you know it was me at the door?" Eliza demanded.

"Oh, that." Helen placed the spoon she'd been working on down on the table, along with the rag. When she looked up at Eliza, her expression was far more normal—amused and lightly teasing. "You, Miss Eliza, have a very peculiar gait."

Eliza's shoulders relaxed, and instantly she felt foolish. Of course. Her mother had always scolded her for loping around like a boy, and after a couple of weeks of living among the other girls, she knew none of them had her plodding steps. She pulled out the chair at the head of the table and rested her hands in front of her.

"I need your help," she said.

"I know," Helen said, picking up a fork and inspecting it in the candlelight. "You need me to help you bring her back."

Eliza's heart thumped.

Helen breathed on the fork, and Eliza could have sworn that the rust stains disappeared before her eyes. Still Helen lifted the rag and polished it anyway.

"None of your spells work on me," she continued, laying the fork alongside the other gleaming utensils. Her eyes flicked to Eliza's locket. "Not a one. I'm under the protection of a charm that makes me immune to witchcraft."

Eliza sat and stared. "A charm?" she blurted stupidly.

"Yes," Helen said as she polished a teaspoon. "I know what those books of yours can lead to. I knew the girl who last owned them." She placed the teaspoon down on the table and slowly turned to look at Eliza. "She was killed by her craft."

Eliza felt as if Helen had just plucked one of the forks off the table and jammed it into her heart. "Killed? Like Catherine was?"

"No, not quite like that," Helen said thoughtfully. "This girl, she let the magic consume her. It became an obsession . . . an addiction . . . and it took over. After she died, we tried to burn those books so that it would never happen again, but it didn't work."

Eliza sat up straight and swallowed hard, attempting to focus. "What do you mean, it didn't work?"

"We threw them in the fire, and they came out an hour later without a mark or a scratch," Helen explained. "They were untouched, Miss Eliza. Unscathed." She pushed the silverware away, her eyes hard. "You're fooling with a power that is not to be trifled with. That is why I have tried to send you those messages all this time. Tried to tell you to turn back when you were about to get yourself into trouble. But you don't seem to want to listen."

Eliza's heart dropped into her toes. "That voice I've been hearing . . . that was you?"

"Yes, Miss Eliza," Helen said, going to work on a serving spoon. "But like I said, you didn't want to listen."

Eliza was stunned, an awful hollowness growing inside of her gut. A feeling that she had started something she could not control. A feeling that if she didn't end it now, it might grow and expand and swallow everything she held dear.

But it had already swallowed Catherine, and she couldn't rest with that on her conscience.

"If you wish to help me so badly, then help me now," Eliza pleaded, scooting her chair closer to the table, angling herself to look into the maid's face. "Help *us*."

"I'm sorry," Helen said simply. "I can't do that."

"But you must!" Eliza protested. "Helen, if you know something of this, if you understand how these spells work, then you *must* help us."

Helen continued to polish the silver, as if Eliza wasn't begging for someone's life.

"We're going to do it with or without you," Eliza said.

Helen paused. She laid down the rag and turned to look Eliza in the eye.

"Fine," she said. "I will agree to help you on two conditions. First, I wish to read this spell first, to make sure there are no mistakes."

"Done. And second?" Eliza asked, laying her palm flat on the table.

"Second, when the spell is done, we bury the books again," Helen said. "We bury them, and you all put this magic where it belongs. In the past."

"Agreed." Eliza reached out and took the maid's hand. "All I want is for this to be over."

Helen sat and stared at Eliza's hand on hers. "All right, then," she said, sliding her hand away from Eliza's. She wiped both palms on her dingy apron. "I'll help you."

"Thank you," Eliza said, her voice thick. "Thank you, Helen." She shoved her chair back and held out her hand to the maid. "Now come along. We must go."

"Go where?" Helen asked, standing.

Eliza looked her up and down. Beneath her blue shawl and brown apron she wore a nightgown of white flannel. *Perfect.*

"The girls are waiting in the chapel," Eliza told her.

Helen hesitated, glancing at the door as if she expected a ghost or goblin to come screeching out at her. "Waiting for what?"

"For you," Eliza said. "It's time for your initiation."

CHOSEN ONES

"The girl who died—her name was Caroline Westwick," Helen said, tugging her blue shawl closer to her body as she, Theresa, and Eliza trailed the other girls back through the woods after her initiation. The sky overhead was lit by the biggest full moon Eliza had ever seen. It glowed an eerie yellow-green against the midnight sky. "That was the name of the girl who died. Odd, isn't it? How she and Catherine have the same initials?"

A chill went through Eliza as she glanced back toward the chapel. Catherine was there, all alone in that basement, her body growing colder by the moment. Eliza felt an ache in her gut over leaving her friend behind once again, but she'd had no choice. She had wanted to do the Life Out of Death Spell right away, as soon as Helen had become a member of the coven, but Helen had insisted they wait another day—long enough for her to study the spell, to make sure it was safe. And that, after all, had been a condition of her initiation, so Eliza had no choice but to agree.

"Check your sources," Theresa said under her breath, glancing ahead at the other girls. Their hushed conversations traveled back to Eliza's ears in furtive whispers. All of them had just seen Catherine's body for the first time, and all of them had been affected. "Everyone knows that Caroline Westwick ran off to Europe to marry some divorced ex-duke and broke her mother's heart."

"That's just what her family wants you to believe," Helen said, looking Theresa in the eye. "But next time you visit their home, walk out to the orchard. At the foot of the easternmost tree, you'll find an unmarked grave. That's where her mother goes every morning to grieve."

Theresa stopped walking. All the color dropped from her face, and she held both hands against her stomach. "How can you possibly know this?"

Helen paused and looked down at her hands. "Because I visit Caroline, too."

Theresa pressed one hand into the trunk of an old oak tree, her breathing ragged. The rest of the girls kept tromping ahead, not noticing their friends' absence.

"Theresa? Are you all right?" Eliza asked, placing her hand on the small of Theresa's back.

Theresa nodded, waving Eliza away, but Eliza kept her hand there as she looked wildly around at Helen. "I'm sorry. It's just . . . she was a friend of the family."

"I don't understand," Eliza said. "Why would the Westwicks lie about something like that?"

Helen removed a handkerchief from the pocket of her nightgown and handed it to Theresa in a perfunctory way. Theresa cupped the fabric over her mouth, closed her eyes, and breathed.

"Think of your own mother, Miss Eliza," Helen said. "Would it be more humiliating for her to say you'd simply fallen in love and followed your silly little heart, or to tell the world that you'd become obsessed with witchcraft, lost your mind to it, and subsequently killed yourself?"

Eliza's mind went suddenly gray. Now she clung to Theresa's arm to steady herself. "She committed suicide?"

"In a manner of speaking," Helen said flatly. "She threw herself off the roof of the Easton Academy chapel, but I don't think she knew what she was doing when she did it."

"How is this possible?" Theresa looked around in confusion, as if hoping Caroline would step out of the trees and explain it all away. "Why did she do it?"

Helen sighed.

"It was Caroline's older sister, Lucille, who originally found the books. She started her own coven, and she invited ten other girls to join, just as you did. Even though I was only thirteen years old, I was one of those she invited. Caroline was not," Helen said.

Eliza narrowed her eyes. "She invited a maid, but not her own sister?"

The moment the words left her lips, Eliza felt ashamed.

"I think that was why she did it, Miss Eliza," Helen said. "I believe that by asking me, she was taunting her sister."

"That does sound like Lucille," Theresa admitted. "She always left Caroline out."

Helen nodded. "Every time our coven would meet, Caroline would follow us. She would hover upstairs in the chapel, and occasionally she would beg to be let in, but Lucille always shunned her. She would laugh about it, like it was all a joke to her. It made some of us uncomfortable. But you didn't argue with Lucille."

Eliza looked at Theresa, wondering if she saw the parallels to her own position at Billings, but Theresa's attention was trained on Helen.

"Everything we did back then was in good fun, or so we thought," Helen said. "It was much like I'm sure it's been for you. We cast fun little spells, helped the girls pass tests, helped them attract certain boys. They even cast a spell to get me out of scrubbing the floors when I had a cold." The moon broke from behind a cloud, bathing Helen in milky light.

"And?" Theresa prompted. "What happened?"

"One night Caroline's frustration got the better of her," Helen explained. "She snuck into Lucille's room and stole the books. She told her sister she would burn them unless Lucille initiated her. So we did. We took in a twelfth. And that, we all later believed, was our mistake."

Helen turned and began walking again, her steps hurried, as if she wanted to get away from these memories. Eliza gripped Theresa's hand, clinging to her as they rushed to catch up.

"What do you mean, your 'mistake'?" Eliza asked.

"Caroline was never invited to join the coven. She forced her way in," Helen told them. "We didn't choose her, the way Lucille chose us. She wasn't meant to be a witch . . . and she couldn't handle the power."

"And that's why she died?" Theresa asked.

Helen nodded. "All Caroline wanted was to be like her sister, so she cast several spells. One to change her hair color, another to make her taller, another to make her smarter, a better musician, a finer artist. All just to be like Lucille. But it was too much. She didn't know what she was doing. And she lost her mind."

Helen paused as they reached the edge of the woods, looking out over the Billings campus. Every window was dark, yet the moon cast its solemn glow over the troop of girls moving swiftly toward Crenshaw.

"After she died, we tried to burn the books—and that was when we realized Caroline's original threat was empty, though she had no idea at the time. When burning them didn't work, we locked them in the chapel basement, then buried the map along with the locket Lucille had commissioned for herself as the leader of the coven," Helen said. Her eyes flicked to the gold locket around Eliza's neck. "The locket you now wear, miss."

Eliza's hand fluttered up to touch the gold trinket. Suddenly it felt heavier than it ever had before.

"If you thought the books were so very dangerous, why bury the locket and the map right there in the garden where anyone could find them?" Theresa asked. "Why make a map at all?"

Helen took a deep breath and blew it out audibly. "The map was Lucille's idea. She said the books were too precious to be lost forever. She said that some future Billings girls would find them, and maybe they would know how to harness their power better than we did." She cast an arch look at Theresa. "Really, I think she couldn't let go. As for the burial spot, it wasn't a garden then, and we were all too terrified to venture back into the woods at night to bury it there."

Eliza looked at the dark windows of Crenshaw House. She wondered which room Caroline had lived in.

"Caroline's last words were what convinced us that we never should have let her force her way in to the coven," Helen said, gazing off into the distance.

Theresa gripped Eliza's hand tightly. "Why?" Eliza asked. "What did she say?"

Helen's eyes shone with unshed tears. "We were all on the roof. We were trying to stop her," she said, her voice thick. "But she wouldn't come down. She turned to look at us—her eyes were so unfocused, so blank. Then, right before she fell, she said, as clear as day . . . she said—"

Helen paused, touching her fingertips to her lips as they quivered.

"What? What did she say?" Theresa demanded.

Helen drew in a ragged breath. "She said, 'I don't belong.'"

THE OTHER WOMAN

Eliza walked into her room that night and fell directly into bed, glad that she was already wearing her nightgown, since she never would have been able to muster the energy to change. She curled into a ball facing the center of the room, but at the sight of Catherine's empty bed, she flung herself around to face the wall.

"It's going to be all right," she whispered to herself. "Helen is clearly a powerful witch. With her on our side, we can't fail."

A sudden scratching noise sounded at her window. Eliza's heart vaulted into her throat and she sat straight up in bed. A long, silent moment passed. Then the scratch sounded again. Eliza whirled around. A pale face hovered outside her window, staring in at her.

Eliza screamed. *Catherine?* Had her roommate come back of her own volition to punish Eliza for letting her fall to her death? But then her eyes focused on the panicked visage.

"Harrison?" she whispered.

He gestured frantically for her to let him in. Eliza jumped out of bed, realizing with a start that she was on the fourth floor, and whipped open the window. Harrison was perched precariously on the one-foot-wide stone lip that ran around the periphery of the building. He clutched both sides of the window and jumped to the floor, crouching for a moment to catch his breath.

"Harrison Knox, *what* are you doing!?" Eliza demanded, closing the windows with a *bang*. "You could have killed yourself."

Harrison stood, blew out a breath, and smiled. "It would have been worth it to see you." He looked her up and down, and the smile transformed into a grin. "And in your nightgown, no less."

Eliza blushed furiously. She reached for the fringed shawl on the back of her desk chair and drew it tightly around her shoulders.

"I'm sorry if I frightened you," Harrison said, stepping toward her. He cupped her cheek with his hand, and she automatically tilted her face into his palm. "But even though you refused my invitation, I simply couldn't stay away any longer."

All Eliza wanted to do was fall into Harrison's arms. To let him hold her and comfort her and chase away all the awful things she'd seen and done. But he didn't belong to her. He was Theresa's. Right or wrong, whether they were in love or not, he had proposed and she had accepted. They were going to be husband and wife.

"Eliza," Harrison said, stepping still closer. That one word was like a plea.

And then he tipped her chin up with his finger and brought his lips down to brush hers. Eliza's skin was on fire, and her mind seemed to experience complete weightlessness. Every one of her reservations was obliterated by that one touch. She moved into him, and Harrison wrapped his arms around her, deepening the kiss. Eliza had never felt so completely loved in her life. So secure, so excited, so absolutely sure. Harrison was the man she was meant to be with. No other person would ever make her feel this way.

And yet—

She pulled away.

"What is it?" Harrison asked, his eyelids heavy. "Eliza, what's wrong?"

"You shouldn't have come," Eliza said, summoning all her strength just to utter that one sentence. She touched her still-tingling lips with her fingertips.

Harrison hesitated. He looked behind him as if someone might be watching. "But I thought—"

"Theresa and I . . . we're friends now, Harrison." Eliza's heart twisted excruciatingly, and she found she couldn't look him in the eye. "And I can't do this to her. I won't be the other woman."

"But Eliza, you know how I feel about you," Harrison begged, his blue eyes entreating. "How I feel about her. Can't we just—"

"No." Eliza forced herself to look at him, and her heart broke, shattering into a million tiny pieces all over her insides. "Go, Harrison. Please."

Harrison opened his mouth to protest but seemed to think the better of it. He stepped past her toward the window, but Eliza grasped his sleeve between her thumb and forefinger. "Out the door, please.

I don't think I could manage having your death on my conscience as well."

Harrison nodded, though he had no idea how much meaning her words held. He paused with his hand on her doorknob and looked back at her. "If I'm caught, I won't tell them who I'd come to see," he said, his expression pained.

"Tell them whatever you wish," Eliza replied, turning away from him. She felt exhausted, suddenly, as if she'd run out of fight. As she heard the door click quietly closed, she would have welcomed expulsion. Anything to get away from here. To put this place and all the people she'd hurt behind her.

She watched from above as Harrison jogged off into the night, headed for the fateful woods and the Easton campus beyond. One lonely tear slid down her cheek, but she told herself she had done the right thing.

Eliza Williams was no one's mistress.

POWERFUL

"Jane and Viola were up all night pressing the figs we got in town for oil," Theresa whispered under her breath as she and Eliza walked to class the next morning. "Are you certain that Helen knows where to find eye of newt? Because we can't afford to waste any more time. That spell has to be done at midnight tonight, or Catherine is lost forever."

They both smiled stiffly at Miss Tinsley as she walked quickly past them.

"Good morning, girls!" the teacher called brightly. "I hope you're ready for a lively translation session this morning."

"Yes, Miss Tinsley," the two girls replied in unison.

The teacher lifted a hand in a wave and disappeared through the front door of McKinley.

"All I know is Helen told me she could get it, and I trust her," Eliza replied.

Theresa paused at the foot of the steps to McKinley Hall and waited for a pair of younger girls to scurry by before speaking.

"And why is that, exactly?" Theresa asked, smoothing an errant lock of hair back behind her ear. "I swear, Eliza, I wanted to stage a protest last night when you walked into the temple with that girl. The only reason I didn't was because we don't have the time to spend searching for someone better."

Eliza rolled her eyes and walked a few steps away from the main path, leading Theresa out of earshot of the other students and teachers.

"You just don't like her because she's a servant," Eliza said through her teeth. "But she's been doing this for a long time. She's probably more powerful than any of us."

"Probably," Theresa said, pursing her lips. "And *that's* what I don't like about her."

Eliza blinked. Was Theresa worried about having her own power usurped, or was she concerned that Helen might somehow turn her power against the coven?

"Ladies."

Eliza jumped and whirled around. Miss Almay stood before her, a pinched, suspicious look on her face. Theresa grabbed Eliza's hand in surprise as Eliza's gaze darted around. Where on Earth had the head-mistress come from?

"Might I ask why the two of you are dawdling here?" Miss Almay asked, looking down her nose at them. "I trust you're not planning anything for which you might find yourselves in my office."

"Of course not, Miss Almay," Eliza stammered.

"We were just discussing our literature exam," Theresa improvised.

"Very well, then. Get to class," Miss Almay ordered, stepping back so that they could step onto the path in front of her. The two girls did so, still clutching each other. They hadn't taken two steps when Miss Almay spoke again, her tone so low and ominous, it sent a quiver of fear down Eliza's spine. "And remember, girls, I've got my eyes on you."

BE GONE

Eliza was breathless but oddly calm as she and the other ten members of their coven approached the chapel that evening. Within the hour, the spell would be cast, and Catherine would be alive.

Provided all went according to plan.

"You remember your promise to me, don't you, Eliza?" Helen asked. She had a dark hood pulled over her hair, and her candle's flame was reflected in her eyes, making her blue irises glow red.

"I do," Eliza whispered. "This will be our last spell. After tonight, we bury the books and move on with our lives."

"With Catherine," Theresa added firmly.

"With Catherine," Eliza repeated.

Theresa paused and lifted the lantern. The imposing, white-walled façade of Billings Chapel rose out of the night before them. Behind the three leaders, all the other girls came to a halt.

"We're here," Theresa said.

"As are we."

Eliza gasped and whirled around. Miss Almay and Mrs. Hodge rushed toward them. Miss Almay shoved through the crowd of stunned girls and came to a stop right in front of Theresa and Eliza. Her skin was ruddy with exertion, and her dark hair had come loose from its bun, but her expression was triumphant.

Eliza glanced anxiously over her shoulder at the chapel. Catherine lay right inside, her chances at survival dwindling with each passing moment. They were so close. So very close.

"Miss Almay," Helen began. "Please, don't—"

"I'll deal with you later, Miss Jennings," Miss Almay snapped, not bothering to cast a glance at her maid. Instead she glared down her long nose at Eliza and Theresa. Eliza's pulse pounded in her ears. She could practically hear Catherine begging her to do something— begging her to save her life. "I don't know how you managed to sneak out of the house so quietly, but Mrs. Hodge caught a glimpse of your candles out the window."

Eliza looked at Theresa, desperate for some sort of a sign that she had a plan. Theresa, however, was looking right at Helen.

"Miss Almay, let me explain," Theresa began. "Well, you know how devout Alice is. She simply must pray inside the chapel every single day. It makes her feel closer to God. Isn't that right, Alice?" She didn't wait for the girl's answer. "But this morning, Alice *missed* morning services because of her, well, monthly . . . trouble."

Helen took Eliza's hand. "Concentrate on Miss Almay and chant with me," she said so quietly Eliza wasn't even sure she'd spoken the words aloud.

"Befuddled, bewildered, be gone," Helen whispered, staring straight at Mrs. Hodge. "Befuddled, bewildered, be gone. Befuddled, bewildered, be gone."

Panicked and baffled, Eliza followed Helen's lead. She stared at Miss Almay's face as she repeated the chant.

"Befuddled, bewildered, be gone. Befuddled, bewildered, be gone."

Eliza focused on the chant, on Miss Almay, on her strength, as hard as she possibly could, but nothing was happening. Her palm began to sweat inside Helen's grip, and her breath grew shallow and still nothing. Theresa, meanwhile, was running out of fiction to tell.

"So we promised Alice that we would bring her up here tonight before midnight so she could pray . . ."

"Befuddled, bewildered, be gone. Befuddled, bewildered, be gone."

Clarissa, who was standing behind Eliza and Helen, suddenly took Eliza's other hand. She started to chant along with them, staring intently at Miss Almay.

"Befuddled, bewildered, be gone. Befuddled, bewildered, be gone."

Soon Jane joined in with them. Then Lavender, Viola, and Bia. Finally Marilyn and Genevieve caught on, dragging Alice with them.

"Befuddled, bewildered, be gone," they whispered together. "Befuddled, bewildered, be gone. Befuddled, bewildered, be gone."

A cold wind kicked up around their feet, swirling up from the ground.

"What? What's this?" Miss Almay demanded, shielding her eyes. "What are you girls doing?"

"It's not working!" Eliza cried.

"Just keep going!" Helen ordered.

"Befuddled, bewildered, be gone. Befuddled, bewildered, be gone. Befuddled, bewildered, be gone."

And just when Eliza was certain that whatever was supposed to happen would never happen without the power of the full coven, without Theresa reciting with them, the wind suddenly stopped. Eliza pushed her hair away from her eyes and blinked through the cloud of dusty dirt that billowed around them. When the haze cleared, she saw Theresa laughing.

"What can you possibly find amusing at this moment?" Eliza demanded.

"Look at them!" Theresa said, pointing to the lawn.

There, in the middle of the moonlit lawn, was a dazed-looking Miss Almay. She staggered from side to side with her arms splayed out in front of her, blinking rapidly and looking around overhead, her chin jerking this way and that as if she was following a rowdy flock of birds with her eyes. Mrs. Hodge was walking into a thick tree trunk over and over and over again.

"Poor Mrs. Hodge," Theresa said. "She'll have a bump the size of Plymouth Rock tomorrow."

Eliza walked over to Mrs. Hodge and, taking her by the shoulders, turned her toward the school. Mrs. Hodge instantly began walking straight ahead, her eyes glazed over like a dead animal's. As Eliza watched her go, Theresa gave Miss Almay a slight shove, sending her after her maid. The headmistress spun in circles as she walked.

"Good work, Helen," Theresa said, turning back toward the group.

"I have no wish for congratulations, Miss Billings," Helen said quietly. "I'd just like to get this done."

Theresa's expression hardened. She picked up her lantern from the ground and strode toward the chapel.

"Your wish, *Miss Jennings*, is my command."

LIFE OUT OF DEATH

Eliza stood in the chapel basement, her palms slick with perspiration, her arms crossed in front of her. One of her hands grasped Helen's, the other Theresa's, as all eleven girls stared down at the lifeless form of Catherine White. Catherine's face had been covered by a swath of white gauze, her hands folded over her chest like a praying angel. As each girl slowly left the circle, one by one, to add her ingredient to the stone bowl at Catherine's feet, Eliza's knees quaked beneath her.

This had to work. It simply had to.

We need you to return to us, Catherine, Eliza thought, closing her eyes as a wave of nerves crashed through her chest. *We need you here with us. I know you want to be here, too. Please, please, please come back to us.*

All around the room the candles flickered and dimmed, then flickered again and glowed stronger. There was a hush among the coven, and the air was thick with desperation, hope, and fear. Jane's shoes scratched the silty floor as she shuffled forward and tipped her bottle of arrowroot toward the bowl. Then, head bowed, she returned to the circle and took Viola's hand. Helen released Eliza, bent to pick up her vial of eye of newt, and slowly, methodically added it to the bowl. The ritual was like a rhythmic dance, each girl doing her part with grace and precision. And then it was Eliza's turn.

As she rejoined the circle, Helen looked Eliza firmly in the eye. Eliza set her jaw, bent over, and lifted the bottle of jasmine from the floor at her feet. She carefully avoided the thick, white candles Lavender had placed all around the body, per the book's instructions. When she arrived at the bowl, she looked up at Catherine's face.

The corpse's eyes were open and glaring at her angrily.

Eliza gasped and took a step back, her heel coming down right on Marilyn's toe.

"Eliza, what is it?" Marilyn demanded.

"Shhh!" Clarissa admonished. "We're supposed to stay perfectly quiet."

"But I—she—"

Eliza gestured at Catherine with her bottle, but when she looked back again, Catherine's eyes were closed. The gauze hadn't been disturbed. The body hadn't moved. It was just Eliza's mind playing tricks on her. She cleared her throat nervously; her pulse was racing through her veins, making her feel lightheaded.

Trembling from head to toe, Eliza took a tentative step toward the body. She checked Catherine's eyes once more. They were still closed. Shaking her head slightly, she opened the bottle and dumped the contents into the bowl's fragrant mixture. Then she slipped the empty bottle into the pocket of her blue dress and returned to the circle, taking Helen's hand.

Theresa stepped forward. The final ingredient was the rosemary. She stepped forward with the sprig in her two hands and slowly, meticulously tore each needle from it, dropping them in one by one. Eliza felt as if she was falling into a trance as she watched Theresa. The room seemed to be growing warmer, and the heady scents of rosemary, lavender, lilac, and jasmine filled the room.

As the last rosemary needle fluttered into the bowl, a light, airy wind filled the room—a comforting springtime breeze. It tickled Eliza's skin and filled her with hope. All around the circle, the girls began to smile.

This was going to work. Every last one of them could sense it.

Theresa returned to the circle and took Eliza's hand. She nodded, and the girls began to recite the spell, which they had committed to memory.

"Powerful spirits, we implore thee, give us the power, hear our plea."

The words had barely escaped Eliza's lips, when every candle in the room suddenly went out. There was no wind this time, no movement—nothing natural that had extinguished the lights. The coven simply plunged into darkness. Eliza could make out nothing, save the white gauze over Catherine's pale face. Fear radiated from Eliza's heart and poured off the others in waves. For a long moment no one spoke. Then Theresa squeezed Eliza's hand and started the next line.

"From the darkness into the light, help our sister travel this night."

The other girls joined in. Instantly, a biting cold chased out the last remnants of warmth, permeating the room and biting at Eliza's skin. Eliza heard Bia moan in fear on the other side of the circle but could feel nothing outside of her own terror and the frigid cold air.

"We witches here will be her guide, to wrest her from the other side."

A crash of deafening thunder filled the room, coming not from outside the chapel, but from within. Bia screamed as the candles blazed to light around Catherine, their flames like a wall of fire between her body and the coven. They licked at the beams in the ceiling and spread menacingly wide, threatening the hems of the girls' skirts. A few girls edged backward, but no one broke the circle. The sudden heat was excruciating, and Eliza turned her face as her eyes began to sting and tear. Together the coven managed to shout the last few words.

"Let her know no pain, let her fear no strife, give us the power to save her life!"

Another crack of thunder leveled Bia as she fainted dead away. Instantly, the flames completely died as if doused by a deluge of water. Someone—Eliza couldn't tell who—shouted in surprise. A few of the candles flickered meekly around Catherine's hands and feet. Smoke plumed from the stone bowl, and the stench of burned herbs filled the air. Jane covered her eyes and began to sob. Marilyn and Genevieve clung to each other. Looking stunned, Alice took a few steps back and fell into a chair.

Eliza, Theresa, and Helen stared at the body. Eliza's chest heaved up and down with her ragged breath. Her locket was white hot against her skin, but she didn't move to adjust it.

Catherine remained still.

"What's going on?" Eliza asked, her voice a mere whisper. "What happened? Why didn't it work?"

"I don't know," Helen said, her eyes wide. "We did everything by the book. You added all the rosemary?" she asked Theresa.

"Of course I added all the rosemary," Theresa replied defensively. "Do you think I wanted it to fail, Helen? Do you think I wanted her dead? What do you expect me to—"

A sudden gasp cut her off, and Eliza hurtled backward, startled so thoroughly that she had to grasp the stone wall to keep herself from joining Bia on the floor. Every girl in the room held her breath.

Catherine White had just sat up.

NOT RIGHT

"Eliza?" Catherine said.

Her voice was a croak, and she stared straight through Eliza as she said her name. Theresa dropped Eliza's hand, and Eliza rushed forward.

"Catherine!"

She whipped away the gauze that clung to Catherine's hair, and enveloped her in a hug. Catherine's arms hung limply at her sides, but Eliza hardly noticed. Catherine was back. Catherine was alive!

"It's a miracle!" Alice said from her chair near the door. "A miracle."

"How do you feel?" Eliza asked. "Are you all right?"

"Are you hungry?" Genevieve asked.

Eliza pulled back and looked into Catherine's eyes. They stared back at her as if unseeing. As if she'd never looked upon Eliza before in her life. A cold slice of uncertainty bisected Eliza's heart.

"Catherine?" she said, holding on to the girl's arm. "It's me. Eliza."

Slowly Catherine's eyes seemed to focus on Eliza's face. Then, suddenly, as if tugged by an invisible string, her head jerked downward in a nod. Eliza felt a rush of relief. There was still no color in her friend's cheeks, and her skin was waxy, but she was moving. She was there.

Then her eyes glazed right over again.

"What's wrong with her?" Viola asked.

"She's been dead for almost two days," Clarissa replied in her know-it-all way. "Give her some time."

"Let's not talk about death, shall we?" Theresa requested with forced brightness. "What's important here is that Catherine is alive. We should bring her home and give her a chance to rest."

Eliza clenched her jaw. She didn't like the fact that everyone was talking about Catherine as if she wasn't there. As if she was still just a corpse on the floor.

"Would you like that, Catherine?" she asked her friend. "Would you like to go back to our room and lie down?"

Catherine stared into Eliza's eyes and again, Eliza felt the chill. Catherine's head jerked side to side, as if she was a marionette being operated by a novice puppeteer. Eliza held back a choking lump of disappointment and fear, telling herself that Clarissa was right. Catherine just needed some time.

"You don't wish to go back to Crenshaw?" Eliza asked patiently, trying to keep the tears out of her voice.

"Here," Catherine said hoarsely. "Stay here."

"But we have everything back in our room for the party," Gene-vieve lamented, biting her lip. "The punch and the sandwiches and the chocolate."

"You planned a party?" Theresa demanded, nonplussed.

Genevieve blushed, and Marilyn reached for her hand and squeezed it. "It was Genevieve's idea. It was meant to be a surprise."

"Well, we can go get all the food and bring it back here," Alice said, her eyes bright. "If this is where Catherine wishes to be, we can bring the celebration to her."

Everyone agreed to this plan, and Lavender, Alice, Marilyn, and Genevieve set off to gather the party things. Eliza held Catherine's hand as they watched the four girls go.

"You," Catherine said. "I wish to stay with you, Eliza."

Eliza glanced at Theresa, whose jaw was set with obvious anger. She felt a thump of trepidation, but she couldn't deal with that at the moment. Catherine was back, and she needed Eliza.

"I'm not going anywhere," she told her friend, taking her hand in both of hers. "We'll all stay right here together. Isn't that right, Theresa?"

Theresa clucked her tongue. "Of course. If I'm even wanted."

Eliza glowered at her. How could Theresa possibly be selfish at a time like this?

"What was it like, Catherine?" Clarissa asked, approaching her tentatively. "Do you remember anything? Anything at all about what it was like to be . . . dead?"

Catherine tilted her head, another jerking action. "Cold. I remember cold."

Clarissa slipped her arm around Catherine's and led her to one of the chairs near the wall. "Come and sit. We can talk all about it."

As soon as the two girls had walked away, Eliza hazarded a glance at Theresa. "What's the matter with you? Aren't you excited? The spell worked!"

"A spell we wouldn't have had to do if it hadn't been for you sneaking off into the woods to meet my future husband," Theresa snapped, the color rising in her cheeks.

"Theresa!" Eliza reeled back. "I thought . . . I thought we were past this. I've told Harrison I can't see him again. Now Catherine's back . . . you have everything you want."

"No thanks to you, Eliza Williams," Theresa said, narrowing her eyes. "I think I'll go see if the girls need any help with their supplies."

Then she turned on her heels, whipped her wide skirt behind her, and stormed up the stairs. Eliza stared after her, feeling so livid she could have spit on the floor. Didn't Theresa understand what she'd given up for their friendship?

"Eliza?" Catherine said, staring blankly across the room. Clarissa, Jane, Viola, and Bia, all of whom had gathered around the girl, turned to look at Eliza as well. "Eliza? Where is Eliza?"

Eliza took a deep breath, trying to calm down. Tonight was about Catherine, not Harrison. Catherine was here, and Catherine needed her.

"I'm coming, Catherine," she said.

But just then, a cold hand closed around her wrist. Eliza's heart hit her throat as she whirled around. Helen Jennings stood before her, her blue eyes shot through with fear. Eliza placed her hand on her chest and tried to catch her breath.

"Helen? What is it?" she asked.

"I must speak with you," Helen said, her fingers curling into fists at her sides. She glanced past Eliza's shoulder at Catherine and the other girls, and something about her expression made Eliza's blood run cold.

"What is it?" Eliza asked impatiently. "Catherine's asking for me."

"This is about Catherine," Helen whispered, ducking her chin. "Eliza, she's . . . she's not right."

A lump of foreboding formed just above Eliza's heart, and she reached up to touch her locket. For the first time she felt the tenderness beneath the pendant, and she winced. "What do you mean, 'not right'?"

"I don't think the spell worked," Helen said, taking Eliza's hand and tugging her toward the doorway, away from the other girls. "I don't know what exactly, but something is not right with that girl."

"How do you know?" Eliza asked, the lump traveling slowly up her throat.

"Her eyes. The way they stare . . . ," Helen whispered furtively. "It's just like Caroline looked before she died. That's not Catherine. At least, not the Catherine you knew."

Eliza hesitated a moment, but then the words filtered through and she found them suddenly ridiculous.

"Not Catherine? What are you talking about? Look at her!" She gestured toward the far wall and was appeased to find that Catherine was, at that very moment, smiling. "She's fine. She's alive. Helen, she's alive because of us," Eliza said, holding both Helen's hands in hers. "I know you don't trust the books, and I know that some awful things happened, but look at what the books have wrought now. They may have killed before, but now . . . now they've given life."

"But Eliza—"

"No," Eliza said. She took a step back, dropping Helen's hands. "There's a difference between what Caroline did to herself and what's happened to Catherine. Caroline used magic for her own vain and selfish reasons. What happened to Catherine was not her own doing. She has been sent back to us because it was not her time, and she is going to be fine."

Just then, Eliza heard footsteps and laughter overhead. Genevieve and the others had returned with the food and drink.

"This is a celebration, Helen," Eliza said. "Why don't you join us?"

Helen clenched her teeth, but remained silent. Then she turned on her heels and was gone. Eliza felt a pang of anger mixed with disappointment.

But then Alice skipped down the stairs and into the room, grabbed Eliza around the waist, and swung her around happily. "This is all because of you, Eliza," she said. She stopped twirling and gestured at Catherine. "Look what we are able to do, all because you brought it out of us! We are all-powerful because of you!" She flung her arms around Eliza's neck and hugged her as the other girls began to unpack the sweets and pour out tumblers of punch for the party.

Eliza laughed as the members of her coven cheered and applauded for her. Alice was right. They were all-powerful. And never had she felt so alive, so free, so utterly unrestrained by expectations and rules and uncertainty. She looked over at Catherine and smiled; her smile was readily returned by her friend.

Catherine was alive again. That was all that mattered. Finally, everything was going to be perfect.

EARLY MORNING VISIT

Eliza knew what she was doing was wrong. She knew that if her mother found out she was sneaking onto the boys' campus at dawn—unescorted, no less—she would be disowned forever. She knew if Theresa found out, she would declare war on her. But she was far beyond caring about right and wrong. The line between the two was so completely blurred at this point that she could hardly make it out. All she knew was that she wanted to see Harrison. No, she *needed* to see Harrison. And so, as soon as the imposing gray brick wall of Ketlar House came into view, she lifted her skirts and broke into a run.

By the time she had flattened herself against the wall beneath what she knew to be Harrison's window, she was panting in a highly unfeminine way. This, she *did* care about. She forced herself to take a few deep, steadying breaths, counted to one hundred, then stooped and picked up a handful of the tiny pebbles that served as a border around the outside of the house. She stepped back, cocked her arm, and threw them at the glass pane two stories up.

Eliza looked up at the window. Nothing. No movement at all. Grabbing another handful of rocks, she took a step back.

"Elizabeth Williams, what are you doing?"

Eliza whirled around, heart in her throat, hand still suspended and full of dirt and pebbles. Harrison and Jonathan both stood before her in athletic pants and sleeveless shirts. Their skin shone with sweat, and their breath was heavy. Jonathan bent at the waist to catch his breath, but Harrison stood straight and took a few steps toward her. Eliza found she could not tear her eyes from the glistening skin of his shoulders.

"What are you ... I ... ?" She tossed the pebbles to the ground and dusted her hands off. "What are *you* doing?" she asked.

"Training," Harrison replied. His expression was hesitant, confused. Not that she could blame him, since she'd so callously tossed him from her room the last time they'd met. "Jonathan and I are trying out for the school's running team."

"You're trying out," Jonathan said, still bent at the waist. He slapped Harrison's chest as he hobbled past, headed for the Ketlar door. "I'm clearly not fit enough for this."

"Where are you going?" Harrison asked.

"To curl up in a corner and die, I expect," Jonathan replied, only half joking. "You two kids enjoy yourselves."

Harrison looked about to protest, but Eliza reached for his hand and he fell silent. The door swung open and slammed closed, and

Jonathan was gone, leaving the couple alone in the dewy pink light of morning.

"What are you doing here?" he asked her. "Is everything okay?"

"Everything is amazing," Eliza said. "It's just . . . I've been up all night long, and when the sun came up this morning . . . all I could think about was you."

Slowly the creases smoothed away from Harrison's handsome face and he smiled, his blue eyes shining with relief. He opened his mouth to speak, but then somewhere nearby, another door slammed. Harrison looked around, then took Eliza's hand.

"Come on. I know a place we can go that's a bit more private."

Harrison led Eliza around the back of the building, then behind Drake Hall and to the back of Gwendolyn. For a moment she thought he was going to take her down into the basement again, but instead he walked her around the side of the building, peeked around the corner, and then mounted the steps. Through the stone archway was a small outdoor room with a bench built into the solid rock wall. The cavelike space cut them off completely from sight. She sunk down onto the slatted wooden bench and Harrison sat next to her, still clutching her hand. As she looked down at their entwined fingers, Eliza was so full of emotion, she felt as if it was choking her.

She was with Harrison. She was with Harrison. She was with Harrison.

"Eliza," he said, searching her eyes. "Tell me you've changed your mind. Tell me that's why you're here before I go completely insane."

"Well, we can't have that," Eliza said with a laugh. "Yes, Harrison. That's why I'm here."

Harrison smiled, his joy so pure it was written all over his face. Then he cupped Eliza's face with both hands and kissed her. Already breathless, Eliza felt as if she might faint as Harrison's lips searched hers. She sunk against him, oblivious to the rules of modesty and propriety. Right then, she wanted to feel all of him and to let him feel all of her. His hands trailed over her shoulders and down her back and he pulled her to him—so close, she felt as if her heart was beating against his.

"I'm so glad you came," Harrison said finally. He kept his arms looped around her waist, his nose practically touching hers as he spoke. "I'm going to break it off with Theresa," Harrison said. "I'll do it today, this morning, right now."

No more did Eliza care about Theresa's feelings. Not after the way the girl had turned on her last night. The girl was capricious, selfish—untrustworthy. "Today will be fine. I'm in no rush."

Harrison lifted a hand and gently smoothed Eliza's hair away from her face. "But I am. I can't pretend not to feel the way I do anymore," he said, his voice a husky whisper. "I love you, Elizabeth."

Her heart caught so deliciously it sent shock waves of delightful shivers all through her fingertips and her toes.

"I think I've loved you since the moment I saw you riding in the carriage," Harrison continued. "Who knew the day you set foot on this campus would be the day my life changed forever?"

Eliza smiled and closed her eyes, solidifying this moment in her memory—the one moment of her entire life that she knew she would never, ever want to forget. Then she opened them again and looked into the eyes of Harrison Knox—the eyes, she suddenly realized, she would be looking into for the rest of her life. Her throat was still full, as were her heart, her lungs, her everything. But somehow, she managed to speak four small words.

"I love you, too."

SOMETHING ELSE

Still dizzy from an hour spent alone with Harrison, kissing, holding hands, and whispering all their hopes and dreams to each other, Eliza snuck back into Crenshaw House, closing the door carefully behind her. The house was deathly silent, all the girls still sleeping after their late night of revelry. Eliza took the stairs at a run, thinking she might wake Catherine when she got back to their room. After all, Catherine had been gone for a few days, and so much had happened. She and Harrison had shared their first kiss. They had said "I love you." And now there was talk of the future—once Harrison spoke with Theresa, of course. Everything was happening so fast, but none of it would be happening at all if not for Catherine.

Arriving at the closed door of their room, Eliza bit her lip and stifled a girlish laugh as the gesture brought the sensation of Harrison's kisses back to her mouth. She quietly turned the doorknob and stepped inside.

But as soon as she did, her heart dropped through the floor.

Catherine sat on the edge of Eliza's bed, her feet planted squarely on the floor, her eyes staring dead ahead, as she slowly, systematically, tore Eliza's copy of *A Tale of Two Cities* to pieces, page by cherished page.

"Catherine!" Eliza gasped, stepping forward. "What are you doing?"

Catherine tilted her head toward Eliza in that odd, jerking way, staring straight through her, but never pausing in her task. She tore a page, dropped it on the floor, then tore the next, then the next, then the next. The action, the staring—it was as if she was taunting Eliza. Torturing her. Eliza felt the sudden urge to grab the girl and shake her for destroying the one and only gift Harrison had ever given her. But she paused and forced herself to remain calm.

"Catherine," she said coolly. "That book belongs to me. Might I have it back?"

She laid her hand out flat, but Catherine continued to rip the pages from the spine. Her eyes were glazed, lifeless, blank. A sliver of fear sliced down Eliza's spine. Helen's words echoed in her mind.

"That's not Catherine. At least, not the Catherine you knew."

No, Eliza told herself. *She just needs time. She's been through so much. Of course she needs time to get back to her old self.*

Screwing up her courage, Eliza walked across the room until she was standing in front of Catherine. The girl's head jerked, following her, but her eyes still stared, unfocused, as if gazing right past her. Eliza's heart gripped with terror.

This was terribly not right.

Rip, toss, rip, toss, rip, toss. One of the pages hit Eliza's foot, and she swallowed back an anguished cry. The book. The precious, precious book. All in pieces.

Just reason with her. She'll be all right if you reason with her.

Eliza knelt on the floor at Catherine's feet, her knees resting on so many fallen pages.

"Catherine, please," she said quietly. "Please, stop. It's me. It's Eliza. Your best friend."

Suddenly Catherine let out a piercing screech, so inhuman it stopped Eliza's heart cold. Eliza froze, her eyes widening in horror as Catherine threw what was left of the book at the wall.

"Catherine! What are you—"

But before Eliza could choke out the words, Catherine hurtled off the bed and threw her entire weight on top of Eliza, curling her fingers around Eliza's throat. Her fingers were like claws of ice, their grip so strong that Eliza's eyes bulged from the strain. The chain of her locket cut into her flesh, and she could feel the pendant begin to burn.

A terrified scream escaped Eliza's lungs, but Catherine's powerful fingers squeezed it into a strangled whimper. Eliza's head slammed back against the hardwood floor, and she grasped at Catherine's wrists with her hands.

"No," Eliza croaked. "No, Catherine. Please." She managed to turn her head to look up into the face of her tormentor. Catherine's teeth were set in a fierce grimace, like some kind of feral animal.

But it was her eyes that stopped Eliza's heart cold.

They were dead. There was no life in them. No sign of Catherine in them at all.

"You did this," Catherine said, her voice a throaty growl. "You. It was you. You did this."

"No! It's not my fault," Eliza whimpered, her voice but a weak rasp. "I didn't know, Catherine. I didn't know."

"You did this to me. You did this," the thing repeated mercilessly.

"I'm sorry! I didn't know. I didn't . . ." Tears streamed from the corners of Eliza's eyes, across her temples and into her hair. "Stop," she pleaded, trying in vain to breathe. "Please, stop."

She did not use Catherine's name again, for she now realized, far too late, that Helen was right. This thing was not her friend.

Eliza struggled to breathe, but no air would come. The thing that wasn't Catherine had a grip like a vise, and it seemed to be growing tighter by the second.

"You did this. You. You did this to me."

I'm going to die, Eliza thought suddenly, an image of Harrison's smiling face floating through her mind. *I'm going to die right here, and he'll never understand why.*

Her vision started to prickle over with colorful dots, and her hands fell away from the thing's wrists as darkness started to take her. It tightened its grip and shook her, banging her head against the floor again, over and over and over, and slowly Eliza began to let go.

"You did this. You. You did this to me. It was you. You did this to me."

Yes, it was me. I killed Catherine, Eliza thought, her spirit giving in. *I brought this thing back in her place. It was me. I did it. I deserve to die.*

And then the door to her room opened.

"Eliza!" Theresa screamed.

The thing was not distracted by the visitor. Its grip merely tightened. But Eliza's eyes popped open in hope. "Theresa," she croaked. "Help me. Help . . ."

Theresa grabbed the first heavy object she saw, Catherine's copy of *Wuthering Heights*, and wielded it over the thing's head.

Do it, Eliza thought. *Please, just do it. Just end this.*

But as Theresa brought the book down, Helen ran in and snatched it out of her hands.

Theresa whirled on her. "What are you—"

"That will do nothing," Helen said, tossing the book aside. She grabbed Theresa's hand. "Repeat this with me: 'Creature from beyond the grave, this is not your home. Return to the darkness from whence you came, and leave this soul alone.'"

At the sound of the spell, the thing lifted one hand from Eliza's neck and pointed at Theresa and Helen. "Curses on you! All of you! Curses on your families and all the fruit you may bear. Curses on you for all eternity!"

Shaking, Theresa and Helen clung to each other and recited the spell.

"Creature from beyond the grave, this is not your home. Return to the darkness from whence you came, and leave this soul alone."

Eliza was just about to black out again when suddenly the grip on her throat was released. The thing that wasn't Catherine stood up and stepped toward Theresa and Helen. Eliza curled into a ball on the floor, unable to do anything but fight for air.

"Again!" Helen screamed.

"Creature from beyond the grave, this is not your home. Return to the darkness from whence you came, and leave this soul alone!"

"Curses! Curses on all of you!" the thing wailed.

It took another step, but this time its legs were quaking. Eliza saw this from the corner of her eye. The spell was working, but it was not strong enough. She reached for Helen's ankle, the only part of her she could hope to touch, and clung to her for dear life.

"Again!" Eliza croaked.

"Creature from beyond the grave, this is not your home!" the three girls shouted together. "Return to the darkness from whence you came, and leave this soul alone!"

The thing made one desperate lunge, reaching for Theresa's throat. Theresa let out a scream, but before the hands could reach her, the thing that wasn't Catherine went stiff and fell over onto the floor. Its eyes stared across at Eliza, and as Eliza watched in horror, they slowly glassed over with a gray fog. Whimpering, Eliza sat up, gagging and coughing and sobbing, her hands at her throat. The locket instantly turned cold, but Eliza could feel that it had scorched her skin. Theresa hit her knees and reached for Eliza as she crawled away from the body and toward the door. They clung to each other as Eliza's body was racked with choking sobs and coughs.

"She attacked me," Eliza heard herself say. "She attacked me."

"Why?" Theresa asked. "Why would Catherine do that? After we brought her back. After all we did for her."

"We didn't bring back Catherine," Helen said flatly, staring at the lifeless body. "We brought back something else entirely."

CRIME

Eliza could not stop crying. Since the moment Theresa had wrapped her in her strong arms on the floor of her dormitory room, tears had been running down her face without pause. Even now, as she, Helen, and Theresa carried Catherine's body through the woods for the second time, the flow was continuous. Tears sluiced down her cheeks and dripped onto the bodice of her dress. She hated appearing weak to Theresa and Helen, neither of whom had shed so much as one tear, but she couldn't stop the flood.

She had no idea how her friends were so unaffected. How could they not be moved by the wretchedness of what had occurred? With every moment that passed, Eliza's misery mounted—another recollection, another realization. She had thought she'd saved Catherine, but all she'd done was bring some fiend to life on Earth.

"Oh, for heaven's sake, Eliza, please stop blubbering," Theresa said through her teeth as they hobbled past the white rock with

Catherine's sagging form between them. Theresa had been walking backward the entire way, craning her neck to see over her shoulder and keep from tripping. "It's almost over."

"No, it's not," Eliza replied, her voice thick with tears. Her throat throbbed mercilessly. Angry, purple, finger-shaped bruises had already begun to form on her neck before the girls had even left Crenshaw. But as unsightly and painful as they were, they were meager penance for everything she had done. "It will never be over. Catherine will always be dead."

"This is not your fault, Eliza," Helen said, running forward to hold a branch aside so that the girls could duck through. "You could not have known this would happen."

But it is my fault that she died the first time. Theresa came after me, and Catherine went after her. If not for me, none of this would have happened, Eliza thought, clenching her jaw. If she hadn't been sneaking around with Harrison behind Theresa's back, none of this would have happened. *That is the crime I will carry with me all my days.*

"Be careful. We're going down," Theresa said.

She backed down the slope into the ravine, her feet sliding on the dry dirt, loosening a few rocks, which bounced down and splashed into the shallow water. Eliza held her breath and gritted her teeth, struggling to keep hold of Catherine's ankles. Her fingers were slick with sweat, and every inch of her body itched from the exertion.

"Lay her here. This is where she first fell," Theresa said.

Carefully, Theresa bent and laid Catherine's head on the rock which had been her end. The jagged surface was still stained with

Catherine's blood. Eliza placed Catherine's feet down, then took a few steps back, trying to catch her breath.

"It's no good," Helen said, looking down at them from the top of the ravine. "She wouldn't be lying so straight."

Eliza gave a sob and turned away. Theresa clucked her tongue in frustration.

"If you want something done right, better to do it yourself," she muttered.

Eliza could hear the girl's feet slipping on the stones, splashing around as she rearranged Catherine's body.

"There. Is that better?" she asked.

Eliza glanced over her shoulder. Theresa had arranged Catherine so that she was on her side, one arm flung behind her, her legs bent as if she was running.

"Yes. That should do it," Helen said.

Eliza covered her eyes and cried. She said a silent prayer, pleading with God to forgive her for all she had done. Then she felt Theresa's arm around her waist.

"It will be all right, Eliza," Theresa whispered in her ear. "Our spell will have broken last night. Today Miss Almay and the instructors will realize Catherine is missing. They'll send out a search party and when they find her, they'll think she simply went for a walk alone and fell. Everything is going to be fine."

Eliza sniffled, swallowed, and nodded, unable to form any words. Unable to understand how Theresa could possibly think anything would be fine ever again. Aside from everything else that had happened, had the girl not heard that thing place a curse on all of them? Eliza knew she was going to live in fear of that curse for the rest of her life, never knowing exactly what it might mean.

"We should go," Helen said.

Suddenly there was a loud crack, like a tree limb breaking nearby. Eliza gasped, and Theresa dragged her down to the ground, pulling them both into the ravine. Theresa's breath was ragged with fear, and Eliza clung to her as if she would have drowned if she let go.

"What was that?" Eliza hissed.

"I don't know," Theresa replied.

"Who's there?" Helen shouted, swinging around. "If you're bold enough to follow us, you should be brave enough to show yourself!"

Eliza clenched her hands into fists, marveling at Helen's courage. She bit down on her tongue and looked at Theresa, who widened her eyes. The venerable Miss Billings was impressed as well. For a long moment, all three girls were silent and the forest was still.

"It was nothing," Helen called down to them. "No one's here."

"Are you sure?" Eliza asked weakly, detesting the tremor in her voice.

"I'm sure. But let's go before someone realizes we're all missing," Helen replied.

Holding hands, Eliza and Theresa scrambled up the sloping bank of the ravine and joined Helen at the edge. All three of the girls looked down at their fallen friend. Eliza closed her eyes.

"Take her to Heaven, oh Lord. She was a good, pure soul," she said.

"Not like the rest of us," Theresa added seriously.

"No," Helen said. "Indeed not."

A PACT

The forest was pitch-black as Eliza, Helen, and Theresa tromped through the underbrush in the dead of night for what Eliza hoped would be the final time. Helen and Theresa carried the heavy trunk full of books between them, while Eliza struggled with the three large, rusty shovels they had borrowed from the storage shed.

"Here," Helen said suddenly, when the girls were about half a mile due north of the chapel. She pointed at a patch of clearing, which was covered over by fallen pine needles. "This spot should be big enough."

"Thank goodness," Theresa said, dropping her side of the trunk. The thud frightened some dozing birds from the trees above, sending them cawing off into the sky.

"Let's get to work," Eliza said sullenly. She shoved the tip of her shovel into the dirt and began to dig.

Together the three girls toiled away, clearing a hole that was about four feet wide and at least six feet deep. The longer Eliza worked, the faster she went, feeling that with each jab of her shovel, each toss over her shoulder, she was somehow excising the horrible events of the past few weeks. Sweat prickled under her arms, above her lip, and along her brow, but she didn't stop to rest or to clear it away. She only worked harder.

"I think that's enough," Helen said finally.

Eliza started. The three of them had been silent for so long, the sound of a voice seemed almost unnatural. She and Theresa were standing inside the hole, while Helen hovered above them. For the first time in more than an hour, Eliza really studied Theresa. She had a streak of dirt across her cheek, and her dark hair was matted with perspiration. The look that passed between them was one of wary respect. Suddenly, Eliza's heart was full. She felt as if there was no malice left in her. She had no space left, no energy left, to harbor such things.

"You saved my life," she said as Helen jumped down into the hole, leaving her shovel behind. Eliza looked from one to the other, her eyes shining with tears. "You both saved my life."

Theresa reached for Eliza's hand. "You would have done the same for me."

"And me," Helen added, taking Eliza's other hand.

For a long moment the three of them stood there, holding on to one another, and Eliza could feel that none of them wanted to let go.

"It's not your fault, Eliza, that he loves you," Theresa said suddenly. She looked at the ground. "I know it's not your fault." She looked up again and shrugged, though her eyes were full of tears. "No one ever loves me best."

Eliza's heart welled, but she found she couldn't speak. How could she respond to that? How could she possibly make it all right?

She squeezed Theresa's hand. "Come on. Let's get on with it."

The other girls nodded. Helen climbed back out of the hole and shoved the trunk toward the edge. Carefully, she lowered it down into the waiting arms of Eliza and Theresa. The trunk was heavy and awkward, with the books sliding and clunking around inside. Once the trunk had been placed squarely in the center of the hole, she and Theresa crawled out and took up their shovels.

"Wait," Helen said, holding out a dirt-covered hand. "We must make a pact. We must swear right now that none of us will ever come looking for this trunk again. That none of us will ever tell anyone where to find it."

"I swear," Eliza said willingly, placing her hand above Helen's.

"I swear," Theresa said, adding her hand above Eliza's.

"Good," Helen said with a nod. "I've had enough witchcraft to last two lifetimes." Then she pushed her shovel into the pile of dirt at her side, and made to cover the trunk.

"Wait!" Eliza said suddenly. "I almost forgot."

She reached up, clasped the locket in her hand, and gave it one good yank, breaking the delicate gold chain that held it. Without a second thought, she tossed the trinket into the hole, where it bounced off the top of the trunk and came to rest on the ground.

"Good riddance," she said.

As she gazed down at the locket, Eliza felt a momentary pang, remembering the day she'd first held it in her palm—that day in the sun with Catherine and Theresa and Alice—the last day of their innocence. But then the memory was gone, chased away by all the horror that had followed. Her lips set in a thin line, and she reached for the handle of her shovel.

"All right, girls," she said. "Let's finish this."

HURT

Eliza stood in her black mourning dress, holding hands with Theresa, both of them still as stone. The sky was a blanket of dark gray clouds, and the air was thick with a humidity that seemed to mute every sound. Eliza stared at the gleaming brown wood of Catherine's casket as it was carried by, feeling numb and exhausted. All her tears had been cried.

It had taken less than a day for the police search party to find Catherine in the woods. Hours of miserable anticipation that had felt like years to Eliza. But now it was over. She tried to take comfort in the fact that Catherine was going home.

"At least she's at peace now," Theresa whispered, squeezing Eliza's fingers.

Eliza nodded mutely, her throat full of emotion. Theresa hadn't left her side since the night of their pact. Theresa had spoken to Miss Almay, and had all of Eliza's things—except for her bookshelf, as it reminded her too much of Catherine—moved into her private room on the top floor of Crenshaw. That way, Eliza would no longer have to live in the room she'd shared with Catherine—the room in which she had almost met her end. And now here they were, roommates, clinging to each other as if they were old friends.

"Thank you, Theresa," Eliza whispered. "For everything."

Theresa simply nodded, giving Eliza a small smile, before returning her attention to the proceedings.

The eight pallbearers loaded the casket into a hearse—a long, black carriage draped with dark purple swaths of fabric—for transportation to the train station and then on to the Whites' farm in Georgia. All of the Billings and Easton community had turned out to pay their respects and say good-bye to Catherine—students, teachers, and staff alike.

Catherine's father and mother had made the trip up to Connecticut to squire their only daughter home. They stood across the dirt road, watching with red-rimmed eyes, as the pallbearers closed the solid black door on the back of the hearse. Catherine's father's hand rested on the shoulder of a small boy with blond hair, whose bottom lip had been quivering all morning. Eliza assumed this was Lincoln, Catherine's younger brother. She could barely stand to look at him.

Finally, Miss Almay stepped forward to shake hands with the Whites and offer her condolences. The crowd along the side of the road stood in awkward silence for a moment before breaking up. Packs of boys turned their steps toward Easton's campus, their hands in the pockets of their starched suits, their heads respectfully bowed.

Alice's sobs grew louder, and Eliza found she could stand it no longer.

"Excuse me, Theresa," she said furtively, releasing her friend's hand. "I need to be alone. Just for a moment."

Before Theresa could respond, Eliza turned and walked toward the elm tree next to Crenshaw House, striding as fast as she could. She paused near the outer branches, unwilling to duck under the canopy and be alone in the secluded spot where she and Catherine had so recently been together. Crossing her arms over her chest, she looked up at the sky.

I just need a moment to myself, she thought. *I just need a moment to breathe.*

The other girls seemed to understand this. She saw them walking past her on their way into Crenshaw. Lavender and Clarissa shot her concerned looks, but no one stopped. Eliza breathed in and out, telling herself it was time to let Catherine go, time to let her guilt go, time to move on. She couldn't go on feeling this weight in her chest. She simply could not live this way.

She just wished she could talk to Catherine one last time. She wished her friend could absolve her—tell her that it wasn't her fault.

Her eyes fell on Harrison, and the moment he noticed her, his brow knit with concern. But Eliza couldn't see him right now. She could not talk to him in this state. She covered her mouth to keep from crying and finally ducked under the thick branches of the elm.

Once inside the privacy of the leaves, Eliza walked over to the tree's trunk, leaned against it, and cried. Her chest heaved as she bent her head forward, letting the rough bark cut into the skin of her forehead.

What had she been thinking? This guilt was never going to go away. Catherine was never going to come back and absolve her. Nothing was ever going to be right again. Nothing.

"Eliza."

Whirling around at the sound of her name, Eliza saw Harrison slipping inside her sanctuary. She shook her head at the sight of him, not wanting him to see her like this.

"Eliza," he said again, approaching her. "I'm so sorry about Catherine. I know how you must feel."

"You don't know anything," Eliza heard herself say, her voice soaked with tears. She backed away from him, moving around the trunk of the tree. "You don't know anything about me, Harrison."

Still he came. He closed the gap between them quickly and pulled her into his arms.

"I know everything I need to know," he said, holding her head against his chest. "And it's okay to cry. I'm here."

"I can't," Eliza said, sniffling. Her chest felt as if it was being crushed by the weight of ten thousand heavy heels. "I can't."

"Eliza, no matter what happens, I'll always be here for you," Harrison said, leaning back. He placed one finger beneath her chin and lifted her face to look into her eyes. "All I want is to be with you. I haven't spoken to Theresa yet because of all that's happened, but I will. I'll make her understand."

Eliza yanked herself away from Harrison's grasp. "I can't, Harrison." She channeled every bit of frustration and misery and regret into the words. "I can't be with you. You belong with Theresa. You should be with her now, not me. She needs you. Please, just go to her. Leave me alone."

The look of hurt and confusion on his face was impossible for Eliza to bear. She had hurt Catherine. She had hurt Theresa. She had hurt all her sisters in the coven. And now she had hurt Harrison, too.

"But Eliza, I thought you said—"

"I know what I said, but I was wrong," Eliza sobbed. "Please, Harrison, just go. Just go to your fiancée."

Harrison still didn't move. Eliza couldn't take the pain in her chest for a moment longer. She ducked under the lowest branches and ran for Crenshaw House, shoving the heavy door open. Nearly blinded by tears, she ignored Mrs. Hodge, who called after her, and ran up the stairs and into her old room, slamming the door behind her.

This, she realized instantly, was a mistake. Catherine's things were still there. Her dresses still hung in the closet. Her books still stood on Eliza's shelves. Her quilt still covered her bed. This was the last place Eliza wanted to be right then. The last place in the world. But as she turned to go, there was a knock on the door.

"Miss Williams?" Mrs. Hodge said tentatively. "Catherine's father has sent some men to pack up her things. May I let them in?"

Eliza's heart pounded. Without thinking twice, she dropped to the floor, yanked Catherine's case of magical items out from under her bed, and shoved it under the one she had slept in. Then she stood up, dried her eyes with her fingertips, and took in a long, ragged breath.

"Come in," she said.

Mrs. Hodge opened the door. The two young men in plain, gray flannel jackets doffed their caps at Eliza but said nothing. They simply went to work, transferring Catherine's clothes from her bureau to her trunk. They plucked her toiletry items from the shelves, removed the linens from her bed, and finally removed the fleur-de-lis from the wall, tossing it on top of everything else. The whole while, Eliza stood in the hall with Mrs. Hodge, at a respectful distance but watching their every move. She held her breath the whole time, waiting irrationally for one of them to spot Catherine's box, to realize that it belonged to her deceased friend and not to her.

"Good day, miss," one of the two men said to Eliza as they carted the trunk out between them.

"Good day," Eliza managed.

Mrs. Hodge gave Eliza a sympathetic smile. Eliza was surprised and touched to be the recipient of such kind emotions from such a hard woman.

"Is there anything I can get you, Miss Williams?" Mrs. Hodge asked.

"No, thank you," Eliza replied, stepping into her old room, now eerily empty. "I'd just like to be alone for a while."

"Of course," Mrs. Hodge said.

The maid reached for the handle and closed the door, leaving Eliza on her own. Trying not to start crying all over again, Eliza sat down on the edge of her bed and stared at the blank side of the room that was once Catherine's.

"I wish you were still here, Catherine," Eliza said aloud. "I wish you were here with me right now."

There was, of course, no reply. But Eliza felt a strange warmth over her shoulders, a glimmer of peace inside her chest. Somehow, she felt as if Catherine *was* there. And that she was wishing she could be with Eliza, too.

It wasn't until the men and the trunk were long gone and the house had gone still that Eliza lay back—and in doing so, caught a glimpse of her bookshelf. Her heart caught and she smiled, for the men had accidentally left her Catherine's most prized possessions: her books.

Wiping the last stray tears from her eyes, Eliza shoved herself up and pulled out the blank book her mother had given her. She opened it to the first page and ran her eyes down the list of girls she, Theresa, Catherine, and Alice had chosen to be members of the "Billings Literary Society." Then she turned to the next page, the one on which each of the girls had personally signed her name. Her fingers grazed Catherine's signature, and her heart caught miserably.

Eliza took a deep, broken breath and sat down at her old desk. She took out a pen, turned to the first clean page in the book, and began to write. Slowly, methodically, she recorded every detail of the past few days. The story of Caroline Westwick, of her sister Lucille, of Helen's involvement in the original coven and Caroline's suicide. Then she tearfully recorded all that had happened with Catherine—her dream about her friend's death, the actual accident, the ritual and the thing it had brought back, and finally the curse. As much as it broke her heart to recall the details, she knew she had to record them—just in case any future Billings girls ever stumbled across the books again. They would have to be warned. They would have to be protected.

Catherine would have wanted it that way.

HELP THEM

"Why must Miss Almay keep such a close eye on everyone?" Theresa asked Eliza as they sat on the wrought-iron bench alongside the Crenshaw garden on Wednesday afternoon following classes. "Does she think we're all going to wander off and meet our doom in the woods?"

"No," Eliza replied, watching as Miss Almay paced the flower beds planted alongside the house's foundation. "She knows something is wrong. She can tell."

"How could she not know?" Helen asked. The maid knelt in the garden a few feet in front of the two girls, pulling out weeds—all the better to hide the fact that the three of them were conversing. "Look at them."

Eliza scanned the area. It was free period, and several of the younger girls had started up a game of jump rope on the lawn. Their laughter and shrieks of joy were in stark contrast to the attitude of the girls from the coven. Alice sat under cover of a wide-brimmed felt hat, reading her Bible diligently, as she had been doing ever since she'd learned that Catherine was dead—again. Jane reposed on a bench opposite Eliza's and Theresa's, staring listlessly into space as she toyed with her hair. Lavender, Bia, and Viola sat together on a picnic blanket not talking to one another. Marilyn and Genevieve were ostensibly watching Petit Peu play with a stick, but they hardly seemed to notice him at all. Clarissa was squirreled away in the library, ignoring the existence of everyone else.

"Well, we're still in mourning," Theresa said. "Of course we'd be listless."

"It's not just listlessness," Eliza said. "It's guilt."

Theresa's head snapped around, and Helen stopped weeding abruptly but didn't turn.

"What do you mean? Why would they feel guilty?" Theresa asked.

Eliza's mouth was dry. "Because we had the chance to save Catherine, and we failed," she said, one single tear spilling down her cheek. "We promised them we could bring her back. We set them up for failure. They believe . . . they believe Catherine is still dead because of them. Because of us. Don't *you* feel that way, Theresa?"

Theresa took a breath. "No," she said. "We tried, Eliza. Most people wouldn't have even done that."

"Well, even if you don't feel it, they—we—do," Eliza said, crossing her arms over her chest as she watched Alice slowly turn the page in her Bible. "That sort of pain doesn't just go away."

For a long moment, none of them spoke. All three of them just watched the others—watched them ignoring one another, watched them not living their lives.

"All right, then. We have to find a way to help them move on," Theresa said finally. "We have to help them put this whole mess behind them and start over."

"But how?" Eliza asked.

Helen stood up, dusted her hands off, and turned to them. "I know we said we were done with magic, but perhaps we need to cast one last spell."

THIS PAIN

Eliza stood in the center of the temple with Theresa and Helen, the other eight members of the coven gathered in a circle around them. It was Saturday afternoon, and Miss Almay had gone off campus for a visit with her sister in Norfolk. If the girls were going to put Helen's plan in motion, now was the time.

"What are we doing here?" Clarissa snipped, hugging herself against the chill. "No one wants to be here, you know."

"Clarissa is right. You don't intend for us to be casting spells again, do you?" Marilyn asked, holding Genevieve's hand.

Bia and Viola stood huddled near the door, while the others eyed Eliza, Theresa, and Helen with suspicion. Eliza ignored their questions. She looked into Theresa's brown eyes and held her breath.

"Ready?" Helen asked. She pressed a single grape leaf into each of their palms.

"Ready," Theresa and Eliza replied.

The three girls clasped hands, their leaves pressing together, and recited the incantation.

"Sleep, sisters, sleep, and dream your fondest dream. Take no note of what we do. Things are not what they seem."

This time, there was no dizziness whatsoever. A warm wind swirled up and out from the tight circle, lifting Eliza's hair straight up from her head. When it died down, she glanced at Helen and Theresa for courage, then turned around.

All eight girls had fallen fast asleep where they stood. Lavender was even snoring. Alice swayed slightly on her feet but didn't tip over.

"Let's get to work," Theresa said determinedly. She walked over to Jane and touched her fingertips to Jane's forehead. "When you wake, you will be free of this pain," she said. And Jane's head nodded forward, her chin ducking toward her neck.

Eliza stepped up to Clarissa and placed her fingers against the sleeping girl's forehead. "When you wake, you will be free of this pain." Clarissa's head nodded forward.

Standing in front of Alice next, as Helen and Theresa worked on the other girls, Eliza took a deep breath. She hoped that when Alice awoke, she would be back to her formerly vibrant, bright-eyed self. She hoped that she would be free of this fear of retribution, this overwhelming guilt that had consumed her. She reached out, touched Alice's forehead, and closed her eyes, channeling all her energy into her friend.

"When you wake, you will be free of this pain."

Alice's head nodded, her red curls grazing her cheeks. Eliza smiled slightly, hoping she had done right by her friend.

"All right. We're done," Theresa said, her long, azure blue skirt swishing about her ankles as she turned. "Let's get them upstairs."

Helen placed her hands gently on Genevieve's shoulders and turned her toward the stairs. Then she took Marilyn by the hand and walked her toward Genevieve. Marilyn went along, being led like a sleepwalking child. Helen lifted Marilyn's right hand and placed it on Genevieve's right shoulder. Catching on, Eliza set about helping form the chain. Lavender's hand met Marilyn's shoulder. Then Clarissa, then Alice, then Viola, then Bia, then Jane.

"I'll take the front, and you girls take the rear," Helen said. Then she walked to the front of the line, placed Genevieve's hand on her own shoulder, and began to walk. Each of the sleeping girls stepped forward as her arm was tugged by the girl in front of her. The chain loped up the winding staircase in silence, never missing a step. Eliza and Theresa stayed behind on the floor of the temple for a moment, looking at each other in awe.

"That Helen really knows her magic," Theresa said.

"Thank goodness," Eliza replied. She took a deep breath and let it out, feeling relieved. If this spell worked, at least her friends would be released from their misery. That was something.

At the end of the chain, Jane started up the first step. Eliza looked around the temple and felt a pang of regret and nostalgia. What they had done here in this room had been exciting. It had opened up so many possibilities. But now, those possibilities were gone forever.

But this is a good thing, she reminded herself. *Then, you looked forward to only happiness and innocent mischief, but look what misery you wrought. Those books are better left hidden.*

"We'd better follow," Theresa said, nodding toward the stairs.

Together they took one last look around their hallowed space. The pedestal and chairs still stood where they'd left them, looking so lonely and bare without the candles and the draping and the books. With one last sigh, Eliza reached for Theresa's hand. The two girls turned as one and climbed the stairs. At the top, Theresa closed the door behind them, and Eliza turned the key with one final, resounding click.

"Never again," Theresa said, looking Eliza in the eye.

Eliza slipped the key into the pocket of her dress, where it came to a rest, cold and heavy at her side.

"Never again."

CAN'T GET ENOUGH OF THE BILLINGS GIRLS?
TURN THE PAGE FOR A SNEAK PEEK OF

OMINOUS

THE NEXT PRIVATE NOVEL, COMING MARCH 2011

I knocked on Noelle's door in Pemberly Hall Friday morning, my eyes puffy and at half-mast—I hadn't slept at all since we'd discovered the Book of Spells in the basement of the Billings Chapel. It took Noelle a moment to answer, and when she did, she grabbed my arm and pulled me inside.

"Wait. Reed just got here," she said into her iPhone. "I'm putting you on speaker."

Noelle placed the flat cell phone atop her dresser and stepped back. She wore a gray wool skirt that came halfway down her calves, paired with heeled black boots and a black ballet-neck sweater. Her dark brown hair was pulled back from her face on the sides, and her makeup was impeccably done, complete with fully lined eyes and lavender eye shadow.

Apparently *she* had slept. I pulled my navy cotton cardigan tighter around my wrinkled long-sleeved T-shirt and stifled a yawn.

"Girls?" Noelle's grandmother's voice came through the speaker loud and clear. Well, *our* grandmother's voice, I corrected myself with a jolt. I had learned just a couple of days ago that Noelle and I were half sisters. "Girls, are you there?"

"We're right here, Grandmother," Noelle said, placing her hands on her hips.

"Reed?"

Noelle knocked me with her elbow.

"I'm here," I croaked.

"Good. Noelle is a bit . . . out of sorts this morning," Mrs. Lange said, sounding displeased. "Perhaps you can help me calm her down."

"Calm me down?" Noelle blurted. "Like that's gonna happen. You sent us out into the snow in the middle of the night to find the quote-unquote *key to our future* and what do we find? A book about witch-craft." She went over to her bed and yanked the thick tome out from under a tangle of bed sheets and silk pajamas, holding it up as if her grandmother could see it. "Is that what you're trying to tell us Gram? Really? That you think we're witches? I'm sorry, but you're either senile or really, *really* bored."

I took the book from Noelle with two hands. Even though I agreed that last night had felt like a pointless practical joke, the book was still real. It had once belonged to Elizabeth Williams, one of the original Billings Girls, and was therefore a precious relic to me.

"Seriously, Grandmother, have you ever thought about taking up mah-jongg?" Noelle continued without pause. "I hear it really helps keep your faculties in order."

"Noelle," I scolded under my breath.

She widened her eyes at me. "*What?*"

Through the speakers, I heard Mrs. Lange take in a deep, patient breath. "Girls today are so skeptical and jaded. But you two—you have no idea the power you could wield."

Noelle rolled her eyes.

"So . . . ?" I said slowly, hugging the book to my chest. "Are you saying that *you've* actually done witchcraft?"

"No," she admitted. Noelle threw up her hands and turned away. She'd been away from school for almost two weeks and her Louis Vuitton rolling case was still open on the floor. She picked it up and turned it over, dumping the entire contents out on her gold and burgundy throw rug. "No one at Billings has practiced in a long time," Mrs. Lange continued. "But the two of you . . . girls, you have no idea how powerful you could be, now that you're together."

I felt an odd chill go through me and I looked over at Noelle. She sorted through a pile of balled-up sweaters, crumpled socks, and tangles of necklaces, her fingers shaking slightly.

"The two of you have a unique opportunity here," Mrs. Lange continued, oblivious to Noelle's silent tantrum. "You might be able to fix certain things, set to right the unpleasant . . . situation that has arisen at Easton."

Noelle stood up straight, her arms falling down at her sides, one hand clutching an Hermès scarf and the other the gold chain strap on a Gucci purse. We looked at one another and I knew we were thinking the same thing: The woman *was* senile. But then, I saw a flash of movement behind Noelle, a blur of color against the stark white snow outside. Stepping over the pile of clothes at my feet, I carefully walked to the frost-laced window and peered out. There, across the quad at the desiccated site of the former Billings House—our former home—was group of people in long wool coats. I recognized the perfect posture of Headmaster Hathaway and the jet black curls of Demetria Rosewell, one of the more powerful Billings alums. They walked carefully around the jagged stone outline that was the footprint of the demolished building, along with a pair of men who pointed and jotted notes on clipboards, and bent their heads together in the bright sunshine.

I felt a familiar hollowing-out sensation in my gut. "What's that about?" I whispered to Noelle.

"I don't know," Noelle replied, coming up behind me.

Chilling words coming from her, since normally she knew everything. Although lately, my know-it-all friend had dropped the ball more than once. The idea of her not always being in charge was going to take some getting used to. I turned and looked at the phone.

"Mrs. Lange?"

"Yes, Reed."

"Do you mean . . ." I kept one eye on the group out the window, their feet sinking into the snow. "Do you mean that we might be able to bring Billings back?"

For the first time that morning, Noelle looked intrigued.

"Now you're thinking, Reed."

There was a glimmer of pride in her voice, and I felt it in my chest. I'd made my grandmother proud. Weird. Noelle and I looked at each other, then out the window. Mrs. Rosewell was shaking hands with Mr. Hathaway, nodding in a satisfied way. The sunlight glinted off Mr. Hathaway's wide smile. There was something foreboding about it. Like someone was making a deal with the devil, but I wasn't sure which side was good and which was evil. All I knew was that I didn't like it.

Noelle and I exchanged a glance. What if we *could* bring Billings back? Wouldn't it be worth it to hear our grandmother out?

"No. No way." Noelle shook her head and stepped away from the window, as if she was shaking herself out of a daydream.

Noelle was angrily tossing her things onto her bed. "We are *not* witches, Grandmother. This is not some CW summer series."

"I don't know what that means," Mrs. Lange said.

"It means this conversation is over," Noelle replied. She plucked the phone off the dresser and held it in front of her mouth. "I'll call you later, Grandmother. We're late for breakfast." Then she ended the call before Mrs. Lange could protest.

"Well," I said. "That was rude."

"She'll get over it," Noelle replied, shoving the phone into the rust-colored Birkin bag she was currently using for her schoolwork. She turned and sat down on the mound of her comforter with a sigh. Her shoulders slumped slightly. "I'm sorry, Reed." She looked up at me tentatively. "For everything. The whole faked kidnapping thing was her idea. She kept talking about birthright and us being sisters and how you needed to go through this test and then we'd have our reward. I thought she was going to ... . I don't know . . . give us the keys to some villa in Spain I'd never heard about so we could bond this summer." She sighed again and her eyes fell on the book, which I still held clutched to my chest. "I never would have said yes to any of it if I knew she was batshit crazy."

"It's okay," I said, releasing my grip slightly so I could look down at the worn cover. "I can see how she could be really . . . persuasive."

A tingling sensation sprung to life in my chest and traveled down my arms, into my fingertips, making the book feel warm in my hands. I would never have said this to Noelle in a billion years, but there was this teeny, tiny part of me that wondered . . . what if Mrs. Lange *wasn't* crazy? What if what she'd said was true and we could wield some kind of power? I'd seen some insane stuff since I'd started school at Easton last fall. Nothing supernatural, of course, but definitely crazy—things I never would have thought were possible even two years ago. What if this was possible too?

"Okay, forget this."

Noelle plucked the book right out of my hands and tossed it back onto the mess of her bed. My fingers felt cold suddenly, and I tucked them under my arms.

"I say we concentrate on more important things," she said, her brown eyes bright.

"Like what?" I said, trying not to look over her shoulder at the book.

"Things based in actual reality." She reached for her black-and-white plaid coat and opened the door for me, but I hesitated. "What?" she asked impatiently.

"Do you mind if I take that?" I said, gesturing toward the book. "I mean, if you're not going to look at it—"

"Seriously?" She walked to her bed, picked up the book, and held it out to me. "It smells like rotting garbage and mold. *Please* take it."

I reached for the book, but she snatched it back toward her shoulder, giving me an appraising glance. "As long as you promise me you're not going to try anything in it. Because I really don't think I could be friends with someone who actually believes in this crap."

I held her gaze. "I promise."

Her eyes narrowed further, but after a long moment, she handed the book over. I stuck it in my messenger bag and pulled the flap down over it.

"As I was *saying*," Noelle said as we stepped out into the hallway, "I think we should talk about throwing you the most kick-ass seventeenth birthday party in the history of birthdays. You're a Lange now. I'd say you're well overdue."

Instantly, my shoulder muscles coiled.

"I'm not a Lange."

I tried to keep the irritation out of my voice, but it didn't entirely work. The thing was, I barely even knew Noelle's dad, and I wasn't even sure if I wanted to. But I was certain that I didn't feel like part of their family. I was a Brennan, and I always would be.

Noelle rolled her eyes again as she started to close the door behind us. "Whatever."

"Actually, Noelle, I wanted to talk to you about that. . . . Can we keep this whole sisters thing between us for now? If that's okay with you," I added quickly.

She froze with her hand on the doorknob. "Why?"

"I just . . . I don't want to deal with all the questions and explanations and everything until I'm a little more used to it," I said.

"Wow. I'd think you'd be kinda psyched to be my sister," Noelle said. Only she would have a big enough ego to say something like that without a hint or irony or self-deprecation.

"It's not that," I told her. "It's just . . . it's kind of humiliating, you know? I'm going to have to tell everyone that my mom cheated on my dad with your dad." I looked at my water-stained leather boots, mottled after days of tromping around campus in the snow and sleet. "There's no getting around that."

Noelle's expression utterly changed. It was pretty clear she'd never thought of the whole thing from my perspective before. "Yeah. Okay. I get it." She closed the door with a bang. "But you still deserve a party."

She had me there. After faking her kidnapping, scaring me to death, and making me jump through multiple hoops to find her over the past couple of weeks, I'd say I deserved whatever good things she wanted to throw my way. A party might be just what the psychoanalyst ordered after everything I'd recently been through.

Her eyes flicked over me as if she was noticing my outfit for the first time, and did not approve. "Where's your coat?" she asked.

I glanced down at my jeans. "Oh. I guess I forgot it."

She shook her head, walked back inside, and came out two seconds later with a wool camel-colored trench. "See? You should *definitely* be psyched to have me as a big sister. I'm already taking care of you."

"Thanks," I said with a smile, slipping my arms into the sleeves. She'd always taken care of me, and we both knew it. Until that last little escapade of hers, anyway.

She closed the door, took in a big breath, and blew it out. "Okay. Let's start with location and date. I'm thinking the city, on your actual birthday. Unless you've got some better plans back in Bumblefart, Pennsylvania."

I tried not to bristle at her insult of my hometown. I'd gotten used to it over the past couple of years, but somehow, now that she was of the opinion that I'd never belonged there, what with the Lange blood in my veins, it felt more personal. I might not have loved my hometown of Croton, Pennsylvania, but it was my home. And I did love my family, including my father, who would always be my dad, no matter what.

"No," I said. "No plans. I think a party in New York would be perfect."

"Good. I'm so on it."

As we walked down the hallway toward the stairwell, I felt the weight of the book knocking against my hip over and over again, and I itched to steal back to my room and open it up—check out those notes Elizabeth Williams had written in the margins, see if I recognized any of the other handwriting. Maybe I'd have a chance to do it later, when Noelle wasn't around. Because even though I didn't believe in spells, I was sure she would tell me I was ridiculous for caring about these girls who had lived almost a hundred years ago.

But I did. And I was dying to know more about them.

"So you bailed from school for two weeks so you could go to some *spa* in Sedona?" Portia Ahronian said, lifting her fur-lined hood over her head as we walked toward the chapel after breakfast. She tucked her thick black hair inside the hood, untangling some strands that had gotten caught up in one of her many gold necklaces. "What about all your homework? And your tests?"

"Hathaway had them e-mailed to me," Noelle lied casually, lifting a shoulder. "Perks of your dad helping the headmaster land his job."

"And why, exactly, did you have to scare the bejesus out of us the night you left?" Astrid Chou asked, popping some contraband cereal from her hand into her mouth. She dusted the sugar from her hands, then slipped on her colorful knit gloves, which she had attached to the sleeves of her purple coat with kiddie-style glove savers, an accessory only quirky Astrid could get away with on an upscale campus like Easton. "I honestly think Amberly almost had a coronary, and as the only one among us who knows CPR, I was not about to go there."

"Hey!" Amberly protested, her pert pink lips twisted into a pout. "You wouldn't save my life?"

Astrid shook her black bangs off her face. "*Maybe.* But only if you promised me that red Chloé bag of yours."

My friends laughed and I could tell none of them were really still angry with Noelle for the prank she's pulled on the night of her "disappearance." Everyone was just glad to have her back, safe and sound. Of course I hadn't had a chance to tell her that I'd told Ivy Slade she was actually at home with her mom, but that was a flub that could easily be glossed over if Ivy started asking questions.

"Sorry about that, guys," Noelle said, returning to the subject as our feet crunched over the salted stone walk. "I was just messing with Reed. I owed her one, and you guys just got stuck in the middle. But I promise. No more drama for the rest of the semester."

"Great. You just jinxed us," Kiki Rosen said, pausing on the third step of the Easton Chapel and turning around to look at the rest of us. A stiff breeze kicked up her hair, half of which she'd recently dyed neon-green. "We are *so* screwed."

She rolled her eyes, but smiled as Astrid hooked her arm through Kiki's and dragged her inside. Together, the two of them looked like a colorful tear sheet from a comic book.

"Speaking of the chapel, Reed, when's the next meeting of the BLS?" Tiffany Goulbourne asked quietly. She'd been bringing up the rear, scrolling through some photos on her camera with Rose Sakowitz.

Tiffany was never without her camera, even though with her perfect warm brown skin, almost six-foot height, and perfect bod, she could have definitely been posing in *front* of one rather than shooting from behind one. She whipped out her BlackBerry as she approached, ready to type the meeting into her calendar. Tiffany had always been one of my more responsible friends, but unlike the rest of them, she seemed to be getting more organized the closer she got to graduation, instead of less. The other seniors had slowly started to slack, copying homework assignments or faking migraines to get out of class. But not Tiffany.

"We're in need of some girl bonding," Rose added, looking a little pale beneath her mass of red curls.

"Um . . . honestly, I hadn't really thought about it." I looked off across campus toward the woods around Easton, where the Billings chapel stood. Suddenly, I itched to skip morning chapel and dash over there. I wanted to check the place out, see if there was anything Noelle and I had missed last night—any more clues to what Elizabeth Williams and her friends had been doing with a Book of Spells almost a hundred years ago.

Ironic, considering that just a couple of days ago I'd been seriously pondering the idea of never coming back to this place. After Noelle had faked her own kidnapping, I'd all but decided I wouldn't be returning to Easton Academy this semester. I was done with all the insanity, the selfishness, the entitlement. But then Mrs. Lange had explained that the whole thing had been her idea, and had lured me back here with all this mystery and talk of what was to come, and I'd fallen for it like a satellite plummeting back to Earth.

"Why don't we do it tonight?" I suggested. "I'll send out a text later."

"A text about what?"

Josh appeared over Tiffany's shoulder and her eyes bulged out like she was afraid we'd just been caught. What Tiffany didn't know was that I'd already confided in Josh about our secret society—back when he'd been trying to help me figure out who'd snatched Noelle. She and Rose didn't need to know that, though. I didn't want them thinking I'd betrayed their trust just because Noelle had taken a spa sabbatical.

"Nothing you need to worry your pretty little head about," I joked, pulling him toward me. We touched noses and I smiled, inhaling that very particular Josh scent of evergreen soap and dried paint.

"I missed you," he said.

"I missed you, too," I replied.

"Ugh. Let's go inside before we catch whatever cheesy grossness has sickened these two," Noelle joked.

She and the other girls jogged up the marble steps as Josh and I kissed hello. He opened his coat and wrapped it around me along with his arms, nestling us together in a warm Josh-and-Reed cocoon. As I cuddled against him and deepened the kiss, I wondered how I ever could have imagined leaving here—leaving him. Next year, Josh would be off to college and we'd hardly ever see one another.

"We need to do something. Go somewhere," Josh said quietly, pulling back. He lifted one hand and gently brushed his fingertips across my cheek. "How long has it been since we've gone on a date?"

I narrowed my eyes, pretending to think. "Since forever?"

"All right, then. With your permission, I'll make a plan," he said, touching his forehead to mine. "ASAP."

"ASAP sounds good," I replied.

"What the hell is she doing here?" Josh said suddenly.

My eyes popped open and I turned around. Headmaster Hathaway strode toward us from the direction of Hull Hall with Demetria Rosewell in tow. My first thought was, *Double H is going to miss morning services.* But I realized in the next second that this was not the pertinent fact here. Nor was Demetria the "she" to whom Josh had referred. Striding along behind them was Paige Ryan. The daughter of the person who had recently tried to murder me multiple times in St. Barth's. Josh shot her a scowl as she walked by, but all she did was grin. A few steps past the chapel, she paused and looked behind her.

"Missy! Are you coming or not?" she asked.

Missy Thurber, my worst nemesis at Easton, jumped away from Constance Talbot and London Simmons and scurried after her cousin Paige. She also gave me a grin as she hurried by, but hers held a lot more meaning. It was an "I know something you don't know" grin.

My heart sunk inside my chest, and I looked back at Constance and London. The two of them turned and hustled inside, avoiding my eyes.

"What was that all about?" Josh asked, entwining his fingers with mine.

"I don't know," I replied. "And I don't think I want to know."

"I love the idea of a party to honor the seniors," I told Amberly that night as we kicked back on the floor of the Billings Chapel. "Do you want to put a committee together?"

"Yes! I'd *love* a committee!" Amberly said, clapping her hands.

I could see a few of the girls wince at the idea of being roped in by Amberly and toiling under her direction, but it was her idea, so they'd just have to deal. We were just finishing up our meeting when Amberly had very formally presented a "piece of new business" as if we were at a board meeting, rather than sprawled out on silk pillows, chenille blankets, and fur throws in a deserted chapel. Rose had provided the refreshments tonight—gourmet cupcakes shipped in from New York City—and there were crumbs, sprinkles, and coconut shreds everywhere. Vienna Clarke groaned, her hand across her flat stomach, a bit of chocolate stuck to the corner of her mouth.

"Okay, if there are no *other* new points of business," I said, "then I'd say we're adjourned!"

The convivial chatter started up as soon as the words were out of my mouth and my friends began to gather up their things. Noelle clasped Vienna's hands and hoisted her off the floor, while Amberly practically jumped Lorna Gross and Astrid, asking them to join her committee.

"You ready?" Ivy asked, lifting her long black hair out of her red coat and letting it fall down her back. It had turned out that her absence that morning was no mystery after all. She'd simply been waiting at the post office for a care package from home.

"Actually, I think I'm going to hang back for a little while," I said, gesturing over my shoulder in what I hoped was a casual way. I had a plan for the evening, and it did not involve going back to campus.

Noelle paused near the door and cocked an eyebrow. So maybe my gesture hadn't hit the mark. "I don't want to leave all these crumbs. We could attract mice."

"Oh. Then I'll help," Ivy said.

She started to put her bag down again and I panicked. "No!" I blurted.

Both Ivy and Noelle were staring at me now, with matching expressions of concern and confusion. Which was interesting considering how much they hated each other. Noelle crossed her arms over her chest.

"It's just . . . I kind of want to be alone," I said. "I've got a lot to think about and I . . . I guess I've never told you guys this, but I like to clean while I think. It helps me relax."

Ivy's brow crease deepened and for a moment I thought she

would put up a fight, but then Noelle turned, gently knocking Ivy with her shoulder. "Come on. Let's leave the freak to her cleaning therapy."

If anyone knew I really *did* have a lot to think about, it was Noelle. Apparently she was taking pity on me. Which kind of made me feel guilty about all the lying.

"Okay," Ivy said slowly. "But I don't *love* the idea of you being out here alone."

"I'll be fine," I promised her. "I've got my phone if I need anything."

The two of them finally capitulated and followed the others outside, who waved and shouted their good-byes as they slipped out into the night. When their voices had finally died off on the wind, I took a deep breath and looked around. Except for the few flickering candles, the chapel was dark. Some of the stained glass windows had been broken long ago, leaving behind jagged, incomplete mosaics, the stars winking outside their busted panes. The pews were polished and buffed—thanks to the members of my secret society—and the wood floors were swept clean, but high in the rafters there were still some heavy cobwebs, and a stray bird's nest.

Quickly blowing out all but one candle, I grabbed my messenger bag and the last candle and walked to the office at the back of the building.

The room was small and square, its basic wood furnishings covered in years of dust and grime. I placed my candle in the holder on the desk, then walked to the bookcase on the west wall. Using both hands, I pried the bookcase away from the plaster. It swung open, letting out a silence-splitting creak of protest. Behind it was a smaller, white paneled door with a brass knob and an old-fashioned keyhole. I tugged the key on its purple cord out of the pocket of my jeans. As I slid the key into the hole, I glanced back over my shoulder to make sure none of my friends had returned. Then I turned the key with a click and the ice-cold doorknob turned easily in my grasp.

Frigid air rushed up from the basement, along with a musty yet somehow cozy smell that made me think of the basement of the Croton library. The dank room housed all the historical books, and older kids were always getting caught making out down there. I reached back for my candle and held it high in front of me as I descended the stairs.

When my foot hit the concrete floor, I paused. My throat was dry as I looked around. The basement room was a perfect circle. Eleven chairs were set up to face the center, and at that center was a podium, plain and sturdy and made of wood. It was on this podium that we had found the Book of Spells last night.

Inhaling a bit of the musty air, I looked slowly around the room and smiled. Elizabeth Williams had hung out here. She'd been in this very room with Theresa Billings and Catherine White and all the other girls mentioned in the BLS book. I wished I knew what they looked like, and wondered why I'd never thought to try to dig up photographs of them before. They'd had cameras in 1915, hadn't they? Tomorrow I would have to check the Easton archives and see if I could find any photographs.

I tugged out the BLS book first and opened to the second page, the one where each of the members of the first Billings Literary Society had signed their names. Then I slowly opened the Book of Spells. Near the front was a list of basic spells, and next to each was a little tick, as if someone had checked them off after completing them. Next to some items there were notes, written in a few different hands:

"Worked on the third try" or "Must be done with two sisters, holding hands."

Some of these notes were in the same slanting script as the BLS book—there was the curled-down tail on the y's and the flourish on the s's. That small scroll to the W or M or N. The handwriting belonged to Elizabeth Williams.

Carefully, I studied some of the other notes, my eyes flicking back and forth from the signature page in the BLS to the Book of Spells. Suddenly, my heart caught. Some of the other notes had been written by Catherine White, Elizabeth's best friend. Her lowercase a's and o's were perfectly rounded, almost like a child's handwriting.

A shiver of satisfaction went through me, like when I figured out a calculus problem. I paged through the Book of Spells, glancing at some of the titles. The Forgetfulness Spell. The Swelling Tongue. Spell to Mend a Broken Heart. Then something caught my eye as I whipped past, and I slowly paged back. Written across the top of the page were the words "The Presence in Mind Spell."

That handwriting was not Elizabeth's, but it looked familiar. I glanced back at the list of signatures and picked it out right away. The strokes were thick and confident, the uppercase letters overly large. The spell had been written out by Theresa Billings.

"This is so freaking cool," I whispered.

I looked around the room again, hugging myself against the cold. I imagined Theresa, Elizabeth, and Catherine at the podium, jotting down notes in the book. Had they really cast spells in this room? Had any of them worked? Was that even possible? Or was it a game to occupy their time?

A sudden and loud bang woke me up from my imagination. I scrambled to my feet, clutching the books to me as panic filled my limbs. Heavy footsteps clomped down the stairs, every creak like an arrow to my heart. I pressed back against the wall, wondering if there was any way to use my candle as a weapon. Then, someone appeared at the foot of the stairs. Her dark hair hung around her shoulders and she looked at me with a wry expression.

"I knew it!"

"Noelle! You scared the crap out of me!" I blurted.

"Which you deserve!" she said, tromping across the room. "What are you doing? Please tell me you're not really taking this stuff seriously."

She wrested the Billings Literary Society book from my hands and looked at it. "What are you, writing a term paper now?"

I grabbed the book back and crouched, shoving it into my messenger bag with shaky hands, along with the Book of Spells. My nerves had yet to catch up to the fact that there was no danger, and my pulse throbbed in my temples. I breathed in and out a few times, closing my eyes and hoping for patience before I stood up again.

"I'm just messing around," I improvised, shouldering my bag. "I was trying to figure out whether those Billings Literary Society girls really believed in this witchcraft crap."

Noelle, to my surprise, looked interested. "Did they?"

"Some of them, I think," I said, lifting my shoulders. For some reason I didn't want to name names and open the girls up to Noelle's ridicule. Which was, of course, ridiculous, since they were all dead.

"Yeah, well, people were a lot more gullible back then," Noelle said, turning and heading for the open doorway. "Come on. There's still a mess upstairs and I am *not* hanging out here again if it's infested with mice."

"I'm right behind you," I told her, picking up the candle.

As I placed my foot on the first stair, a light breeze ruffled my hair. Only there were no openings in the stone wall, no windows anywhere. At the third step, I felt it again. And by the seventh it was stronger still, the wind right in my face. By the tenth step, the flame of the candle died and by the twelfth, I had to squint my eyes to see. When I got to the top I slammed the door behind me, breathless.

"Since when is that staircase a wind tunnel?" I asked.

Noelle's carefully brushed hair stuck out from behind her ears, and some of her bangs stood up straight on her forehead.

"Must be that window," Noelle said, gesturing at the pane behind the desk. The top was completely bare, as if someone had broken it, removed all the shards, and never replaced it. My insides squirmed as I stared at the bending and swaying branches of the trees outside.

"I don't remember that being broken before," I said.

"Well, it is now," she replied. "Come on. Let's clean up and get back to Pemberly. We need to talk guest list for your party."

"Okay."

I tried to sound as excited as she did, but as we walked out I took one last trembling look at the window, half expecting to see Elizabeth Williams's ghost reaching out to me. I closed the door firmly behind me and jogged to catch up with Noelle.

If I really wanted a life with no drama, maybe it was time I stopped walking around in the middle of the night, looking for it.

The PRIVATE series
KATE BRIAN

Welcome to Easton Academy, where secrets and lies
are all part of the curriculum . . . but these secrets
must be kept private whatever the cost.

Set in a world of exclusive boarding schools, Kate
Brian's compelling *Private* series combines the bitchy
snobbery of the elite and wealthy, with secrets,
mystery and satire. Dark, sinister and sexy
– with no parents around to spoil the fun . . .

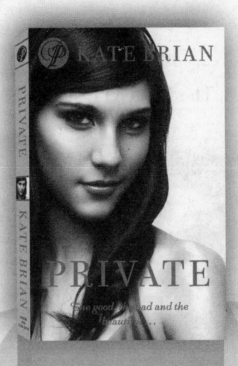

Reed Brennan is delighted when she wins a scholarship to
Easton Academy. But when she arrives at the beautiful,
tradition-steeped campus, everyone is more sophisticated,
more gorgeous and a WHOLE lot wealthier than she is. Reed
may have been accepted to the Academy, but she certainly
hasn't been accepted by her classmates. She feels like she's
on the outside, looking in... until she meets the Billings Girls.

They're the most beautiful, intelligent and powerful girls
on campus. And Reed vows to do whatever it takes to be
accepted into their inner circle. But she discovers much more
than designer clothes hiding in their closets –
there are also plenty of skeletons...